Windy Possibilities

Heather A. Herrick

For Jody Kelly, who convinced me I could be a writer. For Connor and Katie, whose love sparked the earliest inspirations for Charlie and Lilly.

Contents

1.	Chapter 1	1
2.	Chapter 2	9
3.	Chapter 3	14
4.	Chapter 4	21
5.	Chapter 5	31
6.	Chapter 6	42
7.	Chapter 7	54
8.	Chapter 8	64
9.	Chapter 9	76
10.	Chapter 10	84
11.	Chapter 11	93
12.	Chapter 12	102
13.	Chapter 13	110
14.	Chapter 14	115
15.	Chapter 15	128

16.	Chapter 16	135
17.	Chapter 17	141
18.	Chapter 18	153
19.	Chapter 19	160
20.	Chapter 20	166
21.	Chapter 21	176
22.	Chapter 22	183
23.	Chapter 23	189
24.	Chapter 24	201
25.	Chapter 25	211
26.	Chapter 26	222
27.	Chapter 27	233
28.	Chapter 28	240
29.	Chapter 29	244
30.	Chapter 30	255
31.	Chapter 31	262
32.	Chapter 32	270
33.	Chapter 33	279
34.	Chapter 34	284
35.	Chapter 35	296

36.	Chapter 36	301
37.	Chapter 37	305
38.	Chapter 38	314
39.	Epilogue	319
Into the Pacific		325
Gratitude		326
About the author		328
About the Cover Art		330

Chapter One

33° N latitude off the coast of San Diego, California, United States

I carried a steaming mug of peppermint tea up the steep teakwood steps toward the deck. The wood was cool and slightly damp under my bare feet, smelling faintly of salt and varnish. I could hear the rigging humming gently in the pre-dawn breeze, the lines whispering against the mast as *Windy Possibilities* shifted slightly in the calm swell. We were barely moving right now, but I could feel the subtle tug of the wind against the sails, teasing me with the promise of speed. Today would be a good day for sailing. We could make progress. Real progress.

In the soft, pink-gray haze of early morning, I squinted up at the mast. The ropes coiled neatly along the deck, the sails furled but ready, the metal fittings glinting faintly in the sunrise. I loved my 42-foot Jeanneau Voyage 12.5. Every line, every winch, every inch of her teak and fiber-glass felt like home. I'd been sailing on *Windy* my entire life. I'd spent countless hours learning her quirks, her temperament in different winds, her moans and groans as she cut through waves. I'd only started to think of her as "mine" in the past three or four years—

SWIM, SWIM, LOVE YOU, the computerized approximation of my own voice interrupted my thoughts.

Charlie bounded toward me, his chest rising and falling in excitement, tail a blur of anticipation. His amber eyes glimmered with mischief and hope. I smiled, and my chest warmed. Charlie was my best friend. After losing Lilly, I had never thought I could love another dog the way I had loved her. But Lilly had sent Charlie to me in her own way, and he had more than lived up to the impossible standard she'd set. He was loyal, smart, and fearless in the water. Muscles rippled under his chocolate coat as he pranced closer. I could see the stubborn curl of fluff along his neck and back, part lab, for sure, maybe some pit bull, maybe a little husky, possibly something else wild. I'd never know for sure. When I sang along to Jimmy Buffett on the old cassette player, he howled in harmony, a perfect duet, perfect to my tone-deaf ears anyway.

Charlie had pressed buttons on the soundboard I'd made him, a system for communicating. Of course, swimming in open water while solo on a boat wasn't exactly recommended, but when the sea was calm and the wind gentle, I couldn't resist. He'd been begging since sunrise, and this was as perfect a morning as any. The water glistened dark blue, almost black in the early light, smooth except for the tiny ripples brushing past the hull. I knew he wouldn't go far, and I wouldn't either. Still, my stomach fluttered with that familiar mix of excitement and worry that came with leaving the deck behind.

I leaned on the railing and took a long sip of tea, inhaling the salty tang of the ocean mixed with the sweet peppermint. The scent reminded me of my parents, of cold mornings when we had taken *Windy* out on Lake Michigan when I was a kid. It was a bittersweet memory now, but one I welcomed after so much time had passed. I loved this, the quiet rhythm, the constant, small demands of a living, moving home. It was exhausting sometimes, yes, but the reward was freedom.

The sun began to rise over the southern edge of California, painting the sky in pale gold and streaks of pink. Somewhere beyond the horizon, Mexico waited. With a little luck, today, we'd cross into its waters. I took the hair tie from my wrist and pulled my shoulder-length, brown hair back into a ponytail. Some people say dogs and their people look alike. I'm not sure about that, but Charlie's fur was the exact same shade of brown as my hair. Charlie whined softly, nudging my hand with his nose. I laughed. "All right, buddy, let's go for a swim." His tail thumped against the deck in answer, and I felt a surge of joy. Life at sea wasn't always predictable, but mornings like this, with the wind, the water, and Charlie beside me, it was everything.

I jumped into the cold, dark blue water. The chill clamped down on my skin, and for a second, my breath caught in my throat. Then the salt stung my lips, the water heavy and silken as it embraced me. Charlie cannonballed in right after, drenching me with a slap of spray just as I was wiping my eyes clear. I sputtered, half laughing, half choking, then tried to splash him back. But I was too slow; Charlie was already a streak of dark brown fur and paddling paws, his body moving away from me.

I slid my goggles into place, pushed down, and cut through the water after him. The sea was alive around me, lifting me, tugging me sideways, like it couldn't decide if I belonged there. Luckily, humans are generally faster swimmers than dogs. I caught up to Charlie and swerved in front of him, making a wide, exaggerated circle around *Windy*. Bubbles streamed behind me, my heartbeat loud in my ears. Of course, Charlie followed. Charlie always followed.

As I swam, I wondered if I weren't here, where would he go? Would he aim for the horizon without a second thought, muscles burning, trusting instinct long past reason, until exhaustion finally chose for him? The nearest land was miles away. I pictured his paws cutting the water long after mine had given out, amber eyes fixed on some imagined shore that might never come. The image lodged in my chest, sharp and sudden, and I forced myself to breathe past it.

If I let myself linger there, I'd feel it, the hollow truth of how alone I was out here, even with Charlie. Miles from another human. Miles from help. One wrong decision, one bad break, and there would be no one to notice for days. I'd heard that's how people unravel at sea. Not in storms, but in the quiet, the endless distance and isolation. I kicked harder, breaking the surface, unwilling to let the thought finish itself. Better not to linger.

"Well, buddy," I said, treading water, salty drops stinging my eyes, my voice sounding smaller than I expected in all that open blue. "If this wind keeps up, we might just make it to Cabo in five days. Two days early. What do you think of that, Charlie?"

"Arf!" He barked, paddling hard, amber eyes bright and wild with joy.

I grinned. "I probably should have studied dog communication instead of dolphin communication, huh? Would've been pretty cool to know what all your barks and grumbles really mean."

I told him this often, half-joking, half-serious. Even with his soundboard, twenty buttons, each with a word or phrase, I still didn't understand everything Charlie "said." Some days it felt like I understood less than ever. Not that I fully understood the dolphins either, but at least with them, there were moments when the connection sparked, when it felt like something big. And the dolphins were my research subjects. Sure, I cared about them, but I only spent a couple of hours a week with them. With Charlie, I was left guessing at a language with my own best friend.

At times, I thought I should have chosen dogs. Dogs were woven into human life in a way dolphins could never be. Dolphins were exotic, charismatic megafauna that most people only ever see on a tropical vacation. Dogs were family. They were the ones who slept beside us, barked at the door, and grieved when we left.

But science didn't work that way. In my field, the idea that dogs, or most other animals, could use complex language was laughed off as fantasy. Total crap, by the way.

Still, it was hard enough just getting funding to work on dolphins.

I'd been lucky to find Dr. Thatch at UC Santa Cruz, one of the few still carrying John C. Lilly's torch for dolphin communication. He hadn't planned to take another student, not with retirement looming, but I'd worn him down, convinced him to stretch a two-year plan into five. His family threw us a combined graduation/retirement party in May, a bittersweet affair with balloons and cake. A week later, Charlie and I had sailed out toward Cozumel and my new job at the CIMC, the Centro de Investigación Marina Cozumel.

The CIMC was my dream job. I still couldn't believe it. During the interview, both Dr. Andrews and Donna seemed thrilled with my dissertation and research. Dr. Andrews had cautioned that I'd still need to work on other projects that would "pay the bills" at the center. Donna was leaving to take a job at MIT. She was sad to be leaving, but what an opportunity for me. Dr. Andrews seemed straight-laced and a bit old-fashioned, but kind and open to my work on dolphin communication. I couldn't wait to meet him in person. My only concern was the complete lack of response for the past two weeks. I received the job offer two months ago and had been in constant communication since then. But two weeks ago, both Donna and Dr. Andrews had suddenly stopped returning my emails and calls. It was concerning. I wasn't sure what to make of it. I tried not to worry; the sooner I got to Cozumel, the sooner I'd figure out the answer to whatever was going on at the center.

Eight weeks to Cozumel. Six to the Panama Canal, two more beyond that. We'd been gone just over a week, barely a scratch on the journey, and yet already the miles behind us seemed enormous. The sea has a way of stretching time, of making each day feel both endless and fleeting. As I floated beside Charlie, the boat rocking gently nearby, I felt that strange mix of thrill and unease settle deep in my ribs.

I brought my thoughts back to the present as Charlie and I swung back around *Windy's* starboard side. We swam to the swim ladder at the stern. Charlie climbed up first, and I gave him a boost as he hit the last step. I knew he could climb up on his own, but he scrambled on that last step without a little help. I climbed up the ladder, grabbed the freshwater hose for a quick rinse, and toweled off. Charlie shook salt water onto me. I laughed and said, "Thanks for that, buddy. You always shake at the worst times! You're lucky I love you so much." As I said it, I knew it went both ways. Without Charlie, I'd be alone, not just living on a sailboat and sailing to Cozumel to start a new job by myself, but completely alone in life. I hugged him close and inhaled the scent of wet, salty dog. I rinsed us both with the freshwater hose this time.

"Okay, Charlie, it's time to get moving." I unzipped the mainsail cover and unfurled the sail. As I hoisted it up the mast, I realized I didn't even notice the rough rope anymore. I had always had calluses on my hands from sailing, but now they were growing thicker from sailing all day, every day. I thought of my dad, who said you could find a true sailor in any room by the calluses on his hands. I sighed. I still missed my parents so much. I shook my head. I needed to pay attention. Dad also said it was important to pay attention when setting your rigging. As I finished setting the mainsail, I felt *Windy Possibilities* snap to life. She caught the wind and began to move with purpose. Charlie ran to the bow and stood at attention, feeling the wind on his face, ears flapping in the breeze. He loved sailing, especially feeling that first morning breeze.

I went to the helm to check our coordinates. Of course, I used GPS like everyone else today, but I actually love old-fashioned maps. I bought navigational charts for this part of the Pacific before we left, just in case GPS went down, which never happens anymore. I already had charts of the entire Gulf of Mexico and Caribbean because Dad got them years ago. When I was a teenager, he taught me how to plot a course on navigational charts. At the time, I told him it was dumb because "everyone uses GPS now, Dad." But even then, secretly, I loved knowing how to plot a course. It made me feel powerful, like those people in movies standing around a giant table, plotting a course like it actually mattered, yeah, I can do that. I thought of The Martian, when Mark Watney declares that Mars will come to fear his botany powers, and I muttered, possibly even out loud, "The ocean will come to fear my map-plotting skills." Yikes, Marie, maybe don't tempt the sea like that. I hadn't actually plotted a course in about four years.

Chapter Two

33° N latitude off the coast of San Diego, California, United States

Everyone thinks I'm named after Marie Curie, but I'm actually named after Marie Tharp. Don't get me wrong, Marie Curie was a great scientist, and I'd be honored to be named after her. But Marie Tharp has always felt like my kindred spirit. She was a geologist and oceanographic cartographer. She discovered the Mid-Atlantic Ridge; of course, her male co-researcher, Bruce Heezen, got all the credit at the time, but she's really the one. Marie wanted to work on ships and do field work, but as a woman in the 1940s and 50s, she wasn't allowed. She got married, but was only married a few years before getting divorced, which was a big deal back then. She never had kids, also a big deal back then.

I wish I could have known Marie Tharp better. I'd love to get inside her head and understand how she thought. It must have been so challenging to be a woman in that time, to be told you can't do all the things you want to do, and that you're good at, just because you're a woman. I certainly wouldn't have handled it well. Maybe she didn't, maybe no one could have. But I've always been more intrigued by her science than by her personal life, despite that being pretty interesting too.

Marie was a master mapmaker. She took the data collected by men who were allowed to go on the ships and collect data, and she made maps from it. But her maps weren't just charts from single points of data like most maps at that time. Marie took thousands of data points and visualized them to make maps that were representations of the actual seafloor. Where other cartographers saw random bumps and trenches, Marie recognized repeating structures like mountain chains and rift valleys. It's like she could take data points and visualize what they actually looked like underwater.

At the time, the 3D shaded relief maps Marie began making weren't just beautiful and creative; they were groundbreaking. Her maps were meticulous in a way no one had ever seen before. Marie would go back and re-plot data and correct errors obsessively until each map was perfect. They made the invisible become visible. Her maps gave scientists a way to actually see the seafloor, which revolutionized marine geology. There's no way we'd have early-warning tsunami and earthquake systems, undersea internet cables, or even the current hurricane prediction and modeling systems used today without Marie Tharp's maps. Her work is still shaping the world today.

Despite being seen as a hero in science today, it must have been frustrating being a female scientist then. She was super smart and one of the first scientists to theorize continental drift. But it took her years (and another male scientist finally backing her work) to convince Bruce to publish her work on continental drift. Oh, and speaking of publishing, her name wasn't on any publications in the 50s and 60s. I'm pretty sure if it were me, I'd have gotten angry, said what I really thought, and gotten fired pretty fast. I'm just not one to stand by and watch injustice like that.

I've always felt a connection to Marie Tharp. I'm so happy and proud that my parents named me after her. I'm not exactly sure what it is, but like Marie, I love the connections that can be made in science. She clearly loved the connection between art and science, while I love the connection between psychology and science. Or maybe it's just that I met Marie once as a child.

My parents saw her speak once in 1997 when the Library of Congress named her one of the four greatest cartographers of the 20th century. What a huge honor! She was already well into her 70s by then, but she spoke at the event, and my parents both thought she was amazing. So much so that they named me after her.

They named everyone after scientists. Most families trace their history through people; we also traced ours through the dogs who had loved us.

When my parents met, they each had a dog. Mom had a black lab named Edison, and Dad had a shepherd mix named Tesla. Dad always said that he knew he and Mom were meant to be together on their very first date as soon as she mentioned her dog Edison. I guess because they'd started with Edison and Tesla, they named everyone after scientists. The big yellow lab Mom rescued from the shelter as a parvo puppy was named Faraday. Faraday was the dog they had when I was born. He was older by the time I remember him, but I remember cuddling with him when we'd go sailing on cool fall afternoons.

In 2004, Columbia University created the Marie Tharp Fellowship for female scientists. Marie Tharp made an appearance; she was in her 80s by then, but still sharp and witty, according to my parents. My parents totally nerded out over the event, hoping for a chance to meet Marie. They took me to see the ceremony; I was only four, and I don't remember much about it. I'm not sure how we got to meet her, but we did. What I do remember is feeling like Marie truly cared about me. She knelt down and talked with me like I was a grown-up. I can't remember what she said, but she made me feel important. She felt more like a grandmother than a stranger. That felt especially surprising, given that she'd never had children herself.

One of my most prized possessions is a framed photograph of me with Marie Tharp. It hangs in the cabin of *Windy Possibilities* above the small dining table. I'm wearing a frilly, cornflower blue dress, which I'm sure I hated and whined about. Marie is wearing pants, as I pointed out to my parents many times over the years. My parents rarely made me dress up, and from the time I could dress myself, they never complained about my preference for pants over dresses and skirts. In fact, I sometimes think they liked my lack of concern for fashion and propriety. I'm sure they just wanted me to look cute, hoping they'd really get to meet and talk with Marie Tharp and maybe get a picture of me with my namesake.

It's a great picture. Marie Tharp and I are both smiling, she's kneeling down and looking half at me and half at the camera. Every time I look at it, I feel connected to Marie Tharp. Maybe I have some subconscious memory of something she said or did, something my four-year-old brain tucked away. All I know is when I look at that photo, she doesn't feel like a distant scientist I was lucky to meet once. She feels like family.

And maybe that's why I've always carried her with me. She didn't get to go on the ships or lower the instruments into the water, but she still saw the ocean more clearly than anyone else of her time. She took fragments of data and wove them into maps that revealed the world below. She saw the meaning in the hidden patterns, even when no one else did.

That's exactly what I want to do with the dolphins. I can't "see" language the way most people define it, but I can listen, look for gestures, learn behaviors, and build a map of meaning from them. Like Marie Tharp, I believe that if you build enough fragments, piece by piece, the story will come together.

When I look at that photo now, I don't just see a little girl in a frilly dress and a scientist with kind eyes. I see a reminder of what I owe her. Marie Tharp mapped the ocean floor. I want to map the language of the ocean's most charismatic voices. In my own way, I'm still following her lead, searching for connections hidden just beneath the surface.

Chapter Three

28° N latitude off the coast of Mexico

"Engine check time, Charlie."

Charlie sighed from his spot on the deck, already unimpressed. He never liked it when I disappeared into the engine compartment; I think he hated the way it swallowed me up in noise and heat. I shimmied down into the cramped space, knees pressed against metal, the raw heat pressing in instantly. The engine whined steadily, almost like it was humming to me. Boat smell: diesel, sweat, and salt. Not my favorite part of sailing, but necessary.

Dad had always taken impeccable care of *Windy Possibilities*. He was a mechanical engineer, so he loved boat maintenance. Growing up, I'd hated holding the flashlight for him or scrubbing my knuckles raw trying to reach a hidden bolt. Now, I was grateful for every single miserable lesson, and I wished I'd paid more attention. They were the reason I could maintain *Windy* on my own.

The belts looked fine. The oil was clean. For one brief, fragile moment, everything was fine.

Then I saw it. A thin shimmer caught the light, and my stomach dropped. A few drops of water leaked from the gasket on the raw water pump. Just a few. Barely a whisper as they hit the hot engine and hissed into steam. But my heart was already pounding, too loud in the small space.

I knew exactly what this meant.

That pump pulled seawater in to cool the engine. If it failed, the engine would overheat in minutes. Not hours. Minutes. Metal warping, alarms blaring, the smell of burning oil. And then silence. Without an engine, I could still sail, in theory. I always preferred sails to diesel. But an engine wasn't optional out here. It was the difference between sliding into a harbor under control or being pushed sideways into jagged rocks. It was the difference between choices and no choices at all.

It was also a Panama Canal requirement. No engine, no canal. No canal, no crossing. And without the crossing, Cozumel vanished, the job, the plan, the life I'd been building, all of it.

I bit my lip hard enough it hurt. This had to be fixed.

The job itself wasn't impossible. A new cover plate. A new housing. Simple words. But I had never done it before. I imagined taking the pump apart, a bolt slipping from my fingers, vanishing forever into the bilge. I imagined putting it back together wrong, tightening everything down, turning the key... and watching the leak return. Or worse.

My chest tightened, breath shallow, the engine suddenly sounding louder, hotter, closer. One small failure out here didn't stay small for long.

I was past California now, past Ensenada, which meant past the last big port where getting parts would've been easy. I pictured huge shelves stacked with boxes of shiny brass fittings I could no longer reach. My best chance now was Turtle Bay, a tiny fishing village most sailors stopped at out of necessity rather than desire. No marina, no boatyard, just anchoring out and hoping the pangas running back and forth to shore could ferry me to the one shop, or person, who might have the part.

And if they didn't? If the part wasn't there, or worse, I trusted the wrong person to "help" and wound up with a worse problem than I started with? I hated that Dad wasn't here. He'd have been able to fix this no problem. I sighed.

I closed my eyes and breathed, steadying myself against the thrum of the engine. Fear had its place, but panic didn't. Still, for a split second, I heard Aunt Ann's voice in my head—my mom's sister and my only living relative—tight with concern and certainty. You can't live like this forever, Dear. Alone at sea. You're not being sensible. What if something goes wrong? What then? No one would be there to help you.

I shook it off and turned back to the engine. Things always went wrong. You dealt with them. That was sailing.

I climbed back up onto the deck, Charlie pressing close as though he already knew. I scratched his ears with shaky hands and whispered, "Looks like Turtle Bay better have what we need, buddy."

"We're going to need to sail the rest of the way to Turtle Bay. I'm not chancing running the engine. So hope for favorable winds, Charlie!" We were only about a day's sail from Turtle Bay with decent wind.

As I felt the wind changing around me, a memory rose up so sharply it almost felt like a tide pulling me backward. My dad loved sailing. I think he'd even raced some when he was young. He bought *Windy Possibilities* back when he and my mom were dating. He always claimed he bought her to impress my mom. She'd roll her eyes every time he said it, but she'd also smile in that way that told me she'd fallen for him long before the boat ever entered the picture.

Some of my earliest memories are on *Windy*: cuddling into Faraday, our huge, patient yellow lab, his fur warm against my cheek while the cold Lake Michigan wind whipped through my hair. Mom and Dad would tack into the wind together, shouting little corrections over the roar of the gusts, their movements perfectly in sync. I didn't understand it then, but that was their love language: wind, water, and teamwork.

By the time I was five or six, I had my own "jobs" on board. Tiny things like coiling lines or wiping down the cockpit, but Dad made them sound like mission-critical tasks. He'd crouch beside me with exaggerated seriousness and say, "Boat doesn't run without a good deckhand," and I believed him with my whole heart. He made me feel capable before I had any idea what capable even meant.

Mom volunteered at the dog shelter most Saturdays, so it was usually just Dad and me on the water. Two little adventurers playing captain and crew. Later, when we adopted Lilly, she'd curl beside me on the bench seat as though she'd always belonged there. I didn't know it then, but I'd spend my high school years leaning into her warm fur while studying for exams or trying not to cry over teenage heartbreaks that seem insignificant now. Lilly was the last piece of "home" I had after everything fell apart. I only had Charlie because of Lilly.

By the time I reached high school, I spent summers racing Lasers with friends. I loved the precision of it, the controlled chaos, the thrill of heeling the boat right up to her tipping point before she finally dumped me into the freezing-blue water. Lake Michigan was always cold, even in July. Always shocking. Always exhilarating.

Learning on a tiny Laser taught me exactly how far you can push a sailboat before she gives in. It made me braver, and smarter, and honestly a better sailor. Dad saw that shift in me too.

One summer, he started letting me sail essentially by myself. He'd stay below deck, "making breakfast" or "looking for a wrench," while I motored us out of the harbor, hoisted the sails, and trimmed the sheets. He'd poke his head up only when everything was already set, inspecting my work like a benevolent admiral.

At first, I was furious. Why am I doing everything while he sits below? And more than a little terrified of messing up. I triple-checked every knot, every turn of the wheel, every flutter of the telltales. But then, slowly, it dawned on me.

He trusted me.

More than that, he wanted me to trust myself.

And once I realized that? It was exhilarating. I wasn't just a kid anymore; I was the one sailing *Windy Possibilities.*

Thinking about Dad steadied me, but it didn't change the stillness around me.

"Of course," I muttered, "now that we actually need to sail, there's no wind at all." We'd had such beautiful sailing up to this point, and now, with the engine already compromised, the sea went dead calm for the first time since we'd left Santa Cruz. I picked up a tuft of Charlie's hair from the teak deck, dropped it, and watched it fall straight down.

I could run the engine. The thought slipped in un-invited. Just for a few minutes, just enough to keep us moving. But I knew what that really meant. Running it now was a gamble. If the raw water pump failed com-pletely, I wouldn't just be without power. I could cook the engine beyond repair in minutes. One missed warning. One distracted moment. One degree too hot.

I told myself I could watch the gauges closely, shut it down at the first sign of trouble. But the ocean doesn't re-ward "almost careful." If the engine overheated out here, that wasn't a setback. It was a catastrophe. So no. I wasn't willing to risk it. I needed wind, not wishful thinking. I watched the tuft of hair lying on the deck, the stillness pressing in on all sides.

Charlie looked at me with sad eyes. He walked over to his soundboard and pressed: MARIE GOOD LOVE YOU.

"Oh buddy, I love you too. I'm not upset with you, you're a good dog. We're just stuck here, and we have to get the boat fixed. You want to go for a swim, Charlie?"

I walked over to his buttons and pressed: CHARLIE WANT SWIM?

Charlie said: YES SWIM.

We splashed into the dark blue water and swam four big laps around *Windy Possibilities*. "You always know how to make me feel better, Charlie. I love you, you're the best dog." I kissed the top of Charlie's head before we climbed back onto *Windy*.

I was sitting on the deck reading, The Mind of a Dolphin, by John C. Lilly, Charlie lying in the sun at my feet. I'd first found Lilly's work when I was about seven years old, long before I knew anything about ethics, or that Lilly gave dolphins drugs, or the Margaret Howe story. Back then, I'd just been a kid who fell completely in love with the idea of a scientist who believed dolphins could talk, and who thought it was worth trying to listen. Even now, knowing how deeply flawed his methods were, that original spark still mattered to me. The belief that dolphins were minds, not specimens. That communication, not control, was the point.

When the previous page blew back against my fingers, it startled me. I looked up, felt the warm wind brush my face, and couldn't help grinning. I closed the book and jumped to my feet. "Wooo! Charlie, we've got our wind back! Let's go to Turtle Bay."

I unfurled the mainsail, the canvas snapping once before filling, and felt *Windy Possibilities* lean gently into her course. The rigging hummed, the bow lifted, and just like that, we were moving again.

Chapter Four

27.5° N latitude Turtle Bay, Mexico

I hadn't planned on stopping in Turtle Bay, but now we'd have to stop and spend at least a couple of days, depending on how long it took to find the parts to repair the raw water pump.

Charlie and I stood on the bow of *Windy*, squinting into the bright Pacific sun as we sailed toward Turtle Bay. The air was sharp with the smell of salt and diesel as we neared the harbor. Panga boats of every color darted around like water bugs, their outboards whining and sputtering as fishermen headed in and out, sometimes ferrying passengers, sometimes not. Farther out, larger boats rocked lazily at anchor, their hulls flashing white against the huge sweep of turquoise-blue water. The bay felt alive, like a city of its own floating on the sea, noisy and crowded, so different from the quiet stretches of ocean I'd just come through.

I shifted my weight and rubbed the back of my neck, my stomach tight with nerves. I had never seen anything quite like it. Charlie pressed against my leg, ears perked forward, as if he sensed my unease. Leaving *Windy* to climb into one of those pangas and trust it to take me ashore to hunt for engine parts felt like a leap into the unknown. And once I got to town...what then? Would I find a shop that even carried what I needed, or would I end up stranded here for days?

And then the bigger question: did I trust myself to install the new pump, or did I hand over the job to a stranger? I was pretty sure I could do it, but "pretty sure" didn't feel like enough when the Panama Canal lay ahead. Every pump, every gasket mattered on a passage like this. On the other hand, letting an unknown mechanic crawl around inside *Windy's* heart felt wrong too, like letting a stranger touch a part of me.

I tightened my arm around Charlie's shoulders, steadying myself against the roll of the boat. I hoped once I set foot on shore and walked into a shop, the right path would become obvious. For now, though, the decision hung over me like the heavy afternoon heat, sticky and unshakable.

Charlie and I set anchor and hailed a panga. The boat that came buzzing across the water was painted a peeling shade of sky-blue, its little outboard coughing and sputtering as it slowed. The captain was a short, older Hispanic man with weathered skin, wearing a sun-faded baseball cap. He introduced himself as Carlos.

As soon as we climbed down into his boat, he reached out a hand to steady me, then bent to pat Charlie on the head. Charlie leaned against him, tail thumping against the panga's fiberglass hull, his way of giving a hug. I let out a long breath I hadn't realized I'd been holding. If Charlie trusted him, then so did I.

The panga rocked as Carlos pushed us back from *Windy* with one sure shove of his foot. Spray stung my cheeks as we skimmed across the bay, weaving between anchored fishing boats and half-sunk buoys. I stumbled once and dropped a hand to the gunwale, the rough paint gritty beneath my palm. The smell of fuel and saltwater hung thick in the air, sharper here than out at anchor, mingling with faint hints of fish from the day's catch.

In my reasonably good Spanish, I told him I needed to find a boat repair shop and parts for my raw water pump. My words weren't as smooth as I'd hoped, and Carlos's amused eyes told me he understood more than he let on. He answered in English, clear, kind, and far better than my Spanish. "Ah, my nephew, Mateo, runs the best repair shop. But he will need to order parts. You will stay a few days. Have dinner with my family."

Ugh. A few days. My stomach sank. A delay here wasn't just inconvenient, it would mean I'd miss my Panama Canal crossing date. It might mean waiting weeks, circling or stuck in port. That wasn't a margin I could afford. I clenched my hands in my lap and forced myself to take a slow breath. This wasn't the moment to chase the spiral. First came the pump. Then I'd face whatever followed.

For now, I let myself soften into Carlos's easy warmth, the way he already treated me like a friend. Dinner with his family might be just what I needed: to be fed, to rest, to be reminded that even out here, I didn't have to do everything alone.

Carlos took us straight to his home instead of the repair shop. The panga nosed into a sandy stretch of beach, and

Charlie leapt ashore with a happy bark, sending a spray of water flying. I followed more carefully, balancing my pack on one shoulder. The heat hit me as soon as I stepped onto the sand, heavy and humid, reminding me that this place would set it's own pace, whether I liked it or not.

It was just after 4 p.m., but as we walked through a narrow lane and into the courtyard, I realized the party had already started. The place was alive with sound, laughter, children shrieking in a game of tag, the crackle of a grill, someone strumming a guitar. There must have been about twenty people there, and every one of them looked up and smiled as if I were a cousin returning home, not a stranger with broken boat parts.

Carlos introduced me to his wife Rosa, a larger woman wearing a flowered dress. She smelled faintly of hibiscus and woodsmoke. She didn't hesitate for a second, just wrapped me in a big hug, the kind of hug that squeezed the air out of you but left you lighter somehow. She certainly wasn't concerned with an extra mouth to feed or a stranger crashing her party. Charlie adored her instantly, tail thumping, head nudging against her hand for more pets.

Next, Carlos found Mateo and his wife, Ana, and introduced me. Mateo's hands were rough and stained with oil, his handshake firm in the way of someone used to turning wrenches all day. Ana had kind eyes and hair pulled back in a braid that swung down her back. They pulled over a pair of lawn chairs shaded by a lemon tree, and I sank into mine with relief, realizing just how tense my body had been since the engine sputtered.

I told them about *Windy Possibilities*, my raw water pump issue, and my Panama Canal crossing. My voice faltered a little when I admitted how nervous I was about missing my slot at the canal.

"Ah," Mateo said, leaning back, his tone calm and matter-of-fact. "We don't keep many parts here in town. We order almost everything from Ensenada. It takes three or four days to get here. I can't really get anything faster, and no one else here can either. You can call the Canal Port Authority and tell them what happened. They can usually reschedule."

He nodded toward Ana, his voice softening. "Ana can help you if you'd like; she's helped others reschedule."

The way he said it, the way his eyes lingered on her, it was like he was proud of her for something as simple as making phone calls. Proud that they were a team. I felt a tiny pang of jealousy at that look. It would be so nice to have someone look at me like that, to think so highly of me.

I sighed. Three or four days wasn't what I wanted to hear, but I knew it was my only option, and completely reasonable. What I hadn't told Mateo was that I had interviewed and hand-chosen my Panama Canal crossing crew: four English-speaking women with over ten years of boating experience each. These women likely wouldn't be available at a later date; I'd have to take whatever crew was left at the last minute. Most likely, men who didn't speak my language, with little boating experience, not only helping me get through the Canal, but also sleeping on my boat in Gatún Lake. The thought of strangers on

Windy sent a pang through me. But given the situation, I had no other option. I'd just have to figure that out when the time came.

"Ok then," I said, pushing the worry aside, "let's get the parts ordered first thing in the morning, and Ana will you help me call the Canal Authority to get a new date scheduled? Mateo, would you be willing to install the parts for me and give *Windy* a quick check over?"

Ana smiled and nodded her head as Mateo replied easily, "I'd be happy to, Anything for a friend of Tío Carlos."

I laughed. "I just met your uncle an hour ago on his panga."

Mateo grinned, leaning back in his chair as his aunt slid a steaming platter of fresh tortillas onto the table. The warm smell of corn rose up to my nostrils. Suddenly, I was starving.

"We make friends fast here in Turtle Bay. He must have gotten a good feeling from you to invite you to family dinner. He considers you a friend. He's a good judge of character. I trust him."

"I feel that way about my dog, Charlie."

I glanced across the yard. Charlie was sprawled in the dirt at Carlos' feet, his tail flicking lazily while Carlos rubbed his belly with the side of his sandal. The scene made me smile: both of them looked completely content, like they'd known each other all their lives. "If he likes and trusts someone, I do too. And he liked your uncle from the moment we stepped onto his panga. He doesn't always warm up to people so quickly."

"Animals can be like that," Ana said, reaching for a tortilla, her braid swinging forward. "They're not encumbered by all the baggage we humans carry around. They can see others for what they truly are right away. It's a gift to have a dog like Charlie."

"He really is a gift," I said softly. A gift from Lilly, I didn't add, though the thought sat heavy in my chest.

"Salsa verde or roja?" Ana asked brightly, holding out two little bowls toward me, both fragrant with chilies and lime.

"Both, please," I said, and she grinned as she spooned a little of each onto my plate beside the tamales Carlos' wife had unwrapped from their corn husks. The masa was soft and steaming, filled with something that smelled like spiced pork and tomatoes. "Good choice, Tia Rosa makes the best salsas."

Conversation wove easily around me, in Spanish and English, stories tumbling one over the other. The clink of glasses, the scrape of forks, the occasional burst of laughter. I caught words here and there: fish, tides, rain, family. Rosa kept pressing food toward me, as if one plate couldn't possibly be enough, and every time I thought I was finished, something new appeared: a squeeze of lime over fresh ceviche, sweet plantains caramelized at the edges, a slice of flan with a glossy sheen. And margaritas, the margaritas were delicious and endless.

Charlie groaned happily, belly-up, as one of the kids sneaked him a piece of tortilla under the table. I pretended not to notice, though Carlos gave her a mock-stern look.

She dissolved into laughter, and Charlie thumped his tail against the dirt in appreciation.

For a moment, the stress of parts and Canal deadlines slipped away. I felt wrapped in the warmth of the courtyard, the earthy smell of tortillas, the tang of chilies, the salt of the sea still clinging to my hair, and the comfort of being welcomed, fully, into a family I'd only just met.

I wasn't exactly drunk, but maybe just a little tipsy, as I leaned back and looked up at the stars while Carlos steered us across the moonlit bay in his panga. The night was warm and soft, a beautiful quiet, until the sharp sound of an engine tore through it. I blinked into the darkness, squinting at the silhouette of a larger boat moving into the bay. Its bow wave slapped against the hull of our little skiff, rippling the water with a low thrum.

"Who would come in so late?" I asked, turning toward Carlos.

His face was shadowed, the starlight catching only the edge of his cheekbone. "It's best not to ask questions, and to keep to yourself. Especially at night." His voice was low, steady, almost too calm. "This is why Rosa wanted you to stay at our home. I understand why you want to sleep on your boat, but if you are there at night, stay inside. Stay in the cabin. There are strange things happening in this bay. Bad things. We can do nothing to stop it."

I felt a chill, though the air was still warm. "What kind of things?"

Carlos hesitated, his eyes on the dark outline of the yacht as it slid deeper into the harbor, no running lights visible until the last moment. "A man from town tried to interfere," he said quietly. "He disappeared."

My stomach dropped. "What? That sounds like...like drug smuggling in the movies." My voice came out too loud, jittery with nerves and a bit of alcohol.

Carlos sighed, a heavy sound, and shifted his hand on the tiller. "You sound just like Ana. She would not let it go either, until I told her what I know. I sense you won't either."

He was right. I leaned closer. "Tell me."

"They are not smuggling drugs," he said at last. His words were clipped, like he didn't want them in the air. "Animals. For an aquarium in Mexico City. They are capturing endangered animals...illegally."

I felt sick. "For an aquarium? But...why doesn't anyone stop them? Call the police?"

"The government is bribed to look the other way," Carlos said, shaking his head. "Here, the law does not always protect the innocent."

I stared out at the bay, where the sound of chains rattling echoed faintly across the water. My mind spun with flashes of the dolphins, of Lilly, of all the creatures I loved so fiercely. "I knew things like this happened," I whispered. "There was a for-profit aquarium in Texas that got shut down. The owner got caught buying sharks on the black market, and most of their animals had been taken illegally. They were sick, neglected. It was awful."

Carlos nodded slowly. "Sí. For money. For entertainment, but not for the good of the animals."

"It's heartbreaking," I said, my throat tight. "This is why I believe aquariums and zoos should only be public, non-profit. At least then the goal isn't profit, it's care and education."

Charlie shifted beside me, resting his chin on the gunwale, as if sensing my unease. The boat rocked gently beneath us, the salt air thick on my tongue. I wanted to cry, but I forced the tears back. "And here I am, right in the middle of it, with no way to stop it."

Carlos glanced at me, his expression unreadable in the dark. "You cannot fight every battle, Marie. Not tonight."

I swallowed hard and looked up at the stars again, trying to anchor myself in something steady. But the image of that dark ship sliding into the bay, carrying its hidden, stolen cargo, stayed with me long after we reached *Windy's* side.

Chapter Five

27.5° N latitude Turtle Bay, Mexico

Ana and I became fast friends over the four days I spent in Turtle Bay. As promised, she helped set up a new canal crossing date for me. Although, as expected, I'd lose my planned crew. She sighed when I told her how much I'd looked forward to crossing with that group, how each woman had been calm, competent, and kind.

"It makes such a difference who you share a boat with," she said, resting a hand on my arm in that easy, natural way that made me feel like we'd known each other for years. We stood side by side, leaning on the worn rail outside her husband's workshop, watching Mateo's crew work beneath the bright heat. The air smelled faintly of diesel and coconut oil, and sweat beaded at the nape of my neck.

Ana told me stories about the deckhands she'd known, how even the roughest of them still held to a code. "Don't worry," she said with a quick smile, her dark eyes kind. "The men might curse like sailors, but they're more afraid of the police than the sea itself. You'll be safe." Her certainty, her calm voice layered with the low hum of the boatyard, eased something in me.

Later back on *Windy*, I told Ana about my research, her eyes lit up. "You teach them to talk?" she asked, sounding half in disbelief and half in awe. I laughed and showed her Charlie's soundboard. Charlie, delighted by the attention, tapped the button: HELLO and wagged his tail so hard the soundboard rattled.

Ana clapped her hands and kissed the top of his head. "*Ay, qué inteligente*," she murmured. Her delight made me ridiculously happy.

I told her about the dolphins I'd worked with in grad school, Callie and Heidi, and how I'd made them a soundboard much like Charlie's.

"They learned to talk too?" Ana asked, her voice quiet now, reverent almost.

"They tried," I said. "And they understood more than anyone believed."

I could still picture them clearly: Heidi, eight years old, sleek and quick, her skin glinting silver-blue in the filtered light of the research tank. She had a mischievous streak and a smile that always looked half like a dare. Her first word had been ball. The memory of that moment came back so vividly I could almost feel the cool California air, hear the soft slosh of water, and the faint hum of the pumps.

At first, she'd eyed the sound button like it was an alien object, her dark eye fixed on it, then on me, as if to say, You've got to be kidding me. But when I pressed it, said BALL, and tossed her the bright yellow toy, something shifted. The third time I did it, she beat me to it, pressing the button with her rostrum, the smooth, beak-like tip of her snout, and squeaking when I handed her the ball. That sound, pure delight, had made my chest ache in the best way.

Callie, older and quieter, was different. Her curiosity wasn't as playful, but it ran deep. Her first word was PUZZLE. She ignored the ball completely, turning her back to it in that deliberate, dismissive dolphin way. But when I recorded PUZZLE and gave her the chance to match it with her floating toy, she lit up. She pushed the button over and over, clicking softly as if she were testing each sound for meaning. When she finally solved the toy, nudging pieces into place with her beak and fins, she gave a triumphant chirp that still echoes in my memory.

They were magical, both of them. Intelligent in a way that felt almost otherworldly. But even in those beautiful moments, there was always a heaviness underneath, a sadness that came from knowing they lived their lives in tanks, their world reduced to concrete walls and filtered water. I never got much time with them. Everyone wanted time with the dolphins, and my project was never the top priority.

The buttons were challenging for me. When they malfunctioned, the dolphins got frustrated and splashed me, or sometimes rammed the edge of the soundboard with their rostrums so hard the buttons popped off. Their power always startled me, but it wasn't anger so much as exasperation. They wanted to be understood.

It was hard to get time with them. There was always another researcher scheduled, another data collection window I had to work around. Our progress was painfully slow. And of course, I was the only one using the buttons with them, so they didn't have the repetition they needed to really master it.

Still, we got up to about fifteen words, an incredible feat, even if it didn't feel like enough. We could talk about people, things, places, but not ideas. Nothing abstract. Nothing that could tell me what they dreamed about when they slept, or what it felt like when the trainers left for the night and the lights dimmed over the tanks.

I told Ana about it as we sat under the shade of her little porch, mugs of tea in hand, cinnamon for her, peppermint for me. The air smelled of salt and the faint sweetness of hibiscus flowers from her garden. She listened the way some people meditate, quietly, with her whole self.

I was explaining how the boards worked, tracing imaginary buttons in the air with my fingers, when the memory of that morning with Callie came flooding back so vividly I had to stop and breathe.

"She pushed six buttons, all in a row," I said softly, staring past Ana toward the bright shimmer of Turtle Bay. "She said: WANT PLAY PUZZLE MARIE NO JUMPS."

Ana blinked. "She said all that?"

I nodded. "Six words. In perfect order. I was so shocked I almost fell into the tank." I smiled at the memory, though it still made my throat tighten. "Callie was scheduled to work with another researcher that day, James. He was studying jumping height. He wasn't cruel, just..." I hesitated, searching for the word. "Cold. He thought emotions in dolphins were a myth. I guess Callie didn't like his sessions much."

The flash of that moment returned, sunlight rippling across the water, the hum of the pumps, Callie's dark eye locked on mine. I'd crouched by the edge of the tank, the soundboard on the edge of the concrete between us. "I hit: WANT JUMP and said 'no James' out loud," I told Ana, smiling faintly. "She raced around the pool and jumped so high she splashed the observation deck. It was... joyful. Defiant, even."

Ana laughed softly, her eyes bright.

"When she came back, I told her, 'I'm sorry, Callie, I can't change things. I wish I could.' She tilted her head, looked straight at me, and I swear, she understood. Not the words maybe, but the feeling behind them."

A breeze drifted through the open window, carrying the faint cries of gulls from the harbor. For a long moment, neither of us spoke.

"I wanted to publish it," I said finally, "but no one would have believed it. They wanted data points and measurable behavior, not meaning. And building a real device, a communication system they could use freely, was way beyond what I could manage. I didn't have the engineering background or the funding."

Ana reached out and touched my hand, her skin warm against mine. "But you understood them," she said. "That's more important than any machine."

Her words sank deep. I looked out toward the bay again, where *Windy Possibilities* rocked gently at anchor, her white hull gleaming under the afternoon sun. Maybe

Ana was right. Maybe the dolphins didn't need perfect technology. Maybe they just needed someone who was still listening.

What I was able to publish wasn't earth-shattering, not in the way I dreamed it would be, but it was enough. Enough to get me a PhD. Enough to carve out a sliver of credibility in the tiny, fiercely competitive world of animal communication. Enough to prove, to a few open minds, at least, that animals weren't just reacting to instinct but using intentional signals to share their world.

There were conferences where I stood in front of rooms filled with skeptical professors, my palms slick against the remote as I clicked through slides. My stomach would knot, breath catching in that dry, recycled air. I'd scan their faces, raised eyebrows, arms folded, expressions unreadable until the moment a spectrogram aligned perfectly with a recorded behavior. Sometimes, a small flicker of surprise, or the briefest lean forward in their chairs. Those were the moments that kept me going. I learned to argue with data, to defend nuance with precision, to anticipate every counterpoint before it landed.

Slowly, the field began to shift. My work joined a small but growing chorus, scientists from around the world uncovering what animal lovers already knew in their bones: that creatures feel, think, and communicate in ways we've barely begun to understand. I still remember the dizzy, almost guilty joy of reading about a new bill restricting animal testing, or that first court case where "animal welfare" wasn't just a footnote but a ruling. It wasn't everything I wanted, but it was something. A start.

It was enough to keep me believing that empathy could be data.

When Ana asked how I felt about dolphin captivity, I hesitated. It was a question I always dreaded. I hated what humans did to animals in confinement, but I also knew how easily humans ignored what they didn't understand. And how could we protect creatures we never truly listened to?

Still, after my time with Callie and Heidi, it was hard to condone captivity in any form. They were brilliant souls trapped in an artificial blue world. I could still see them, gliding slow circles around the pool, Callie's dorsal fin tracing the surface like a sigh, Heidi pressing her melon against the concrete wall as if she could feel something beyond it. When I stood at the edge, clipboard in hand, they'd turn their eyes toward me, dark, liquid, impossibly aware. Callie would sometimes whistle softly, a question or a greeting, and I'd whistle back, my voice shaking, wishing I could translate the ache in both our hearts.

Their whistles weren't random; I was sure of it. There was pattern, purpose, sometimes even humor. Once, after a long morning session, Callie clicked and spun in place, spraying me with saltwater as if she knew exactly how tired I was. I laughed out loud, but the sound felt hollow. Behind the laughter, there was guilt. No matter how carefully we studied them, they were still prisoners in a tank too small for their minds.

That memory clung to me even now, as I looked out at Turtle Bay. The air tasted like sea spray instead of chlorine. The sound of the waves felt like freedom. Here, the dolphins chose to come and go as they pleased, wild, un-tethered, unmeasured. It gave me hope that this work, this version of science, might be different. That my new job at the CIMC would be the beginning of something better. That understanding didn't have to mean ownership.

When I told Ana that, she smiled, a slow, knowing smile that reached her eyes. We sat together on overturned buckets outside the repair shed, her hands smelling faintly of oil and sea salt. She passed me a cup of thick horchata instead of our usual tea, and we watched the sunset stain the water gold. We'd only just met, but it felt like I'd known her for years.

We also talked about what I'd seen that night after the party when Carlos took me back to *Windy*.

Ana knew more than I expected, about the aquarium in Mexico City, about the quiet corruption that floated beneath the surface like an oil slick. She told me how the men behind it had money, power, and no conscience. How one neighbor who'd started asking too many questions had disappeared, presumed dead. Her voice dropped low when she said it, as if the sea itself might be listening.

She had been quietly digging around and learned that several politicians had taken bribes from a multi million-aire who owned aquariums across Latin America. The man's newest obsession was rare marine life, dolphins, sharks, even sea turtles. Endangered species stolen from the wild, packed into crates, and shipped off to gleaming glass prisons to be displayed under artificial lights at his newest aquarium in Mexico City. The image made my stomach twist. I could almost hear the hollow click of a dolphin's sonar bouncing off the curved acrylic walls, confused, desperate, unanswered.

Ana and I talked for hours about how to stop it. Protests, petitions, press coverage, education, none of it fast enough to save the animals suffering right now. The weight of it pressed between us like a storm cloud, heavy and gray, until one of us said something about how clever dolphins were, and the mood shifted.

Sometimes we'd sit on the worn wooden benches of their tiny courtyard when we were on shore, sipping our cinnamon and peppermint teas. The bougainvillea climbed over the walls in a tangle of magenta blooms, and Ana's cat wove around our ankles like a silent witness. Charlie loved her, even letting the little cat curl up beside him when they napped in the sun. We talked about the small things, recipes, the way sea air curled our hair, but somehow the conversation always found its way back to animals. To empathy. To communication.

I told her more about my research, about Callie and Heidi. She listened as if she could picture them right there with us. I told her how Callie used to whistle differently depending on who entered the gate, and how Heidi once refused to participate in a test until the researcher she liked best returned. How I used to feel something almost telepathic when they looked at me, like we were meeting halfway between languages.

But even in those moments of connection, there was sadness. The pool was too small. The air too still. Sometimes at night, when the lab was quiet, I'd hear their faint whistles echoing off the concrete walls, soft, plaintive sounds that made my chest ache. Ana reached over and squeezed my hand when I said that. She didn't say anything, just nodded, her dark eyes reflecting the same grief I carried.

Mateo would laugh when he found us deep in conversation. "You two must be long-lost sisters," he'd say, shaking his head. Maybe he was right. There was something about Ana that felt familiar, the same quiet strength I used to feel from the dolphins when they surfaced beside me, eyes full of knowing.

By the time *Windy's* raw water pump parts finally arrived, Mateo had installed them, and I was preparing to leave Turtle Bay, I felt like I was leaving more than just a friend. It felt like leaving a little slice of home I hadn't realized I'd been missing. I never thought a breakdown could lead to something so beautiful.

We stood on the dock in the late afternoon light, the sea a sheet of molten silver behind her. The wind tugged at our hair as we hugged, and she pressed a folded piece of paper into my hand, a list of contacts, people who might help expose the trafficking ring. We both knew it would be slow going, a long-term project, but one we would carefully work through together.

"Keep me updated," she said. "And be careful." "I will. You too."

As the panga motored toward *Windy Possibilities,* Ana's figure grew smaller on the dock until she was just a silhouette against the sun. I looked out over the water, half expecting to see a dolphin surface beside me, just a brief shimmer of gray before slipping back beneath the waves.

A reminder that connection, once made, never really disappears. It just changes form.

Chapter Six

9° N latitude Panama Canal

Our first glimpse of the Panama Canal was stunning. Well, at first, it was just a hazy stretch of coastline and a cluster of faint vertical lines, but even from miles away, I knew I was looking at something monumental. Panama City shimmered in the distance, more skyscrapers than I ever expected to see in Central America. It looked almost like San Francisco, the glass towers catching the late afternoon sun, their reflections slicing the air in streaks of gold and silver.

And the Bridge of the Americas, wow. It rose across the skyline like a giant steel arch, its shadow stretching over the water, dwarfing everything else. Even from here, I could imagine the vibration of tires and the hum of traffic rippling through its cables.

As we sailed closer, the ocean changed color beneath us, from the deep sapphire of the Pacific to a murky greenish-brown, thick with sediment and streaks of oil. The closer we got, the louder everything became, horns blaring in long, low moans, engines churning, radios crackling with overlapping orders in English and Spanish. The air smelled of diesel, tinged with metal. It caught in the back of my throat, sharp and industrial.

After weeks of quiet ocean and sleepy harbor towns, the chaos felt almost violent. Every sound, every movement pressed in.

Charlie felt it too. He paced across the deck, nails clicking in quick, anxious rhythms. His tail was low, ears pinned back, his whole body tense as he glanced from the cranes to the massive tankers that loomed like moving apartment buildings. Every splash made him spin in a quick circle, uncertain where to look first.

"I know, buddy. It's a lot," I murmured, running my hand along his back. His fur was sun-warmed and salty, the familiar feel grounding me in the middle of the noise. "But we made it."

The sails came down, and I switched to the engine. The hum of it steadied me, something I could control. I was grateful, now more than ever, for an engine I trusted. Around us, the water churned with the wakes of enormous ships, their steel hulls glinting in the sun. *Windy Possibilities* seemed impossibly small among them, a single heartbeat in an iron sea.

We motored toward the Balboa Anchorage, weaving between tankers and yachts ten times our size. Their wakes rocked us gently but persistently, like the ocean reminding me to stay alert. I kept repeating the same thought: people take boats like mine through every day. Still, a thin thread of worry wound tight in my stomach.

This hadn't been the plan. I'd expected a seasoned all-female crew, each with years of Canal experience and fluent English. I had trusted that plan. But the plan had fallen through. Now, it would be a crew of unknown faces and uncertain skill. I'd have no control over who stepped on board tomorrow morning.

I exhaled and hugged Charlie, pressing my face into his fur. He smelled familiar, like Charlie, with a hint of salt, comforting, solid. His heart beat fast under my palm, but steady.

"It'll be okay, Charlie. We can do this."

He tilted his head, eyes meeting mine for a heartbeat, as if he understood, then resumed his nervous patrol of the deck.

By the time we reached the Anchorage, the sun was dipping low, turning the water to liquid bronze. The Bridge of the Americas framed the skyline, glowing orange as if lit from within. *Windy* swayed in the wake of a passing freighter, her mast creaking softly.

I'd always thought she was a large sailboat, but surrounded by these colossal ships, she felt like a toy in a bathtub. Their hulls towered so high I could barely see their decks, their engines thrumming through the water like the pulse of something alive and ancient.

There were a few polished luxury yachts nearby, their chrome railings gleaming, but mostly we were among container ships and tankers stacked with rainbow-colored boxes that looked almost cheerful in the evening light. The cranes moved with slow, mechanical grace, lifting, swinging, releasing, over and over, like the heartbeat of a city made of steel.

I tried to relax as I waited for the admeasurer. I'd read every rule, checked every safety item twice. *Windy* was ready, Mateo had made sure of it. Ana had helped me double-check my paperwork before I left Turtle Bay. Still, my stomach wouldn't unclench. If the admeasurer found even one thing out of place, he could delay or cancel my crossing altogether.

Charlie finally settled beside me, his body warm against the deck, ears flicking at every sound. I ran my fingers through his fur as I watched the harbor shimmer in the dying light. The air smelled of diesel and oil, but beneath it came faint whiffs of something sweet from the city, maybe fruit from the market: bananas, mangoes, papayas. That small reminder of life beyond the steel and noise made me smile.

For a moment, I let myself breathe. We'd come so far. We were here.

Then the radio crackled. A launch was approaching.

The admeasurer's boat nudged up beside *Windy*, the diesel rumble vibrating through the hull. "Permission to come aboard?"

"Permission granted," I said, relieved he'd asked. Few things irritated me more than someone stepping on board without invitation.

"I'm Captain Torres. I'll be inspecting your boat for crossing." He was short and broad, wearing a spotless white uniform, his expression stern and impassive. Charlie sniffed him, tail wagging tentatively, but Torres didn't even glance down.

"*Mucho gusto, buenas tardes,*" I said, trying to sound confident.

He frowned. "I speak English. There's no need for you to attempt Spanish."

The words landed like a slap. I bit the inside of my cheek and nodded. "Understood."

He moved briskly, testing cleats, inspecting the head, pulling out a tape measure to check dimensions. I stood quietly, hands clasped behind my back, resisting the urge to hover. The whole time, I could hear the faint squeal of cranes and the distant crash of containers meeting steel.

Finally, I handed him the completed forms and check.

"Everything is in order. You'll need to hire a Canal Advisor, three line handlers, and rent lines and buoys, yes?"

"Yes. Is there any way I can request crew who speak some English?" I asked, hopeful.

"No. That's impossible."

"I understand."

"Your crew will board at 0600. Your crossing begins at 0800."

"Thank you, Captain."

Without another word, he stepped off and vanished into the hum of the harbor.

As his boat pulled away, I let out a breath I hadn't realized I was holding. Charlie yawned loudly beside me, as if echoing my relief.

"Well," I said, rubbing his ears, "that went... fine. Let's hope our crew is a little friendlier than him."

Charlie's tail thumped once against the deck.

The light was fading fast now, the air thick and heavy with heat and diesel, but under it all was a flicker of excitement, the feeling that, ready or not, we were about to cross from one ocean to another.

****

I was awake at 4:30 the next morning without an alarm, excitement and nerves coursing through me like a slow electric current. Today was the day we'd cross the Panama Canal. I didn't love the idea of strangers on *Windy*, she'd always been my safe space, my world, but it was a necessity. No one transited the Canal solo.

I tiptoed into the galley, careful not to wake Charlie. The air was thick and warm even before dawn, carrying that faint, metallic tang of diesel from the harbor. I started the kettle for peppermint tea and sat at the little galley table, the hum of the generator and the occasional slap of water against the hull the only sounds in the stillness.

A moment later, I heard the click of toenails on wood. Charlie padded out of the berth, shook himself, and leaned his solid weight against my legs.

"Morning, bud. Sorry I woke you. Want breakfast now or a little later?"

He looked up at me and put a paw on my knee, his usual vote for now.

"Okay, now it is," I said, smiling. I filled his bowl, the dry food clinking softly as the kettle began to whistle. Steam fogged the porthole for a heartbeat before vanishing into the warm air.

I made my tea, grabbed some yogurt and berries, and we headed up to the deck to watch the sunrise over the Canal. The horizon glowed pink and gold behind a line of anchored ships, their hulls etched in silhouette. A few seabirds wheeled and cried above the quiet harbor.

Charlie walked over to his soundboard, pressed two buttons with his paw: HAPPY MORNING.

"Yeah, Charlie, it's a nice morning, isn't it?" I said, stroking his head. "Let's hope the rest of the day goes as smoothly as this."

At 5:45, a small boat pulled alongside *Windy*. The outboard's growl broke the morning calm as four men prepared to board.

First came Juan, our Canal Advisor. He was short and wiry, probably in his late forties or early fifties, with sharp eyes that missed nothing. He'd be captaining my boat through the locks today. The thought made my stomach tighten. I wasn't used to giving up control of *Windy*, but I knew enough about the Canal to understand that I needed him.

Charlie sniffed at him, decided he wasn't particularly interesting, and went back to watching the sunrise.

Next was Javier, tall and lean, maybe early twenties, with a baby face that made him look sixteen. Charlie gave his pockets a suspiciously thorough sniff, and I half wondered if the kid was hiding snacks.

Then came Luis, a stockier man in his thirties with a warm smile and eyes that crinkled kindly. He reached down to pat Charlie's head, but Charlie danced just out of reach. I smiled. He always took a little time to decide if someone was worthy of affection.

The last to board was Gabriel, mid to late twenties, tall, muscular, and carrying himself with the relaxed ease of someone who'd spent his life around boats. Charlie trotted right up to him, pressed his shoulder into Gabriel's shins, and leaned in hard, giving what I called a "Charlie hug."

Gabriel laughed, a low, warm sound that rolled like a wave over the deck. For no good reason, the sound made me smile too. Charlie wagged his tail against his legs, his body language loose, trusting, like he'd already decided Gabriel was safe. I wasn't sure what bothered me more—that Charlie trusted him so quickly, or that part of me wanted to.

"Charlie, come here now," I called.

Charlie looked back toward Gabriel but, after a brief pause, trotted obediently toward me. His nails clicked against the deck as he came, tail wagging in slow, uncertain sweeps. I didn't want him getting underfoot or annoying the crew, though I couldn't quite understand what he was doing in the first place. He was usually slow to warm up to strangers. Still, Gabriel didn't seem to mind. He looked down at Charlie with a grin that softened the sharp lines of his face.

In my best Spanish, I introduced myself to the Advisor and crew, welcoming them aboard *Windy Possibilities*. Juan, the Advisor, would be with us for the day and then head home that evening; the three crew members, Gabriel, Javier, and Luis, would stay aboard through the full crossing, sleeping in the second cabin that night on Gatún Lake.

Juan wasted no time settling into his role as captain for the day. His voice was calm, authoritative, the kind of tone that automatically made everyone pay attention. He explained how we'd rig the heavy lines and buoys, how to move in and out of each lock, and how to catch and secure the "monkey's fist" lines thrown from the linemen stationed high above on the canal walls.

I nodded along, trying to absorb every detail while my heart thudded faster than I wanted it to. I'd read about this process, watched videos late at night in my cabin, but seeing it about to happen, knowing it was my boat in those videos now, made the reality sink in. Those monkey's fist knots were about the size of small apples, packed tight and weighted to help the linemen throw them farther. According to YouTube, they could knock someone out cold if you weren't careful. I swallowed hard, hoping I looked calmer than I felt.

I exhaled, flexing my fingers like I was bracing for impact.

Then I felt Charlie press into my shins, his warm weight steadying me like an anchor. I reached down and rubbed the top of his head.

"That's better, Charlie," I murmured. "Come give me your hugs, not that random new guy."

He leaned harder, sighing in that deep, contented way only dogs can. Around us, the early light shimmered on the water, and I tried to hold on to that little pocket of calm before everything started moving.

"I've got it, Rie!" Gabriel called as the monkey's fist sailed just over my head, narrowly missing my skull before landing neatly in his hand.

My chest seized. Not fear, but something sharper, more intimate. The deck tilted, just a fraction, and for a heartbeat I couldn't remember where I was or why my hands were shaking.

Rie.

No one had called me that in years. Not since my dad.

Heat rushed behind my eyes, fast and unwelcome. I tasted salt and iron and had the sudden, overwhelming urge to fold in on myself right there on the deck, to disappear into the familiar shape of grief I thought I'd outgrown.

But I couldn't. Not here. Not now. *Windy* needed me upright, not unraveling over a single word from another life.

I blinked hard, trying to focus on the task at hand, but my voice came out sharper than I meant. "Gabriel, my name is Marie. Or Dr. Mercer. Never call me that again." I heard the edge in my voice and didn't soften it. "I expect respect on my boat and will not tolerate anything less."

The words hit the air like thrown stones. Gabriel froze, then lifted both hands in mock surrender. "Wow. Okay. Sorry."

Wait, he spoke English?

Juan and the other crew exchanged wide-eyed looks. They might not have understood every word, but they didn't need to. Tone alone said enough. Even Charlie sensed the tension. He slunk between us, tail low, eyes soft, as if he wanted to smooth it all over.

"Ugh, don't make me feel bad, Charlie," I muttered, rubbing my temple.

Rie. The name echoed again in my mind, gentle and warm, the way Dad used to say it. He always said it with this quiet joy, as if the world itself softened for him in that moment. No one else had ever called me that. No one else could.

They probably thought I was overreacting, but it didn't matter. They'd be gone in two days, and I'd never see them again. Still, the word clung to me like salt on my skin.

I brooded as we moved through the first lock, trying to shake the sting of memory. But Charlie kept wandering toward Gabriel, tail wagging, looking up at him like an old friend. And Gabriel, to his credit, met every bit of that attention with easy patience.

Eventually, I couldn't help it. I let the edge slip from my thoughts. He hadn't meant anything by it. How could he have known? And honestly, having at least one crew member who spoke English was a small relief, even if his timing and word choice was terrible.

By the time we cleared the Miraflores locks, my pulse had settled. The afternoon sun hit the concrete walls, and the water shimmered as it rose beneath us, lifting *Windy* in a slow, surreal ascent. Watching those massive gates creak open felt like stepping into another world, a heavy, mechanical breath releasing us onward.

It was almost cinematic, the way the old iron doors parted and sunlight poured through the gap. For a moment, I just watched the water swirl and thought about how tiny we were in this system of steel and tide.

How strange it was that a single word could unravel me more completely than any late night of data crunching and disappointment back in grad school.

Chapter Seven

9° N latitude Panama Canal

I watched from the bow as Charlie grabbed a ball, took it over to Gabriel, and then danced toward his sound board. He pawed at the words: PLAY CHARLIE PLAY BALL.

Gabriel froze, his body stiff with surprise. "Wow, you're a talking dog! That's impressive, Charlie. You want to play ball?"

Charlie tossed the ball lightly into the air toward Gabriel. He caught it, laughing, and threw it back. The ball bounced once, skittered across the deck, and Charlie tore after it, nails clicking on the teakwood, tail wagging so hard his back end wobbled.

I smiled, watching him race back and forth, the late morning sun glinting off the canal water in a shimmer of dull gold. I loved seeing him so happy, but I couldn't quite figure out why he liked this stranger so much. Charlie was usually more cautious.

As we motored through the brown, murky water of Miraflores Lake toward the Pedro Miguel locks, I walked over to where Gabriel and Charlie were still playing. The hum of the engine vibrated through my feet.

"He likes you," I said simply.

Gabriel grinned, giving Charlie another toss of the ball. "He's a really cool dog. How did you teach him to talk?"

I smiled. "I have a PhD in animal communication, but long before that, I knew a dog trainer who introduced me to buttons like Charlie's. She believed dogs behaved better when they could express how they felt. She and Charlie inspired my whole line of research. So yeah, I think he's really cool too."

I could still remember the first time Charlie said LOVE YOU.

He'd been learning his buttons for months, slowly building from simple words like OUTSIDE and BALL to phrases that strung together meaning in a way that felt almost human. That night, we were in the living room, the rain soft against the windows, the smell of wet earth drifting in. I was exhausted from studying for midterms my senior year in undergrad. My head ached, my tea had gone cold, and I'd snapped at him earlier for pawing at my notes.

Charlie had gone quiet then, lying on the rug near the soundboard, his fur dark and still damp from our earlier walk. After a few minutes, he got up, stretched, and pressed one button: LOVE YOU. Then another: MARIE.

It wasn't perfect, the timing was off, his paw hit the edge of the MARIE button twice, but the words came through, clear enough that I froze.

My throat went tight. I sank to my knees beside him, buried my hands in his warm fur, and whispered, "I love you too, Charlie."

He leaned his weight into me, that familiar heavy warmth against my chest, it didn't matter that he was a dog and I was a human. For that moment, it felt like he understood me better than most people ever had.

My dog told me he loved me.

Gabriel threw the ball again, and Charlie bounded after it, panting happily, bringing me out of my memories.

"They told me it was impossible to get crew members who spoke English," I said, the unspoken question hanging between us.

Gabriel shrugged. "I'm from California. Not sure why they don't list English on the roster forms. Maybe because I haven't been here long, just about nine months. And I'm Gabe. No one calls me Gabriel except when I'm working with new crew. And you're Marie or Dr. Mercer," he said with a wink.

"Yeah, sorry about that. I might have overreacted a bit." Wait, why was I apologizing? I wasn't sorry. I barely knew this guy. I was acting like Charlie, being way too friendly for no good reason. Still... it was nice to have someone to talk to.

He held out his hand. I hesitated for a heartbeat, then shook it. His hand was warm and steady. He smiled and brushed his hair away from his forehead. Something inside me, that tight knot from earlier, loosened just a little.

We motored through the Pedro Miguel locks like a well-oiled machine. The crew moved with practiced ease, ropes coiling and releasing in rhythm, voices calling out in both Spanish and English over the echo of rushing water. It felt like a dance we'd rehearsed a hundred times. Juan handled *Windy* like he'd known her for years.

Even I was starting to feel comfortable, catching the monkey fists cleanly, tying them off with quick confidence. We were laughing now, and Luis was teaching me jokes in Spanish. I was fairly certain I was saying things I shouldn't repeat, but who cared?

Charlie had made friends with everyone, especially after realizing that Javier really did have dog treats in his pockets.

"*Para mi perrito*," Javier said with a grin, handing Charlie another treat meant for his own dog.

Windy Possibilities hummed forward through the canal, and for the first time all day, the whole boat felt light.

The final Pedro Miguel lock doors groaned open, and we eased into Gatún Lake. The lake stretched out before me, its surface a patchwork of greenish-brown murkiness that shimmered faintly in the afternoon sun. Thick walls of vibrant green vegetation pressed close along the shorelines, a wild tangle of tropical trees, vines, and palms so dense it looked impenetrable. The water's edge seemed to swallow the land whole.

Despite the constant hum of traffic through the canal, here the water was calm and still, broken only by the occasional ripple of a distant boat. Only a few vessels dotted the horizon; most passed straight through to the Gatún Locks, skipping an overnight stay on the lake. I'd chosen otherwise, wanting a break between long stretches of work and eager to soak in this mysterious place. After the mechanical clatter and tension of the locks, the natural silence here was almost overwhelming.

Until the monkeys screamed, sharp, raucous calls that echoed through the trees, bouncing off the water like nature's own alarm clock. Birds twittered and darted through the canopy, their songs weaving with the deep, rhythmic croaks of unseen frogs hidden among the foliage. The noise wasn't silence. It was a vibrant, living soundtrack, utterly different from the metal clangs and diesel growls of the canal and city.

Charlie stretched out on the deck, his heavy body melting into the warmth of the wood as he let out a slow, contented sigh. His ears flicked at every sound, the monkeys' chatter, the splash of fish, the rustle of leaves. And his tail thumped a lazy rhythm against the deck. The tension that had been knotted tight in his muscles began to unwind. Around him, the crew relaxed too, their faces softening as they leaned against the rails, eyes drifting over the lush shoreline or scanning the vast lake.

I took a deep breath, the humid air filling my lungs with the scent of wet earth and fresh greenery. The slight tang of algae and moss floated faintly on the breeze, mingling with the distant sweetness of tropical flowers. I let the breath out slowly, feeling the tightness in my chest ease just a bit.

"It feels good, doesn't it?" Gabe said beside me, his voice low and easy.

"It really does," I replied, letting myself truly believe it.

I started the grill up on the deck and went down to the galley to grab ground beef, corn on the cob, and a few other essentials for a late lunch. The small space filled with the the faint sweetness of corn husks. Ana had told me once that cooking for your crew was good practice, a way to show appreciation and keep morale up. She was right. I felt grateful; today had actually been...fun.

I'd been so nervous about the last-minute crew change, but these guys were easygoing, competent, and, surprisingly kind. The tension I'd been holding onto since leaving Panama City had loosened with each successful lock, each shared joke. I could almost let myself enjoy it.

By the time I made it back to the deck, the air was heavy with humidity and the faint tang of lake water. I shaped the burger patties and dropped them onto the hot grill. The sizzle was instantly satisfying, followed by the smoky smell curling into the air, mingling with the warm, earthy scent of the rainforest. Charlie thumped his tail lazily against the deck, nose twitching at the smell of meat.

Gabe appeared beside me, wiping his hands on a rag. "Where are you headed after the Canal, Dr. Mercer?"

"Cozumel," I said, flipping the burgers. "I'm starting a job there."

He looked startled, meeting my eyes sharply. "Cozumel, really?"

"Yes, really," I said, smiling a little at his reaction. "Is that hard to believe?"

"Only because that's my next destination," he said. "I'm heading to Cozumel to divemaster."

"You scuba dive?"

"Yeah, since I was a kid. My grandpa taught me." He paused, then looked at me with sudden earnestness. "Listen, I know you don't really know me, but I'd be willing to pay and work as a deckhand for the rest of your trip to Cozumel if you'd give me a ride."

For a second, I just stared at him. It would be nice, having company for the long sail, an extra set of hands for the rougher stretches. But then the thought slammed into me like cold water: this was how women got hurt. Or worse. Absolutely not.

"Let me think about it," I heard myself say.

I am a total idiot. What was I thinking?

We all sat down to lunch on the deck, too captivated by the view to eat inside. The air was soft and heavy, carrying the scent of grilled corn, damp wood, and something faintly floral from the jungle. The sun shimmered across the surface of Gatún Lake, turning the water a deep greenish bronze that shifted and rippled with each passing breeze. All around us, the jungle pressed close, dense walls of tangled vines, giant-leaved trees, and flashes of color from orchids and bromeliads clinging to their branches.

In the distance, I could hear howler monkeys calling across the canopy, their guttural voices rolling like thunder. Birds flashed like streaks of color through the trees, brilliant blue, flashes of red, something white and graceful gliding low over the lake. It felt ancient, untouched. For a moment, I could almost imagine the whole world ending beyond this expanse of water, leaving us here alone in a wild green universe.

These guys might see Gatún Lake every week, I thought, but this might be my only chance. I wasn't going to waste a second of it.

I asked, "*¿Con qué frecuencia disfrutan del Lago Gatún?*" How often do you get to enjoy Gatún Lake? I expected them to say "often," or at least "every few days."

Luis answered first. "This is a rare treat. Many people are in a rush to transit, so we go straight through and do not stop to enjoy."

Juan nodded, his voice low and warm. "I have done this job for many years. This is the first time in months I will be spending the night on Gatún Lake. It's why I took this assignment. I wanted to see the lake at night again."

Gabe leaned back in his chair, balancing it on two legs as he looked out over the water. "I've been working the canal for almost a year, and this will only be my third overnight on Gatún Lake. I like it, but it's not as peaceful as you'd think. It's noisy with animals. I was sleeping on deck one time; it was like trying to rest in a jungle concert. It's nice that you've got bunk space for all of us on *Windy Possibilities*."

We ate in companionable silence after that, chewing slowly, gazes drifting out over the lake. The air shimmered in the heat, insects hummed lazily, and somewhere in the distance a splash echoed, something big slipping into the water.

Then, from near the soundboard, I heard: CHARLIE SWIM ?

He pressed the buttons carefully, his paw hesitated just a moment over question mark. Charlie had a question mark button for asking questions on his soundboard. He didn't always use it, mostly when he was uncertain or a little confused. My heart squeezed a little at how earnest he seemed.

I looked toward the lake, the dark, murky water, the quiet ripples moving toward the trees at the shoreline. I could almost see what he imagined: the two of us swimming side by side, the cool water washing away the heat of the day. But I'd read enough and seen enough to know better. I was pretty sure there were crocodiles in there.

"Charlie, we can't swim here. It's not safe," I said softly, walking over and scratching behind his ears. "We'll swim when we reach the Caribbean. The water there will be clear and warm, you'll love it."

He wagged his tail once, slow and thoughtful, then went back to watching the lake. I followed his gaze, the stillness of the moment sinking into me.

The crew was speaking rapidly in Spanish about Charlie talking. My Spanish was good, good enough that I usually followed conversations easily, but they were talking over one another, laughing, their excitement bubbling too fast for me to catch every word. I caught perro que habla, "talking dog," and inteligente. I smiled.

"He is a smart dog," I said.

Javier slowed down a little, his curiosity shining through. "Did you teach him to talk like that?"

"Yes, I did. When he was a puppy."

He grinned. "Then you are very smart too."

"Thank you," I said, though the words caught in my throat. I couldn't remember anyone ever saying I was smart for teaching Charlie. People were always amazed by him, not by the long hours I'd spent shaping his vocabulary, button by button, waiting for the moment he'd finally understand that words could mean things. Somehow, that simple compliment landed deeper than I expected.

The conversation flowed easily after that, shifting to the canal itself, the locks, the gates, the way the water rose and fell to lift entire ships through the isthmus. I followed most of it, nodding along, asking a question here and there. They spoke with pride, their words carrying the hum of history and admiration for the place. The air smelled faintly of algae and jungle, blending with the heat.

When Gabe began describing how the locks were engineered, the vocabulary grew faster, more technical. I lost the thread for a few moments until I heard *ingeniería oceánica*, ocean engineering, and looked up.

He spoke animatedly, hands moving as he explained some structural detail of the locks, something about pressure and flow, but I wasn't really listening anymore. An ocean engineer, working as a deckhand? That didn't add up. I watched him for a moment, the way the sun caught the side of his face, the easy way he fit among the crew.

I couldn't help wondering what story he wasn't telling.

Chapter Eight

9° N latitude Panama Canal

The night air on Gatún Lake was still and heavy, the kind of tropical quiet that presses against your skin and makes your thoughts feel louder than they should be. Charlie slept curled against my hip, his tiny snores lost beneath the distant croak of frogs and the soft lap of freshwater against *Windy's* hull. I lay awake, staring at the stars, foreign constellations I still didn't know, and somewhere between the ripples and the creaking lines, my mind slipped backward.

I must have been about seven when Mom came home from the shelter smelling like dog shampoo and sage hand soap, her volunteer scent. She dropped her purse by the door, sighed, and said, almost to herself, "I had a very interesting day."

That was Mom-speak for something emotional had happened.

"A man came in with his dog," she said, kneeling to untie her shoes. "Before he even spoke, he just... hugged her. Like he was holding himself together with both arms." She shook her head softly. "He looked up at the receptionist and said, 'I think I have to give up my dog.' And then he broke down."

I sat on the couch, legs swinging, trying to picture it. A grown man crying over a dog. I didn't yet understand how deep that kind of love runs.

"Teri told him there's a two-week wait for owner surrenders," Mom continued, "and he just... folded. So I brought him and his dog, her name is Lilly, into the quiet adoption room."

I remembered that room: the soft chairs, the little table with dog treats, the warm lamp that made even scared animals feel a little bit safer.

Mom's voice softened. "He sat down, patted his lap, and that big gray girl, sixty-five pounds of pure muscle, climbed right up like she was a Chihuahua. He held her and said, 'I have terminal liver cancer. They say I have three to six months.'" Mom swallowed. Even now, in memory, I could hear the hurt in her voice. "He said, 'She won't understand. She'll think I'm abandoning her.' And all I could think was... he's not wrong."

My chest tightened, recognizing now what I hadn't then: Mom had come home carrying someone else's heartbreak.

"So..." Mom said finally, looking squarely at Dad, "no pressure, David, but what do you think about taking in a big, one-year-old pit bull in the next few months?"

Dad smiled that crooked half-smile he only used when his heart was already made up. "We haven't had our own dog in awhile. I think it's about time." He added with a wink, "Her name doesn't fit our naming system, but we'll survive."

I shot upright. "Yes it does! John C. Lilly is a famous dolphin researcher!"

Mom and Dad shared that concerned parent glance, the one I learned much later meant: Is this the scientist who gave dolphins LSD? (He was. I didn't know that part then.) It was the beginning of my obsession with dolphin communication. My parents had no idea how far I would take it.

A few days later, Trevor, the man from the shelter, came for dinner with Lilly trotting beside him. She was beautiful, a storm-gray pit bull with golden-brown eyes and a tail that wagged so hard her whole butt swayed. Trevor told Mom, "She loves kids," and Mom gave me the nod.

We played fetch in the backyard until the sun dipped low behind the fence. Lilly always brought the ball straight back, fast and proud, like a pro athlete who lived for applause. Most of our foster dogs wandered off mid-game; Lilly never did. She locked onto me instantly, like she'd chosen me before we'd even adopted her.

For months, Trevor and Lilly visited often. The grown-ups talked softly in the living room, voices low, while I romped around the yard with Lilly, oblivious to the quiet grief unfolding only a room away. All I cared about was that Lilly was fun, gentle, and already felt like mine.

Then one afternoon, Mom came home with Lilly's leash looped around her wrist.

"Well, sweet girl," she told her, scratching behind her ears, "this is your home now."

I ran to hug Lilly, burying my face in her warm fur. "Hey, Mom, where's Trevor?"

Mom hesitated just a fraction. "Trevor won't be visiting anymore."

"Okay. Can I take Lilly out back?"

"Yes, sweetheart."

I didn't realize until years later what that conversation truly meant. At seven, all I knew was that Lilly was staying, and Trevor wasn't. My world was small and simple. Love was love, and Lilly was mine.

We'd missed having a dog on *Windy Possibilities*. Faraday, our yellow lab, had died when I was five. I remembered him only in snapshots. Mom always said foster dogs didn't need to learn the chaos of sailing, but Lilly? Lilly got a full tryout.

That first weekend, Dad said, "Let's see about your sea legs, Lilly." Mom even came, bundled in her warm coat. She pretended it was to help, but I think she wanted to witness Lilly's debut.

At the dock, Lilly hopped aboard with a curiosity so intense she practically hummed. She sniffed every inch, the cockpit cushions, the coils of line, Dad's toolbox, the teakwood steps. When Dad started the engine, her ears shot up. She froze, staring at the motor like it was a dragon waking from sleep, then tilted her head, offended and perplexed.

We burst out laughing.

Once we motored out to open water, Dad cut the engine. Lilly watched us uncover the mainsail and run the lines through the blocks. When the wind filled the canvas and *Windy* heeled just a little, Lilly stood tall, braced her paws wide, and lifted her face into the breeze with the biggest pit bull grin I'd ever seen.

Lilly was a born sailor.

Years later, after the crash, Lilly was my rock, the only family I really had left. She came to live with me at college as my emotional support dog. Mr. Cunningham, the counselor, was a friend of Dad's. He was the one who told me about the crash, and immediately did the paperwork for Lilly so she was allowed everywhere on campus, even the cafeteria.

Then, one cold November morning, my senior year, Lilly didn't get up for breakfast.

That alone was wrong. Even at fifteen, even with white fur softening her dark gray muzzle and a slower gait, Lilly never missed breakfast. I called her name down the hallway. Nothing. For a moment I told myself she was burrowed in blankets, avoiding the early chill that had crept into the townhouse overnight.

But when I walked into my bedroom and saw her curled in her dog bed, I knew. Before she even looked up at me, I knew.

Her eyes, those warm, honey-brown eyes that had watched over every version of me, were wide with pain and confusion. She tried to lift her head and couldn't. When I reached to help her stand, she let out a sound I had never heard from her before. A raw, startled yowl that cut straight through me.

"Oh, baby... I'm sorry. I'm so sorry."

My breath spun out of control. I was shaking, crying, trying to be gentle but terrified of hurting her. Lilly, even then, even in agony, licked my hand once. Trying to calm me. Because that's who she was.

My roommates helped me slide a piece of cardboard under her, turning it into a makeshift stretcher.

I carried Lilly to the car, whispering to her the whole time, telling her she was okay, even though we both knew she wasn't. I drove like the world was ending. When I pulled into the parking lot, I couldn't move. I just sat there with the engine ticking, the heater blowing lukewarm air, my hand reaching back to stroke her soft gray fur. Lilly's breaths were short and shallow.

I pressed my forehead to the steering wheel and the truth hit me like a physical weight: I was not going to leave with her.

For years, I had kept her safe, through the plane crash, through the grief that hollowed me out. She had been the steady heartbeat beside me when everything else in my life shattered. But I couldn't protect her from this. I couldn't stop time.

"Lilly," I whispered, turning to her, "I love you. I love you more than anything. You're the best girl in the world."

My voice cracked, but she blinked slowly at me, trusting me the way she always had.

Two techs came and gently helped me lift Lilly out of the backseat. I walked beside them, one hand on her fur the whole way, like letting go even for a second would break me open.

In the exam room, everything smelled like bleach, cold tile and endings. They brought towels, laid her down softly. I sat on the floor with her head in my lap, the same way she had always rested her head when she comforted me, and stroked her ears, whispering every good memory I could think of. I wanted her last moments to be a blanket of love she could sink into.

The vet came in quietly. Her face said everything before her words did.

"I'm so sorry, Marie. It's liver cancer. Her organs are shutting down. We can't stop it. The kindest thing we can do is help her pass."

I nodded. I don't know how I did, but I did.

I leaned over Lilly, burying my face in the warm curve of her neck. "You've done everything for me," I whispered through tears. "You can rest now, sweet girl. I love you so much. You're such a good dog."

Her breathing slowed. Then stilled.

And even now, years later, floating on a lake in the middle of Panama, I could feel the warmth of her fur beneath my hands. Even now, with Charlie asleep at my side, I still missed Lilly desperately.

Then I remembered the dream. I still remember every detail, every feeling as if it had happened yesterday, even after almost six years.

I felt Lilly pressed into my side.

For a blissful second, I didn't question it. The warmth of her body, the steady pressure of her ribs rising and falling, it was so familiar, so right. I rolled toward her, burying my hand in the soft gray fur of her shoulder.

"Please take me to the shelter with you today?" she asked.

Her voice was calm, gentle, exactly how I'd always imagined it might sound, and somehow not startling at all, as if my dreaming mind had been waiting for this moment.

"Of course," I said. "Should we eat breakfast first?"

"Yes, please."

We sat at the small kitchen table, Lilly crunching her kibble while I ate. Morning light slid through the windows in golden streaks that felt warmer, softer, not quite real.

"Why do you want to go to the shelter?" I asked. "You know some of the dogs there are sick and sad."

Lilly lifted her head, her eyes impossibly deep. "I have something to show you."

We were walking down a hill toward the marina, though it wasn't any marina I knew, the colors were too bright, the shadows too soft. *Windy Possibilities* waited at the dock like she'd been summoned. I tied her to a tree—a tree—because of course that made sense in this dream logic world.

We sailed down the river, the Mississippi, but somehow, not quite the Mississippi. Mist curled low over the water, glimmering like it held stars inside it. Lilly sat beside me at the helm, ears pricked forward, watching the banks slide past.

When we reached the shelter, everything felt both familiar and strange. The hallway stretched too long, the doors slightly out of place. Lilly led me, purposeful, steady, into a room I didn't recognize. The air shimmered, warm and humming.

Inside was a rolling incubator holding newborn puppies, barely hours old. Tiny bodies, pink bellies, impossibly small paws kneading the air.

Lilly stood on her hind legs, peering inside. She touched one tiny pup with her paw, impossibly gentle.

"This one," she said. "He's meant to be your dog."

She turned to me then, and her eyes locked onto mine with an intensity that made everything else fall silent. Something tugged at my awareness, pulling me upward.

"Lilly... wait," I cried as the room blurred, colors smearing like wet paint. "Please!"

She held my gaze until the last possible moment, and then...

I woke with a gasp, arms wrapped around a pillow instead of her warm body.

Gray morning light filtered into my real bedroom. No *Windy Possibilities*. No talking dog. Just the ache of missing her so deeply it felt like an empty room inside my chest.

Lilly had visited me in dreams before, running alongside me, curled at my feet, but she had never spoken. Never shown me something so specific. So vivid.

As I dressed, I wondered, ridiculous as it seemed, if I would ever actually meet the puppy from the dream. If

Lilly would come to me again. If dreams could be more than memories.

I drove the usual fifteen minutes to the shelter, wishing for a moment that it really was just over the hill and that I really could tie *Windy Possibilities* to a tree.

Dreams bend the world into shapes that feel impossible and true at the same time.

I walked through the shelter's front door, and before I could even sign in, two volunteers rushed toward me.

"Marie! Come with us," one said breathlessly. "A dog came in last night. You need to see her puppies."

Something in my chest fluttered, a warm echo of Lilly's voice: I have something to show you.

I knew the moment I looked into the incubator.

These were the puppies from my dream, the same tiny bodies, the same little pink paws kneading the air. Déjà vu hit so hard I had to grip the edge of the rolling cart to steady myself. A dog had been brought in the night before, malnourished and half-frozen, in labor. She'd held on just long enough to deliver her puppies, then slipped away before morning.

I didn't tell anyone about the dream. I'd just lost Lilly, telling the staff she had led me to this puppy would've sounded unhinged. So I placed my hand gently on the same puppy Lilly had touched in the dream and said, as casually as I could manage:

"I'll foster this one."

I named the tiny chocolate-colored puppy Charles Darwin. The name was far too big for something that fit in the cup of my palm, but Lilly had shown him to me. He would grow into it.

My roommates fell in love instantly, cooing over him as he wriggled like a little brown bean in the blanket I'd wrapped him in. He was still too small to bark or cause trouble. All he did was sleep, squeak, and curl into my neck like he was trying to become part of me.

A few days later, I took him to my appointment with Mr. C, the counselor. Charlie slept tucked inside my jacket, warm against my chest.

Mr. C frowned the moment he noticed the puppy. "Marie, you can't keep that dog in campus housing."

"Yes, I can," I said. "He's my emotional support animal. You already approved the paperwork."

"Lilly was a special case," he said gently, folding his hands. "But this is an abandoned neonate. Not an ESA. This isn't sustainable. When you move for grad school, you'll have to give him up."

His words hit like ice water down my spine, the same cold, helpless fear I had felt the day Lilly died. Something in me hardened.

"I am never giving him up," I said, standing so quickly, the chair scraped the floor.

I left before he could answer, holding Charlie tighter as hot tears burned behind my eyes.

The next days blurred into a loop of alarms every two hours, tiny bottles warmed under the faucet, and stumbling half-asleep through my senior-year assignments. I was exhausted, stretched thin, emotionally frayed. Raising a newborn anything was hard, doing it while grieving and finishing college was nearly impossible. But every time Charlie finished his bottle and pressed his warm little face into my hand, something in me steadied. Something healed.

I didn't know how I'd make it work when I moved to California. I didn't know how I'd manage the next week. But I knew one thing with absolute certainty: I would never give up this puppy.

I blinked back into the present, the dream-memories dissolving like mist. The hum of *Windy's* battery fan replaced the newborn squeaks of Charlie, and the soft lap of Gatún Lake brushed the hull.

It was almost four a.m. I lay in bed, Charlie pressed against my side, wondering how a whole lifetime of love could rise so sharply in the dark.

Chapter Nine

9° N latitude Panama Canal

"Your degree is in ocean engineering? But you're working as a deckhand on the Panama Canal? And you want to get a ride with me to Cozumel to work as a Divemaster? Are you running from the cops or something?"

Gabe laughed quietly, the sound low and warm in the little galley, and for some reason I thought he'd have a nice singing voice. What a weird thing to think.

It was just after four in the morning, still dark except for the small yellow glow of a single light above the counter. The world outside was hushed, broken only by the distant call of a howler monkey echoing across the water and the soft slap of waves against *Windy's* hull. The air smelled faintly of wet earth and jungle, overlaid with the sharper, bitter-smooth scent of fresh coffee. I don't like drinking it, but I've always liked the smell. It was the first thing I noticed when I woke.

He was already sitting at the small table, shoulders relaxed, hands curved around his mug. I made myself peppermint tea, the steam warming my face in the chill predawn air, and slid into the bench across from him. Charlie flopped onto the floor between us, immediately snoring softly, his paws twitching like he was chasing something in a dream.

Gabe was in a chatty mood. He told me about growing up in California, summers with his grandparents in Mexico, and said that's where he learned Spanish. As he spoke, I noticed little things: how he leaned forward when he got excited, how he brushed his thumb absently over the handle of his mug, how his eyes caught the light when he smiled.

"I went into ocean engineering thinking I could build things to help the environment, make the ocean cleaner and better," he said, voice lowering a little. He looked down at his coffee then, the sparkle dimming. "But I found that ocean engineering is only about exploiting the ocean for money, and I hated everything about it." He shifted back in his seat, one hand raking through his dark hair before he rolled his shoulders, like he was trying to shake something off. Then he glanced up again, and just like that, the warmth was back in his eyes.

"So here I am. I love working on boats. I love being near the water, meeting different people. People who are crossing the canal are always interesting." He winked, the corner of his mouth curving up. "How do a woman and her dog end up sailing through the canal to Cozumel for a job?"

I watched him take another sip of coffee, steady and unhurried. I still didn't know if I trusted him, but he was growing on me. And that degree in ocean engineering? That could be an opportunity for the sound buttons.

I began telling him my story, not my entire story, just the part about the dolphins and communication.

"Like I said before, I work in animal communication, specifically dolphin communication. I'll be the lead researcher, the only one, really. So I'll be able to run the program. I'll have all the time with the dolphins I want, which is pretty much my dream come true."

As I spoke, the boat shifted slightly under us, a gentle roll that made the spoons in the drying rack clink together. Outside, the lake was starting to wake up, an occasional fish splashed nearby, and the faint calls of parrots drifted from the jungle. Peppermint steam curled against my cheek, sharp in the cool morning air.

"In grad school," I continued, "I could only get a few hours a week to work with the dolphins because there were so many different researchers wanting time with them, so it was tough to make progress. So I'm super excited about this opportunity. My challenge is the technology. I have this device, but it's not waterproof enough. If I could make buttons and a board that could go underwater, it would be easier for the dolphins to use. I could snorkel or even scuba and talk to them for longer periods of time, ask more questions, and introduce more complex concepts. That could help progress my research faster and help me better understand the ways dolphins communicate."

Charlie let out a soft sigh on the floor, shifting in his sleep, his nails clicking faintly against the wood. Gabe leaned his elbows on the table as I spoke, chin resting lightly on one hand, the other circling his coffee mug, steam curling up between us. He had the kind of stillness that made you think he was actually listening, not just waiting for his turn to speak.

"My end goal," I said, lowering my voice a little, "is really to further John C. Lilly's work and help humans come to 'a time when all killing of whales and dolphins would cease, not from a law being passed, but from humans understanding that these are creatures with tremendous intelligence and enormous life force.'"

As I quoted John C. Lilly, I realized I was rambling and probably overwhelming him. My words felt big and heavy in the small galley. I mean, I could talk about my research for hours, but he didn't want to hear about it.

"So you had dolphins talking to you with word buttons like the ones Charlie uses?" he asked, his voice curious rather than skeptical. "Did they know as many words and talk as well as he does?"

He tilted his head slightly, dark hair falling across his forehead, eyes catching the faint glow of the galley light. Outside, the first hint of pink crept into the sky, brushing the treetops of the jungle.

Wow, he's actually interested! That's cool.

"Oh, they had about twenty words. Charlie has about thirty, and both the dolphins and Charlie understand more words than they have buttons for. Especially on *Windy*, it's hard to have a big soundboard. The buttons are always getting damaged from salt splash, so it's tough to keep them working well." I shifted my mug between my palms, steam curling under my chin as I spoke. Outside, something splashed, maybe a fish or a crocodile. I felt good about not letting Charlie swim in the lake. A bird trilled once, then fell silent.

"But I try really hard," I went on, "because Charlie loves using his buttons and being able to communicate with me more easily. It relieves a lot of frustration for both of us. He doesn't have to just bark at me. He can actually ask for what he wants. And you saw, when I explained to him that we can't go swimming in Lake Gatún? I think he understands. At least he seems to."

Charlie snuffled in his sleep, his paws twitching once as if he were dreaming of running. The galley light glinted off Gabe's coffee mug as he leaned back, the chair creaking softly under his weight.

"Your biggest challenge is making buttons like Charlie's that can be underwater in saltwater?" Gabe asked. His voice was still low, quiet enough not to wake the others, but curious, carrying a slight rasp from the coffee.

"Yes," I said, nodding. "I had a couple of different people working with me in grad school, but we just never got very far. So the sound board stayed at the surface, and the dolphins had to bring their heads out of the water to hit the buttons. It works, but it's not the easiest for them. I really think if the soundboard were underwater, their communication would be so much more natural."

Outside, the first gray of dawn was beginning to creep across the lake, soft light catching on the edges of the jungle trees. I noticed Gabe tracing a finger absentmindedly along the rim of his mug, his dark hair a little mussed from sleep, eyes bright despite the hour.

"What if I knew someone who might be able to help with that?" he said after a moment. "I promise I'm not trying to be weird about it. I'll still pay you for taking me to Cozumel. But this sounds like an interesting project. I'd love to be able to use my degree for something good, and I'd love to help you." He smiled, quick and almost shy.

Oh my god. Was I really going to take this guy I had known for two days with me all the way to Cozumel? I'd been sailing alone for over a month. Letting someone aboard felt riskier than that. A distant howler monkey's call rose from the tree line, low and echoing, like a warning, but then faded. Charlie shifted again and gave a little sigh, his tail thumping once against the floor. I trusted Charlie's judgment of character. He liked Gabe. And I wanted to know what he could do to help with my soundboard. He seemed genuinely interested in my research.

Charlie stirred, stretched with a grunt, then popped upright, suddenly wide awake. He sat up in front of me, perfectly still, eyes locked on mine like a statue. His ears were forward, his whole body humming with silent insistence.

"He wants his breakfast. He has some kind of inner alarm clock," I explained, sliding past Gabe to reach for the kibble. The faint rattle of the food in the scoop made Charlie's tail thump like a drum against the galley floor.

"He's a really cool dog. How old is he?" Gabe asked, watching as I poured the food into his bowl. The metallic clink of kibble against stainless steel filled the quiet.

"Yeah, I think he's really cool too." I smiled as Charlie dove into his bowl with gusto. "He'll be six in November."

"Have you had him since he was a puppy?" Gabe leaned back a little, cradling his coffee, his dark eyes curious in the dim galley light.

"I got him when he was two days old, when his stray mom froze to death in an ice storm." I hesitated, thinking about telling him the dream I'd had, when Lilly showed me Charlie before I met him, but I thought better of it. I had only ever shared that with my college roommates, and I'm pretty sure they thought I was crazy.

Instead, I went with the more tangible truth. "Having a newborn puppy who needed bottle-feeding every two hours while I was a senior in college was... beyond challenging." I gave a rueful laugh. "The only thing harder was having a twelve-week-old puppy I didn't know how to train."

Charlie finished eating, licked the bowl clean with an exaggerated scrape, then padded back to me. He flopped down and lay his heavy head on top of my feet with a satisfied sigh. His fur was warm against my skin, and I scratched behind his ear, feeling him melt into the touch. Definitely worth every sleepless night.

"He's not pure lab is he?" Gabe asked, looking at Charlie more closely. As he cocked his head to one side, studying Charlie, his dark hair fell over his forehead, almost to his eye. His eyes were the same dark brown color as Charlie's fur.

"No, I'm pretty sure he's a mix, but I'm not sure what. His mom looked like a full lab. No one ever saw Dad. People sometimes guess a pit bull mix, which would make sense since he's pretty muscular and super loyal. I think maybe some husky since he's fluffier than a lab and he howls sometimes. He likes to sing along with the radio. He likes Jimmy Buffett a lot." I shrugged. "I could do one of those genetic tests for him, but I never have."

The sun was beginning to shine into the galley now and I heard the rest of the crew waking up.

"I'll start some eggs. Looks like you made enough coffee for everyone, thanks. I think we should eat up on deck and enjoy the morning. I didn't realize we missed sunrise." I was disappointed to have missed sunrise on Gatún Lake, but I had enjoyed talking with Gabe. Time had passed more quickly than I'd realized.

"Want me to get some bacon going?"

"Trying to earn your keep already?"

"Just doing my part Dr. Mercer." He pulled bacon out of the small freezer and took it up to the grill on deck.

"Well Charlie, what do you think? I don't know why I'm asking you. You've already decided you love him. I don't know why, but I always trust your judgment." I sighed.

Chapter Ten

I sat alone at the galley table, the hum of the engine steady beneath my feet, remembering the early days with Charlie.

When Charlie was twelve weeks old, I knew I had to do something. He barked and howled incessantly every time I left him alone. The sharp, high-pitched yips echoed through the townhouse walls, frantic and fearful, as if he thought I had vanished forever. He shredded socks into confetti, and he stole whatever he could reach from my roommates' closets. Looking back, I couldn't believe I'd once thought Charlie was mentally unstable.

That might have been manageable, except one morning while I was brushing my teeth, I heard a sharp, panicked shout, "Charlie! No!" My stomach dropped. I bolted from the bathroom, toothbrush still in my mouth, foam dribbling down my chin, and found him with my room-mate's brand-new noise-canceling headphones clamped in his jaws. His eyes were wild with mischief, tail wagging furiously, like he'd just uncovered buried treasure.

I looked at my roommate. Her face was pale with fury, but she was calm enough to act. We knew what to do: she edged toward him from one side, me from the other, and we slowly backed him into a corner. My heart was pounding, my mouth still full of toothpaste, as I reached in. One hand grabbed his collar, the other wrestled the headphones from his stubborn little jaws. His puppy teeth scraped my fingers before my roommate finally helped me pry them loose.

"Sorry," I blurted, clutching the slimy, drool-covered headphones. "I'll replace them if they're damaged."

"It's fine." Her voice was tight, not fine at all.

I knew both of my roommates had had enough. Honestly, they'd already given me more grace than I deserved. They knew I had just lost Lilly, and that it hadn't been long since I'd lost my parents. They were sympathetic. But still, they shouldn't have to live with shredded socks and stolen belongings, or risk finding their electronics mangled by sharp little teeth. But sympathy didn't excuse chaos, and Charlie was chaos embodied.

And it wasn't just normal puppy chaos. Sometimes the look in his eyes when he chewed or barked had an edge of desperation, as if something inside him wasn't wired quite right. I couldn't stop worrying that he had some kind of disorder I didn't understand.

I knew a little about dog training. There was a trainer on staff at the shelter where my mom volunteered. Of course, having a trainer on staff costs money, and our little shelter in Rock Island couldn't afford such a luxury.

I googled dog trainers in the area. I'd never worked with one before; my parents had always trained our dogs themselves. I had an idea about the basics: Charlie should sit, stay, come when called, walk nicely on a leash, drop things when told. But knowing what he should do and actually teaching a frantic, sock-shredding, headphone-destroying puppy were two very different things. I didn't know how to get there with this crazy dog who seemed half wild.

I found a trainer named Laura, who ran a small business called Barks & Wags.

I pulled up to the address she'd given me and saw an open-air barn in her side yard. It was big. Big enough, I thought, that you could ride horses in it if you wanted. A corrugated metal roof covered the space, but there were no real walls, just a short fence of three wide wooden planks running around the sides, with gaps between each plank. The gate bore a large white sign painted in dark blue: Welcome to Barks & Wags.

I opened the car door.

Charlie exploded out, nearly dislocating my shoulder as he hit the ground in a gangly leap, paws scrabbling on the gravel. "Charlie! You have to be good!" My voice came out high-pitched, pleading. I looked around quickly. Laura must already be in the barn, thank goodness she hadn't seen that humiliating display.

I tried to walk him toward the barn. But Charlie's leash jerked tight as he lunged after a single brown leaf tumbling across the driveway. His whole body quivered with the effort of pursuit, like the leaf was the most interesting thing in the world.

If I thought getting him out of the car was bad, I hadn't seen anything yet.

The second I opened the gate and stepped inside the barn, Charlie saw the sawdust floor and completely lost it. His paws hit the ground and he launched into a frenzy: bouncing, spinning, barking at nothing, then flopping sideways onto the sawdust like he intended to wrestle it into submission. He rolled and kicked and scrambled, sending up tiny clouds of dust that made my throat scratch. His leash tangled around my wrist and yanked hard enough that I stumbled forward, mortified.

And then I saw her.

Laura stood just a few feet away, leaning casually against the fence rail, arms folded, watching the whole spectacle. She had clearly seen everything: the leaf chase, the meltdown in the sawdust, all of it. My face burned hot.

I was sure she was about to tell me that Charlie was not right mentally, that he was broken in some fundamental way and there was no hope of fixing him. I could already imagine her voice, calm but firm: This dog isn't trainable. You should think about giving him up.

I froze, holding the leash in both hands while Charlie spun and barked at invisible enemies. For a moment I couldn't move, couldn't even think. Then slowly, I looked up at Laura. My throat felt tight, my eyes prickled, and I tried so hard not to cry.

But Laura didn't look appalled. In fact, the corners of her mouth curved into something dangerously close to a smile. She stood there steady and calm in her worn jeans and dusty cowboy boots, like she had all the time in the world. The whole setup felt more like a horse arena than a dog training space, the wide, open air, the metal roof pinging softly as the morning sun warmed it, the tang of sawdust and hay hanging in the air. And Laura, with her easy confidence, looked more like she ought to be training colts than trying to tame my frantic puppy.

She stepped neatly around Charlie, who was still doing his best impression of a hurricane, spinning midair before plowing nose-first into the sawdust. Without missing a beat, she put out her hand to me. "Hi, I'm Laura. Looks like you've got a typical, happy, high-energy lab puppy on your hands."

"Hi..." I managed, though my voice cracked. "Typical?" I repeated, clinging to the word like a life raft.

Laura nodded with the kind of calm assurance that made me want to believe her instantly. "This is a brand-new and very interesting place for him. Let's let him explore, burn off some energy while we talk for a minute. Is it okay if I take off his lead?"

"Uh, sure," I said, then winced. "But he doesn't come back when called."

"That's okay," she replied lightly, as if that wasn't a red flag at all. She crouched, unclipped Charlie's lead, and in an instant he was gone; a brown streak at top speed. He tore wide arcs around the barn, sending little dust clouds into the air, then flopped to the ground only to roll himself into a fresh coat of sawdust like a sugar doughnut.

Laura leaned against the fence rail, completely unfazed, while my heart sank lower and lower. She said calmly that Charlie was very normal for a young lab puppy.

I heard the words, but it was like my brain short-circuited after normal. Not deranged. Not broken. Not a disaster. I felt my shoulders sag with such relief I almost cried right there in front of her. My puppy was not insane.

Laura spoke for another minute or two, but honestly, I barely caught a word. My head was still buzzing with relief, my palms damp from clutching the leash too tightly. Then, with an easy clap of her hands, she announced it was time to get Charlie.

I stared at her in disbelief. "Uh... how? We usually corner him at home." The wide-open barn stretched out around us like an escape artist's dream. Charlie was galloping laps like a racehorse, no end in sight.

But Laura didn't move to chase him. Instead, she walked over to a big wooden box by the fence, lifted the lid, and revealed a treasure trove of dog toys in every shape and color imaginable. The faint scent of rubber and slobber wafted up.

She glanced back at me with a little smile. "Does he have a favorite toy or game?"

I fumbled. "He... likes tennis balls, but he won't bring them back or drop them."

"That's okay," she said with the kind of certainty I didn't yet understand.

Charlie was at the other side of the barn sniffing something. Laura called "Charlie." When he looked up, she threw the ball. It landed halfway between us and Charlie. He ran toward it, grabbed it and took off running again.

I sighed, "Charlie"

"Run slowly away from him with me," she said. "And don't look back."

We ran away from Charlie. I didn't look back, but I could hear him running toward us. Laura tossed me another tennis ball.

"Offer him this one," she said, "but only throw it for him when he drops the first one."

I held out the new ball, to my complete and utter surprise, Charlie dropped the first ball. So I threw the other one. "Everything is a game to a puppy, so use that to your advantage. You have to be more fun than the distractions around you, that might mean people stare sometimes, but play is really the best way to bond with a dog. This time, show him the ball and hold it about chest level, and move it out, so it's directly above his nose."

As I did this, Charlie sat down. I smiled. I'd tried to teach Charlie to sit every day for a week, with no success. I had been using the exact same gesture. Why hadn't I thought to get his attention with a ball? I looked over at Laura, she smiled again.

"It's a great feeling, isn't it?" We talked more while throwing the ball for Charlie, one ball, then the other and he kept bringing them back. "This is really good, he's driven, so he'll be easy to train. You can use treats too, but in my experience, young dogs who are wound up sometimes do better with toys. The most important thing to remember is that you want to be the most fun game in his entire world. That will help you form a bond. Once you have a strong bond, he'll do anything for you."

I looked at Laura with shiny eyes. "My last dog Lilly..." I swallowed hard to hold back the tears. "I'd do anything to have a bond with Charlie like I did with Lilly, anything."

"Well, let's continue with some lessons once a week. I think you'll be pleased with how quickly Charlie progresses. He's lab," she said slowly, eyeing Charlie thoughtfully. "Do you know what he's mixed with? Pit bull, I'd guess. Both of those breeds tend to form powerful bonds with their people, so I think you and Charlie have potential here."

I was so happy to hear that my puppy wasn't actually insane and that we had potential that I threw my arms around Laura in a tight hug.

"Oh, thank you! We'll be back next week, and I promise I'll work with Charlie every day!"

As promised, I worked with Charlie every day. We both loved the training, and he progressed quickly. By May, Charlie was only seven months old, but he was already impressing everyone with his focus and obedience. Then one afternoon, Laura brought out something new: a small plastic mat with a row of bright, round buttons.

"They're programmed with words," she explained, setting it down on the floor. "Let's see what Charlie does with them."

The buttons were labeled in block letters: PLAY. ALL DONE. BALL. CHARLIE. MARIE. Each time his paw hit one, Laura's recorded voice spoke the word in a clear, tinny tone. At first, he flinched, confused by the sudden sound. But when Laura guided him to PLAY and tossed his favorite ball, something clicked. He already knew the words. Now he could make the sounds. His tail wagged furiously, and within minutes he was bouncing between

PLAY and BALL with a big grin, as if realizing the world had just given him a way to talk back.

It was thrilling, and a little strange. I could see the light in his eyes when he pressed MARIE and then looked straight at me, tail sweeping the sawdust on the floor. My name, from my dog. I laughed so hard I almost cried.

Laura thought of it as training, and maybe that's all it was for most people. But even then, I saw communication. I couldn't shake the bigger questions it raised. If Charlie could learn to communicate this way, what about other animals? What about dolphins? What if we could give them the tools to tell us what they were already thinking? I didn't know it then, but those simple word buttons would change everything about the course of my research and my life.

The memory faded as a faint splash sounded outside on Gatún Lake, maybe a fish, maybe just the water shifting against the hull. Charlie stirred in his sleep beside me, one paw twitching, as if chasing something in a dream. I reached down to rest my hand on his head, smiling. Whatever wild energy he'd had as a puppy, he'd turned it into something extraordinary. I got up to start the eggs for breakfast.

Chapter Eleven

13° N latitude off the coast of Nicaragua

I had to admit, it felt nice having another human on the boat. After the Canal, I'd expected to go back to just Charlie and me. Bringing Gabe along had been a total surprise. I still couldn't believe I'd agreed to it. But after three days at sea, he was growing on me in ways I hadn't expected. He was a good sailor, and I enjoyed his company. After weeks of talking mostly to Charlie and the sea, hearing another voice felt almost strange in the best possible way.

The morning was clear and impossibly blue, the horizon stretching in every direction like glass. Charlie and I jumped into the warm, pale Caribbean water, sunlight glinting off the ripples as we splashed down. The water wrapped around me, buoyant, soft, alive.

For the first time in a long time, I didn't have to worry about leaving *Windy* unattended. It felt absolutely luxurious knowing Gabe was aboard, keeping an eye on things. Charlie and I could swim as long and as far as we wanted without that anxious tug in my gut. I rolled onto my back, staring up at the sky so bright it almost hurt to look at, and let the waves cradle me. Charlie paddled a lazy circle around me, then barked sharply, sending droplets across my face.

"Okay, okay, I'm coming," I laughed, the sound echoing strangely over the open sea. The water was so clear it was like floating in the air. Schools of small silver fish shimmered below us, darting in synchronized bursts of movement. I could have stayed in that water forever, suspended between sky and sea.

But we did need to get moving. After about thirty minutes, I swam back toward *Windy's* stern, the gentle slap of water against the hull greeting me like a familiar heartbeat. Charlie clambered up the ladder first, dripping and proud, while I hauled myself up behind him.

Gabe was waiting on deck, holding out a towel like some kind of tropical concierge. His hair was wind-tousled, the sun reflecting off his sunglasses.

"I could get used to service like this," I said, wrapping the towel around me.

He winked. Again. Ugh, that wink. Why was he always doing that? And worse, why did it make me feel... off balance?

Charlie and I rinsed off with a quick splash from the solar shower, then Gabe and I got to work setting the sails. It was amazing how much faster it went with two people. He didn't know *Windy's* quirks yet, the way the jib sheets sometimes tangled or how the starboard winch handle stuck, but he clearly had sailing experience.

I watched from the helm as he hoisted the mainsail efficiently, using his back, not just his arms, exactly how Dad had taught me years ago. The wind filled the sail with a low, satisfying whump, and *Windy* leaned gently into her course.

I wondered why Gabe hadn't mentioned his sailing background during the canal crossing. It would have been a clear point in his favor for me to bring him along to Cozumel. Maybe he didn't want to pressure me too much.

As *Windy* settled into her stride, slicing through the turquoise water with a soft hiss, I felt that rare, quiet peace that only came from being exactly where I belonged, somewhere between sea and sky, wind and wave, trust and uncertainty.

Once we got underway, the rhythm of the open sea settled in. *Windy* cutting through the turquoise water, the mainsail taut and humming. The deck creaked softly beneath us, and every now and then a spray of salt mist caught the light like shattered glass. Charlie trotted from port to starboard, tail wagging, keeping an eye on flying fish that darted just out of reach.

We had time to think about Cozumel. I pulled out the binder I'd made with details on each of the dolphins Donna had told me about. The pages were smudged at the corners from overuse, the plastic sleeves warm against my sun-soaked fingers. I wanted to recognize and understand a little about each of them before I met them. Seven main dolphins came to the lagoon pretty much every day, and a few others came once in a while. Honestly, I already had every image and word of the binder memorized. But I loved looking at it. It was my reminder that soon I'd get to be with these dolphins in real life, hear their clicks and whistles in person, feel that spark of recognition when they turned an eye toward me. Just thinking about it made my heart lift a little higher than the horizon.

"Dr. Mercer, you busy?" Gabe asked lightly as he stepped over a coil of line and stopped beside me, blocking the sun from my binder. His shadow rippled across the page.

"You can call me Marie," I smiled up at him.

"This is about business," he said, one corner of his mouth twitching in a half-grin that didn't quite give itself away.

"What's up?"

"I'm working on the soundboard. I unpacked what you brought, just to get a look at it. I don't have all the tools I need to work on anything here on the boat, but I think I know what I need to do to waterproof it once we get to Cozumel. I'll have to buy a few tools and supplies, but if I can find everything I need, it should only take me a few weeks to make all the changes and have a prototype ready to test underwater."

The wind gusted, snapping the jib tighter. I pressed one hand on my binder to keep the pages from fluttering away. "Wow, that's awesome, Gabe!" I said, and I meant it.

The idea of finally having something that could bridge the gap, make it easy for the dolphins to use, and give me a chance at real, working communication, sent a rush of excitement through me. If this worked, it would be a game-changer. I was sure of it.

"So tell me about these dolphins," Gabe said, pointing to the binder in my lap.

"Oh, I can't wait to meet them! They're actually wild dolphins who choose to come to the research center every morning for a free meal in exchange for participating in some projects. I find it fascinating that they choose to come back every day. I made this binder to help me get familiar with the dolphins who show up most often. There are some who come less frequently, but these are the regulars. There's Tursi." I rolled my eyes. "The most unoriginal name ever."

"Tursiops truncatus, I get it," Gabe said.

I smiled. "Right, but Donna felt like she was the most interested in communicating with people, and she seems to be the leader of the—"

PLAY BALL, blared from Charlie's soundboard as he pranced over and dropped a soggy tennis ball squarely in Gabe's lap.

Gabe laughed, wiping a splash of salt water from his shirt. "Well, who am I to argue with a talking dog?"

Charlie wagged so hard his whole body wobbled, tail thumping the deck like a metronome.

"Go play ball, I need to study anyway," I said, pretending to be absorbed in my binder. Truthfully, I was watching them, the easy way Gabe threw the ball, the arc of it against the bright blue sky, the joyful yips as Charlie leapt after it. Neither appeared to have a care in the world.

The sails billowed above us, murmuring as the wind shifted, and the steady creak of rigging blended with the rhythmic pulse of waves against *Windy's* hull. The sun glinted off the water in brilliant flashes that made me squint, and a faint trail of salt dried on my skin. The air smelled of ocean and something faintly metallic from the boat fittings.

I sighed, running my thumb absently over the edge of the binder. I'd lost too much in my life to ever feel quite that free.

But watching them, Gabe's easy grin, Charlie's unrestrained joy, something in my chest loosened, just a little. Maybe, somewhere between Panama and Cozumel, I could learn how to breathe again.

***

20° N latitude approaching Cozumel, Mexico

We'd been at sea two for weeks since the canal. The water began to change long before we could see the island itself. The deep blue of the open Caribbean softened into bands of turquoise and jade, a signal that the bottom was creeping closer.

Soon, the reef revealed itself, patches of coral heads scattered like islands beneath the surface, darker clusters teeming with life. Even from the deck, I could see fish flashing below, quick darts of silver, yellow, and electric blue. The colors were so vivid they almost looked artificial, as if someone had turned up the saturation on the world.

Cozumel rose slowly on the horizon, not as a looming landmass but as a sun-bleached ribbon. Flat, dry, edged with scrub and low palms. The reef, not the island itself, was its real treasure. It ran along the shoreline like a living wall, where waves tripped and broke in white ribbons over coral ridges.

The air grew hotter the closer we came, the wind heavy with salt and the faint mineral scent of limestone. The sunlight was so bright it painted everything in sharp relief, the sparkle on the water, the white caps flashing like scales, even the slow arc of a frigatebird soaring high above.

Looking at the clarity of the water, at how the sunlight reached all the way to the sand, it was easy to understand why the reefs here were legendary. If I hadn't been so eager to reach CIMC and meet the dolphins, I would've been tempted to anchor and dive.

Gabe clearly was tempted. He leaned over the side, watching the reef pass beneath us like a moving mural.

"Careful," I called. "You might fall in."

"You'd come back for me if I did, right?" He grinned, sunlight catching the edge of his jaw.

"You'll have plenty of time to dive soon enough. You'll be divemastering on these reefs every morning."

"Maybe," he said. "But I might need to wait a few weeks, make sure your soundboard's working properly underwater first. Don't want to leave you hanging without the right equipment."

He winked again. That wink. I didn't know what to do with it.

We hadn't talked about what would happen once we docked, whether he'd move into a room on shore, or if he was planning to stay aboard for a while longer. I wasn't opposed to the idea of him helping with the soundboard. I did need the expertise. But I also didn't need a roommate. Especially one who kept finding new excuses to wink at me.

Before I could answer, Charlie barked sharply, tail whipping in circles. He bounded to the bow, paws braced against the railing, his entire body quivering with excitement.

"What's up, buddy?" I followed his gaze over the bow, and froze.

A trio of dolphins had appeared off the starboard side, slicing through the water in perfect synchronization. One leapt, suspended in a moment of pure sunlight before crashing back into the sea with a joyous splash. Then another joined, and another, racing *Windy's* bow, cutting through the turquoise like living silver.

Charlie barked again, high and thrilled, his front paws dancing. One of the dolphins turned its head slightly, and for a heartbeat, it felt like they were looking right at him.

"They're welcoming us," Gabe said quietly, leaning on the rail beside me.

I couldn't speak. My throat tightened, not from salt air but from something deeper, recognition, awe, hope. I had dreamed of this moment for years. To see them here, so close to where I'd be working, it felt like a sign. Maybe everything—moving to California, all the hard work in grad school, *Windy's* breakdown, the delay in Turtle Bay—had brought me exactly where and when I needed to be.

The dolphins swam with us all the way toward the marina, weaving in and out of *Windy's* path, surfacing and diving again. Their whistles carried faintly through the air, mingling with the wind and the low hum of the engine.

As we neared land, they peeled away, vanishing beneath the water. Charlie whined softly, his ears drooping as the last tail fluke disappeared.

I crouched beside him, resting a hand on his back. "It's okay, buddy. We'll see them again soon."

The island stretched out ahead of us, white sand, palm trees, and the promise of a new beginning. The dolphins were gone for now, but I could still feel them, like an echo thrumming through the water, calling me forward.

Chapter Twelve

20° N latitude Cozumel, Mexico

The *Centro de Investigación Marina Cozumel* (Cozumel Marine Research Center)—CIMC—had its own pier, large enough for *Windy Possibilities* to dock. That's where we were headed.

I steered her carefully toward the concrete pier as the turquoise water turned shallower and clearer beneath us, sunlight flickering across the sand like molten glass. Gabe jumped easily onto the dock, line in hand, and looped it neatly around the heavy cleat. The soft thud of rope against metal echoed through the still air. I cut the motor. The silence that followed felt monumental. We had finally arrived.

"Hey Charlie, we made it! Can you believe it? We sailed all the way from Santa Cruz to Cozumel! That's pretty cool, buddy!" I grabbed his front paws and lifted them into a clumsy dance. His tongue lolled happily as he licked my cheek, tail wagging fast behind him. His breath smelled faintly of salt and kibble.

"That really is pretty cool," Gabe said, his tone filled with genuine pride.

"Thanks," I said, though I suddenly felt shy about it. The long miles, the repairs, the delay, it all hit me at once. The relief. The exhaustion. The fear I'd been too busy to feel until now.

"Okay," I said, shaking it off. "Let's go check this place out."

I expected a world-class research facility. Donna had told me about the CIMC in glowing detail. It was small but well-funded, with three full-time staff who loved their work and their dolphins. She'd spoken with particular warmth about Dr. Andrews, the center's director. I couldn't wait to meet him. He hadn't answered my recent messages, but I'd left word that I was on my way. I told myself he was just busy.

We crossed the pier, our footsteps echoing on the hot concrete. The afternoon sun shimmered off the white buildings clustered near the shoreline, low stucco walls, red tile roofs, all quiet except for the faint creak of palm fronds in the wind. The air smelled of seaweed and something metallic, old salt mixed with disuse.

Inside the main research lab, the silence deepened. My sandals stuck slightly to the tile floor. The lights were off, the air heavy and still. Dust clung to the countertops. I stepped forward, peering around at the empty workbenches, the stainless-steel sinks, the faint chemical tang of long-evaporated disinfectant.

"Gabe?" My voice sounded too loud in the quiet.

He pushed open a door and frowned. "The freezers are off."

I stopped in my tracks. "What?"

He motioned for me to look. The digital displays were dark. No hum of compressors. Just silence. My stomach twisted. In any lab, refrigeration was sacred.

"This place looks abandoned," Gabe said softly. "I thought you said there were three staff feeding the dolphins every day?"

"I thought there were," I said, hearing the unease in my own voice.

We exchanged a look. The weight of what wasn't happening here pressed in from every corner, the absence of sound, of people, of motion.

"What do you think we'll find in those freezers?" Gabe asked.

I swallowed hard. I didn't answer. I already knew.

None of it made sense. Just three months ago, I'd been hired to manage the research program. Donna told me things were running smoothly, no new grants recently, but steady progress. I'd promised Dr. Andrews that grant writing and funding would be my top priority. He'd seemed relieved, even excited.

So how could everything fall apart in such a short time?

I thought of my last conversation with Donna, how she'd sounded distracted, distant. I'd assumed it was just stress about relocating. Maybe it wasn't. Maybe something had been happening here all along. And Dr. Andrews' silence? The unanswered emails, the voicemails left at sea? I'd brushed them off then. But standing here, surrounded by unmoving air and dead machines, that quiet now felt ominous.

We went into the main office. Dust motes drifted in the slanting light from the half-open blinds, and the faint smell of stale coffee and paper filled the air. The room was tidy but still, as if someone had simply walked out one afternoon and never come back.

On the desk—my new desk—sat two envelopes. One was crisp and official-looking, addressed to me at my California address and stamped Return to Sender. The other was a single sheet of paper folded neatly in half, my name—Marie—written across the front in looping, careful handwriting.

I reached for the handwritten note first. The paper was soft from humidity, the ink slightly smudged at the edges. It was written in Spanish, so I handed it to Gabe to translate.

He read slowly, his voice steady:

"Dear Marie, I'm very sorry. The new owner is not a good person. He fired me. He says he does not care that no one will be here to feed the dolphins; they are wild, and they can hunt. He says he can't make money, so he's going to close the center. I told him you would bring in money, but he won't listen to me. I hope you can convince him. This is a special place. We cannot let him close it. Please call me when you get here. —Isabel"

I exhaled, the air catching in my chest. Isabel. Donna had told me about her, one of the caretakers, the kind who always arrived early and stayed late, who talked to the dolphins like family. The kind of person who couldn't just walk away.

I turned to the other letter, the official one. My stomach was already braced for bad news.

"Dear Dr. Mercer: This letter is to inform you of a change of ownership of the *Centro de Investigación Marina Cozumel* (CIMC). The center has been sold to Mr. Rafael Calderón, who will be taking over immediately. I apologize for the inconvenience. Your position remains secure..."

I stopped reading. Secure. Sure. Donna must have known, and maybe that explained her strange tone the last time we spoke. That mix of guilt and distance I couldn't quite place.

The pieces began fitting together. Dr. Andrews selling the center, Isabel being fired, unanswered messages. The silence made sense now, but that didn't make it better.

"I need to see how bad this is," I said. "We'll start with the lagoon."

Gabe nodded. "Let's go."

Outside, the air felt heavier, the tropical humidity wrapping around us like a damp blanket. The facility itself was heartbreakingly beautiful. Whitewashed walls gleamed in the sun; hibiscus bushes flared red and pink along the pathways. But beneath the beauty, there was neglect, grass overgrown at the edges, the faint creak of a gate swinging loose in the breeze.

We walked down the manicured sidewalk toward the main dock. The rhythmic crunch of our footsteps mingled with the distant hiss of waves breaking against the outer reef. Charlie trotted ahead, tail high, his paws padding lightly across the walkway. The dock stretched out before us, long wooden planks faded gray by salt and sun. I stepped down carefully, the boards warm beneath my bare feet. The lagoon spread wide and quiet, the water like greenish glass, rimmed with mangroves and coral rubble.

I stood there, staring out over the expanse where the dolphins had come every morning for the last five years. The air was thick with salt and the vegetal scent of algae.

Without the hum of boat engines or the familiar whistles of dolphins, the silence pressed hard against my chest.

I sighed. "Without food, who knows if they'll come back?"

Suddenly, I caught a flicker of movement in the water, a quick, silvery flash that vanished as fast as it appeared. I leaned over the edge of the dock, my breath catching. There it was again, closer this time, a sleek gray shape cutting effortlessly through the green-blue water. A dark, liquid eye broke the surface and locked directly onto mine. For an instant, everything—the heat, the salt air, even the sound of waves—fell away.

"Look at that," I breathed, a laugh of pure amazement slipping out. "I guess you're not all gone, are you?"

The dolphin lingered, her smooth head rising higher through the rippling surface, skin glistening like wet silk in the fading afternoon light. Her gaze was steady and unflinching, curious, intelligent. She turned her head slightly, studying me, then Gabe, then Charlie, each of us caught in her quiet orbit. A puff of air broke the silence as she exhaled, sending a spray of mist into the sunlight. The sudden sound startled us all, and we laughed.

"You're Tursi, aren't you?" I said softly. I would have recognized her anywhere, the lighter gray along her rostrum, the half-moon scar on her dorsal fin. I'd stared at her photos in my research binder for weeks. But nothing prepared me for the reality of her, the awareness in her eyes, the way she seemed to fill the space with presence alone. "I'm Marie," I said gently. "And this is Charlie... and Gabe."

"She's amazing," Gabe whispered, his voice hushed, almost reverent.

"She really is," I said, still watching her, unable to look away.

Charlie crept closer to the edge of the dock, his nose quivering with excitement. Tursi tilted her head, fixing her gaze on him, and began making a series of sharp, musical clicks that vibrated through the air like bubbles.

"Has Charlie ever met a dolphin before?" Gabe asked quietly.

"Yeah," I said, smiling at the memory. "During COVID, he came with me on feeding days at the university tanks. I didn't want to leave him alone for so many hours. Heidi and Callie adored him. At first, they were curious, but soon they started playing. They'd toss basketballs out of the tank, and he'd push them back with his nose. It became their favorite game."

As if she understood, Tursi gave a playful toss of her head, splashing water toward Charlie. He barked once, bright and surprised, then crouched in a play bow, front legs braced on the dock, tail waving high in the air.

I laughed and sank down beside him, letting my bare feet dangle into the cool water. "Tursi," I said softly, "have you ever met a dog before? I bet you haven't. But if you hang around, you can play with Charlie more."

She floated just below the surface, her eye flicking between us, listening.

"I'm sorry I don't have any fish for you right now," I said. "But I promise I'll get some tonight. If you're here in the morning, I'll have breakfast waiting. I'll make sure you have food for as long as I'm here."

I didn't know how much of my words she understood, but I hoped she could feel my meaning, the promise behind the sounds.

For a moment, she lingered, holding our gaze. Then she rolled gracefully onto her side, the sunlight sliding like liquid silver across her skin, before dipping below the surface and disappearing into the green depths. The ripples spread outward until the lagoon was motionless again. I sat there, water lapping softly against my calves, heart full and aching at once.

She was real. And she'd found us first.

The lagoon went still again, but I couldn't shake the feeling that Tursi's visit was more than chance. I stood, brushing the salt from my legs. Time to call Isabel. I had to understand what had happened, and how to fix it.

Chapter Thirteen

20° N latitude Cozumel, Mexico

Isabel offered to meet me at the center when I called her. She seemed as eager to talk as I was. She arrived about fifteen minutes later, carrying a small handheld cooler. She was shorter and younger than I expected, no more than twenty, with long dark hair pulled into a neat French braid. Her T-shirt was sun-faded and salt-stained at the edges, but her eyes were bright, determined, full of that fierce compassion I recognized instantly, the kind that belongs to people who love animals more than themselves.

I smiled, already knowing what was in the cooler. "Should we talk on the dock?" I asked in Spanish.

"Yes," she said, smiling back, her dark eyes twinkling. "I have only been here three times since Rafa fired me, but every time I bring fish for the dolphins. I want them to keep coming back."

Oh, I liked her already. A lot.

"I want them to keep coming back too," I said, returning her smile. "Where are you getting the fish?"

"My father is a fisherman. I only take a few, so he doesn't notice." She looked down, almost embarrassed, shifting the cooler in one hand.

"Well, I'll be happy to pay your father for fish so the dolphins can eat," I said gently. "And I plan to get some grant money very soon, so let's not worry about that."

Relief softened her face. She exhaled, shoulders dropping slightly.

"Can you tell me about Rafael Calderón?" I asked.

Her smile vanished. "He's... not a good man," she said carefully. "He says he loves dolphins, but he loves money more. He wanted to make the center into a show for tourists. When the government said no, he fired everyone. He said the dolphins are wild and can hunt. But I'm not sure they can hunt enough to survive anymore."

Her voice cracked on that last line. I felt a tightness in my chest.

"You've done a good thing, Isabel," I said softly. "You kept them alive and kept them wanting to come back. I'll take it from here, but I may need your help."

She nodded, blinking quickly. "You will have it. Always."

***

By the time I reached the Intercontinental Hotel that evening, the sun was sinking low over Cozumel's western horizon. The sky flamed coral and gold, and the air smelled of salt and sugar, ocean spray mingling with the caramel scent of grilled plantains from a street vendor outside. The hotel's glass doors whooshed open, spilling me into a world of polished marble and artificial cool.

I glanced down at myself, blue sundress, flip-flops, hair still wind-tangled from the boat, and immediately felt out of place among the linen suits and expensive perfume.

Rafael had agreed to meet to "discuss the center's future." On the phone, he'd been dismissive. "My dear, research like this is outdated. Surely you'll find a more lucrative career elsewhere."

So why buy a dolphin research center at all?

I didn't have to wonder long. He spotted me almost instantly and came striding across the polished floor, white linen suit crisp against tanned skin, an amber drink glinting in his hand. His smile was practiced, but his eyes were cold. Calculating.

"Good evening, Dr. Mercer," he said smoothly. "A pleasure to meet you."

I forced a polite smile. "Thank you for taking the time."

We sat in the plush lounge chairs, and he motioned for a waiter with a flick of his fingers. "What will you drink, Dr. Mercer?"

"Just water, please."

Rafael's brow lifted slightly, a look that said how quaint.

He leaned back, swirling his drink. "So, tell me, Doctor, what brings such passion to a doomed project?"

"I wouldn't call it doomed," I said evenly. "Just neglected."

He smirked. "Neglected? Perhaps. But I was tricked. The CIMC cannot be profitable. It is a money pit. I was not told the dolphins were wild. I did not know I could not have shows for tourists every day. Did you know the government forbids such things? Wild dolphins! What good are they if they cannot perform?"

I clenched my hands in my lap until my nails bit into my palms. I smiled instead of screaming.

"The point of a research center," I said evenly, "is not to make a profit, it's to make progress."

He laughed, sharp, humorless, already bored. "Progress doesn't pay for fish, *mi querida doctora*. And that ridiculous girl has been feeding those dolphins... what a waste."

The waiter brought my water. I took a slow sip to steady myself.

"What if there were other ways to make money?" I asked. "You own a respected facility, in one of the most biodiverse regions in the world. With the right grants and partnerships, the CIMC could easily support itself."

His eyes narrowed, interested. "Go on."

"I'm a strong grant writer," I said. "If you keep the center open for six months, fully operational, I can bring in the funds to cover its costs for at least two years, probably longer. Salaries, maintenance, dolphin care, everything. It just takes time."

He studied me for a long moment, then leaned forward. "You promise much, Dr. Mercer."

"I deliver much," I said.

A slow smile spread across his face, not reaching his eyes. "You have six months," he said like it was already over. "I expect a tight budget and measurable progress. And I will visit often to see that my investment is being... handled properly."

"Deal," I said, sounding more confident than I felt.

I stood, heart pounding with adrenaline. "Thank you for your time, Mr. Calderón."

He waved a dismissive hand. "Rafa, please. I insist."

I forced another smile. "Of course. Rafa."

Outside, the sun had finally slipped below the sea. The first stars pricked the deep violet sky, and the air buzzed with life, the hum of mopeds, the laughter of children, the rhythmic pulse of salsa drifting from a nearby bar. I drew in a long breath of the real world again, humid and alive, and felt something in me unclench.

I slipped into the line of taxis out front. The music from the bar spilled into the street, and without thinking, I moved a little to its rhythm, the smallest bounce in my step.

The night felt full of promise. Tomorrow, with a little luck, Isabel and her father would bring fish. And if I was very lucky, the dolphins would come back for breakfast.

Chapter Fourteen

20° N latitude Cozumel, Mexico

I was wide awake by 4:30 the next morning. I had to know if Isabel's dad had caught enough fish to supply the dolphins' breakfast. I texted her. She replied immediately, "He's not back yet, but that's a good sign," followed by a smiley face.

I took that as a good sign too and hopped out of bed, Charlie close behind, his nails clicking on the cabin floor. I threw on my usual swimsuit, shorts, and a soft T-shirt, then padded to the galley to make my peppermint tea and coffee for Gabe. The familiar scent of the tea grounded me a little. Gabe was planning to go to town today to look for a divemaster job and an apartment. He'd said he couldn't "take advantage of me" by living on *Windy* any longer. I'd wanted to argue, but I didn't. I knew he needed both a real place to live and a job. I would miss his company, having a person to talk with... even his winks. I hoped he'd still have time to help with the soundboard.

My mug warmed my hands as Charlie and I stepped off the boat and padded down the pier. The predawn air was thick and warm, the world hushed. A single star flickered over the mangroves, and the water in the dolphin lagoon looked like glass, inky dark, still, and endless. Even the mangrove leaves hung motionless, their reflections perfectly mirrored in the surface.

We sat on the edge of the dock, our feet and paws dangling just above the water. The wooden planks beneath me still held a trace of heat from the previous day, and the faint tang of salt and fish hung in the air. Somewhere offshore, a heron gave a low, croaking call.

I leaned into Charlie's shoulder, his fur cool and damp with the night air. "I hope I made the right decision bringing us here, Charlie," I whispered. My voice sounded too loud in the stillness. "I really do think the dolphins will come back, but if Isabel can't get us fish, if I can't get grants or make real progress, if Gabe can't get a fully waterproof soundboard..." I trailed off, staring into the black water that hid everything below. "It's a lot, Charlie. I didn't think it would be so much."

He pressed his head against my arm with a soft sigh, as if agreeing, or reminding me that we'd figure it out together.

"I wonder if Rafa will show up today," I said finally. "I hope he won't be difficult to work with."

The first hint of sunrise touched the horizon, turning the water silver and revealing ripples near the far edge of the lagoon. My heart caught. Maybe, just maybe, they'd come.

It was so quiet that I could hear a truck rumbling to a stop outside. My stomach flipped. Dare I hope? Who else would be here at 5:15 in the morning? The air was heavy with salt and humidity, cool against my bare arms.

Charlie's ears perked up, and his tail began to wag as if he already knew.

We walked out to the street and saw Isabel barreling out of the truck toward us, her braid bouncing, her smile wide enough to erase the dawn shadows. She crashed into me, giving me a huge hug that smelled faintly of sea spray and fish. "Seventy-five pounds of fish for us this morning!" she exclaimed, eyes bright.

"Awesome." I said, trying to match her enthusiasm, but my voice came out thinner than I wanted. Seventy-five pounds sounded like a lot, until I did the math again in my head. It was enough for today. Maybe tomorrow if I stretched it. It wouldn't last long. We didn't need to feed them entirely, but it had to be worth their time to keep coming back.

"You're amazing, Isabel! Let's get these fish inside and into the freezers." I hoped they wouldn't have time to freeze before the dolphins showed up. I needed them this morning, proof I hadn't made a colossal mistake moving here.

Isabel's dad climbed out of the driver's side of the truck. He looked older than he probably was, his skin deeply lined, the kind of tan that only years at sea could give. His hands, thick and scarred, looked like they could wrestle a marlin. "I am glad to sell you these herring," he said, his accent soft and musical. "We catch them almost every day, and they are not worth much. The dolphins and this center make my daughter so happy. It's a blessing to have you here, Dr. Mercer. We hope you will stay."

Something in his tone, steady, sincere, unraveled the tight knot in my chest. "Thank you so much, Mr. Gutiérrez." Maybe, just maybe, I could make this work.

After unloading all the fish, Isabel disappeared into the small break room just off the lab. The hum of the freezer mixed with the scent of salt, metal, and the sharp oiliness of herring. At the stainless steel counter, she filled the coffeemaker with water and dark grounds. "Coffee, Dr. Mercer?" she asked hopefully.

"Oh no, I don't drink coffee."

"What?" The horror on her face made me laugh.

"I've never liked it. I prefer peppermint tea."

"Well, I don't think we have any of that here," she said, rummaging through a cabinet full of mismatched mugs.

"I'll bring some over from *Windy*. I have tons of it."

"What's it like living on a sailboat?" she asked, eyes going dreamy, like she was picturing some romantic adventure novel instead of bilge pumps and salt-crusted rigging.

"Sometimes it's awesome," I said. "I've seen some of the best sunrises and sunsets in the world, but it's a lot of work too. On the way here, I had a mechanical issue and couldn't use my engine—" I froze. "Do you hear that?"

We both went silent. A faint, high-pitched whistle carried through the still air, followed by the slap of a tail against the water.

We ran out to the dock, forgetting about coffee and sailing, and Charlie bounded ahead, barking once before stopping short at the edge of the lagoon, his tail wagging furiously. The water rippled near the far side, the soft curve of a dorsal fin cutting through the dark surface like a promise.

They came.

It was still early, the lagoon gray and hazy in the pre-dawn light. A heavy stillness hung in the air, broken only by the gentle slap of tiny waves against the pilings. I could see a few ripples out in the lagoon, too wide and deliberate to be from the wind, and then slowly, a dorsal fin rose just above the surface, slicing through the gray water toward us.

Isabel gasped, then giggled, bouncing on the balls of her feet like she might lift right off the dock.

"Go fill a bucket with fish," I whispered, my voice barely a breath.

Charlie lay down beside me, head resting on his paws, his golden eyes locked on the fin gliding closer. My heart pounded in rhythm with the soft whoosh of water against the boards.

Tursi's sleek head broke the surface, her skin glistening in the dim light. She exhaled with a hollow puff, sending a fine mist into the cool air. "Good morning, Tursi," I murmured, my throat tightening. "Thank you for coming back."

I'd told myself I knew she would come, but I hadn't realized how much tension I'd been carrying until it dissolved all at once, the relief leaving me lightheaded. Her being here meant everything. Without her, all of this might have been for nothing.

Isabel came running back, breathless, a five-gallon bucket of herring swinging from her hand. She tossed one fish toward Tursi, who caught it midair in a graceful arc, barely rippling the surface. The toss seemed to break some invisible seal, suddenly the lagoon erupted with movement. Six more dorsal fins appeared, dark shapes spiraling closer, some moving fast in playful circles, others gliding steadily toward the dock.

"Tursi, did you bring them all?" I laughed. She answered with a cascade of clicks and squeals that rippled through the water like laughter. I didn't know what it meant yet, but I couldn't help smiling.

"Breakfast time!" Isabel called out joyously, waving a fish in the air like a flag.

A sleek gray head popped up in front of me, and a dark, mischievous eye met mine. Before I could react, a strong jet of water shot from his rostrum, drenching my shirt.

"What the—! I didn't even know dolphins could do that!" I sputtered, half laughing.

Isabel giggled. "That would be Jax. He's kind of a jerk."

"Jerk or prankster?"

"Is there a difference?"

"Sometimes," I said, grinning down at Jax, now twirling in tight circles and clicking triumphantly.

Tursi swam back to the dock, hovering just below the surface, waiting patiently. I crouched and gently placed three fish into her open mouth. She clicked again, her gaze flicking toward Charlie.

"I think she likes you, buddy." Charlie tilted his head, ears perked, panting softly but never breaking eye contact.

Around us, the lagoon came alive. Dolphins sliced through the surface, bodies gleaming silver in the growing light. Some arced high into the air, twisting before splashing down, others breached slowly, exhaling clouds of mist that caught the early sun like halos.

I tried to match each dorsal fin to the photos in my binder, but they moved too quickly, weaving and leaping, a blur of joy and motion.

When the fish ran out, three dolphins lingered. They swam in lazy circles, close to the dock, their eyes bright and expectant. "They want to interact," I said softly, mostly to myself.

I rummaged through a storage box at the end of the dock, uncovering a rainbow of faded plastic balls, ropes, and puzzle feeders. I chose two bright balls and a puzzle toy, tucking a small fish inside before snapping it closed.

Behind me, I could hear the dolphins' soft bursts of breath, the gentle slap of their tails against the water, and Isabel's quiet laughter. The lagoon felt alive.

I threw a red ball, the size of a basketball, into the water. A gray blur shot up beneath it. Then a dolphin leaped high into the air, sunlight catching the droplets that sprayed off his sleek skin like scattered diamonds. He landed with a splash that sent a mist over the dock.

"Is that Kai?" I asked Isabel.

"Whoa, this is great!" a voice called from behind me.

I turned to see Gabe walking down the dock, wearing blue board shorts instead of his usual flowered ones, and a crisp white T-shirt that made his skin glow warm in the morning light. His hair was combed and neatly parted at the side, a first since I'd met him.

"You look—"

"Presentable for once," he finished for me, grinning.

I'd wanted to say pretty, but guys didn't like being called that, did they? Handsome sounded too formal. Nice was probably safer. Jeez, had it really been that long since I'd thought a guy looked good?

"Good luck at the dive shops today," Isabel said brightly.

"Yes, good luck," I echoed, trying to sound enthusiastic, though I didn't want him to go just yet.

"Thanks, ladies, looks like you've got all the luck in Cozumel today. Look at those happy dolphins!"

Kai breached again, twisting midair, the red ball still clutched in his jaws.

"It's the best!" Isabel squealed, her voice almost musical.

"It really is," I agreed softly, eyes on the dolphins. "Now to build a new soundboard and introduce it."

"No pressure." Gabe winked.

I opened my mouth to explain, but he lifted a hand. "I know, I'm just kidding. But I do need to get going."

As he headed off toward the road, a soft smile tugged at my lips. I turned back to the lagoon.

Isabel was kneeling, peering into the clear water. "We have Kai jumping and Tursi here watching us. Who's the third one?"

She squinted, pointing toward a larger dolphin circling near the dock. "I think maybe Maris, she's bigger, and she likes people a lot."

I flipped open my mental notes from the binder. Maris, curious, playful, a quick problem-solver. She loved puzzles. Perfect. I tossed the puzzle toy with the fish inside into the water.

Maris darted forward and caught it neatly in her rostrum, then disappeared beneath the surface. A few seconds later, bubbles rose as she flung the toy around, turning it with her nose and teeth. She surfaced briefly, tossed it into the air, and dived to catch it again.

"She really loves that thing!" Isabel exclaimed, practically glowing.

"Have you seen her work it before?" I asked.

"No! Donna only ever gave them the really easy ones. I've never seen this one. It's way more complex."

"I hope she doesn't get too frustrated," I said, watching as Maris rolled onto her side, studying the toy like she was thinking it through. "I might get in and help her if she seems agitated."

"You're going to get in with them?" Isabel's voice was full of awe.

"Do you want to get in too?" I asked, catching the hopeful flicker in her eyes.

"Oh, could I? I never have before!"

"Never?"

She shook her head, her dark braid swinging. "No, I had the least seniority. I mostly cleaned and did prep work. I watched them every day, but I never got to be in the water with them."

"Well," I smiled, "let's change that right now."

I tugged off my shorts and T-shirt. The air was cool against my skin, the faint scent of salt and sun-warmed wood mixing in the morning stillness. Isabel hesitated, then pulled off her own shirt, revealing a sports bra.

"I'm not wearing a swimsuit," she admitted sheepishly.

"You won't make that mistake again," I grinned.

I slid into the water, the temperature wrapping around me like silk. Tiny ripples spread out, and I held still, not wanting to startle the dolphins. Isabel followed, in her shorts and sports bra, mimicking my quiet entry.

The water went quiet around us, glassy and alive. Then, Tursi glided in, slow and curious, her eye level with mine. Her breath broke the silence with a sudden, musical puff. The sound vibrated through my chest. Kai surfaced nearby, clicking softly, and Maris circled beneath us, the shimmer of her body like quicksilver in the light.

I could feel the energy in the water, intelligent, playful, almost sacred. I reached out instinctively, my fingertips brushing a swirl of bubbles where Maris had just been.

Charlie barked once from the dock, tail wagging furiously.

"I think they like us," Isabel whispered.

I nodded, still half in awe. "Yeah," I said softly. "I think they really do."

I swam toward Maris, who was holding the puzzle toy in her mouth and shaking it violently, sending tiny sprays of water across my face. "Hi there, Maris. Can I help you with that?" I held out my hand, a foot away from her mouth. She eyed me cautiously but didn't let go of the toy.

"You don't trust me yet, I get it. Why would you?" I thought back to training Charlie as a puppy years ago, remembering the patience it had taken to earn his trust.

I swam back to the dock and ran over to the toy box. I pulled out one of the easier puzzle toys Isabel had been talking about, slipped a small fish inside, and got back in the water. Maris's attention flickered immediately to what I held in my hand.

"Would you like to trade?" I asked her gently. She clicked and whistled, a quick, sharp sequence, and Tursi swam over, clicking back to her. Maris dropped the first puzzle toy and took the easier one from my hand. Isabel swooped in to catch the difficult puzzle before it sank to the bottom of the lagoon.

Maris worked on the easier puzzle, rolling sections with her nose and rostrum until the fish popped out. She squealed and clicked triumphantly. "Great job, Maris!" Isabel and I cheered, and even Charlie barked from the dock, his tail wagging like a metronome.

I reset the latch on the difficult puzzle to make it easier, remembering the similar one Heidi had mastered in grad school. I handed it back to Maris. She eyed me suspiciously.

"Just try it," I said softly.

She nudged, twisted, and finally, with a small triumphant squeal, opened it. Water droplets sparkled in the morning light as she tossed the puzzle slightly before bringing it back to the dock.

We celebrated quietly, Isabel, Tursi, Maris, and I, united in our shared thrill. Even Charlie seemed to grin, sitting on the dock with his tongue lolling out.

Next, it was time for the first soundboard. I decided to start simple with highly motivating objects. I recorded my voice on two buttons, BALL and PUZZLE, and velcroed them onto a two-by-three-foot plywood board. I rested it just above the water's edge on the dock.

I pressed BALL and threw Kai's ball into the lagoon. He shot after it like a torpedo. I pressed the button again as he grabbed it.

"Does he notice the board?" Isabel asked.

"It'll take a few tries," I replied.

Next, I hit the PUZZLE button and tossed the easy puzzle to Maris. She grabbed it, solved it, and swam back to us, glancing curiously at the soundboard.

"Or maybe Maris will notice it right away," I observed.

"She's so smart! Do you think she'll hit a button today?" Isabel asked.

"Probably not today. It takes time to teach them what the buttons mean." I placed another fish in the complex puzzle, pressed PUZZLE, and threw it toward Maris. She swam off to work it out.

While Kai and Maris were busy, Tursi approached the board. Her head cleared the water, glistening droplets catching the light, and Charlie sniffed at her from the dock.

"He likes her? He's not scared?" Isabel whispered.

"Nope, he's used to dolphins," I said.

Tursi nudged the PUZZLE button with her rostrum. My voice burst from the board. Tursi startled, swimming a few yards away. I'd tossed the easy puzzle near her head the same moment she hit the button. It was clear she was exploring, figuring out what the board could do. She didn't understand the words yet, but she was curious.

She picked up the puzzle, swam to the dock, and dropped it into a net. Her gaze returned to the board, slow and deliberate. Again, she pressed PUZZLE and looked at me. I quickly handed her the toy. She let out a squeal, tossing it back into the net.

Her attention sharpened. "Isabel, grab a couple more balls!" I urged. I hit the BALL button. Isabel threw a ball toward her. Tursi shot after it, tossed it high into the air, and tapped it back with her rostrum toward Isabel.

"Impressive," I whispered, heart racing. "I think Tursi likes to interact." I didn't want to project meaning where there might be none, but this felt like more. This was far beyond what I could have hoped for on day one.

Chapter Fifteen

20° N latitude Cozumel, Mexico

Concrete words like Ball, Fish, Jump, Play, and even names like Tursi, Marie, and Charlie were proving surprisingly easy to teach. Each dolphin had their favorite words, mostly tied to preferred activities, and watching them learn was like seeing a puzzle slowly click into place. But Tursi... she was different. Her favorite activity seemed to be communicating itself. Every new button I introduced caught her attention immediately. She leaned in, nosing the board with curiosity, her clicks and squeals bouncing back at me from the water. She was quickly becoming my star pupil, and I couldn't wait for Gabe to finish the new underwater soundboard so we could take our lessons even deeper.

Isla was sweet but shy, always hovering at the edges of the lagoon until another dolphin was near. After almost two weeks, she was the only one who hadn't come to the dock to check out Charlie. I worried she might be afraid of him. I'd coaxed her to warm up to me with fish, my soft praise, and gentle guidance. Of course, FISH had been the first button she learned. Any time Charlie wasn't at the dock and Isla was nearby, I led her to the soundboard, pressed the FISH button, and handed her a reward. It felt subtle, but after a few repetitions, Isla swam to the board, lifted her rostrum above the water, and pressed FISH herself. I tried not to get too excited, but inside, I was celebrating. Even shy Isla was communicating. Even she was part of the magic.

Jax, on the other hand, remained a challenge. He wasn't cruel, but mischievous—a trickster who seemed intent on testing every limit. He rarely interacted with the soundboard, and toys held little interest for him. Instead, he splashed and darted through the lagoon, sometimes nudging other dolphins off their game. Watching him was like managing a class clown, and many days left me feeling exasperated. Yet he never challenged Tursi. Occasionally, I could entice him to hit a button, FISH or PLAY, and for a moment, that mischief turned into participation.

Charlie was an unexpected star for the dolphins. Every dolphin seemed intrigued by him, save for shy Isla and playful Jax, who delighted in teasing him. Luma, however, was transfixed. Every time Charlie was on the dock, her eye followed him, her body moving in slow, careful circles just below the water's surface, as if she were memorizing his every move. The sight of a dog and dolphin sharing curiosity, two entirely different species connecting, was almost too magical to believe.

By the end of those first two weeks, I could feel the rhythm of the lagoon: the clicks, whistles, and splashes mingling with Charlie's panting and the soft slap of fish hitting water. Every interaction carried a little victory, every button pressed a tiny triumph. And through it all,

I felt a deep, growing wonder, a sense that the dolphins were not just learning, but choosing to connect with us, on their own terms.

Of course, no one enjoyed the work more than Charlie. He'd taken it upon himself to become our self-appointed dolphin ambassador.

But one afternoon was extra special. Charlie padded onto the dock, toenails clicking against the boards, tail swishing like a metronome gone wild. He stopped at the edge, head cocked, ears perked, and let out a low woof as if to say, Well? Where's my dolphin?

Right on cue, Luma surfaced in a spray of silver droplets, clicking and whistling in a flurry of excitement. She hovered just below the dock, craning her head up at him. Charlie's tail wagged so hard his whole back end wiggled, and then, before I could stop him, he plunged straight in with a big brown splash.

I gasped. "Charlie! You're supposed to wait for me!" But he was already paddling toward Luma, water sheeting off his shiny coat.

Luma circled him instantly, her movements tight and playful. She darted ahead of his paddling paws, then swam back under his belly, brushing him just enough to make him spin in the water, confused and delighted all at once. Charlie barked through a mouthful of seawater, a garbled, joyful sound that made Luma whistle back so loudly it echoed against the dock.

Then something happened I hadn't seen before. Luma slowed down. She rose right up beside Charlie, keeping pace with his doggy-paddle, her dorsal fin cutting the surface only inches from his shoulder. Charlie stopped paddling so hard, just floated, his big brown head bobbing as he panted. Luma nudged him gently with her rostrum, almost like she was steering him.

For a moment, they just drifted together, side by side, my goofy, waterlogged dog and this sleek, wild dolphin, moving as if they were meant to be a pair. Charlie's tail wagged under the surface, sending little ripples across the water. Luma whistled softly, then rolled to show her pale belly right in front of him. Charlie barked again, softer this time, and pawed at the water as if to reach for her.

I stood there with my mask in hand, completely forgetting to get in the water. My throat tightened. This wasn't just play. This was... something else. Affection, recognition, maybe even a kind of love.

When Charlie finally dog-paddled back toward the dock, shaking himself off in a shower that drenched me completely, Luma followed and hovered near the ladder. She stayed there, watching him with a steady, intent gaze, as though waiting for him to come back.

"Guess you've got a girlfriend now, Charlie," I murmured, scratching behind his ears. His tongue lolled out happily, but his eyes were fixed on the water, on her.

Before I could say anything else, Luma darted toward the soundboard. My heart skipped. Luma only used the soundboard when I prompted her. But now, she went straight for it, her sleek body twisting to line her rostrum up with the buttons: CHARLIE.

Charlie's ears pricked at the sound of his name. He barked once and trotted over to the edge of the dock, tail thumping against the boards.

Luma pressed again: CHARLIE PLAY.

I froze. "Did you hear that, buddy? She asked for you."

Charlie let out a high-pitched, eager bark, the one he usually reserved for tennis balls. His whole body vibrated with excitement, and I swear if he had words, he would've said, Yes! Yes! Let's go right now!

Luma chirped and pressed: CHARLIE one more time. Then she floated just below the surface, eye-to-eye with him.

I pressed a hand to my mouth. This wasn't data I could dismiss as coincidence. This was intent, preference even. And it wasn't just about toys or food or puzzles. It was about connection.

I leaned down to Charlie. "You realize you just became a research subject, right? You and Luma..." My voice trailed off as I watched them staring at each other. His amber eyes, her dark, liquid gaze. A dog and a dolphin, telling each other something I didn't quite understand.

For once, I wasn't the translator. I was just the witness. Moments like this were pure magic, the kind that made the rest of the world fall away.

But the magic didn't erase reality.

It wasn't all sunshine, saltwater, and dolphins learning new words. Behind every playful morning was a long afternoon hunched over my laptop in the dim office, the air heavy and still, the hum of the old AC unit cycling on and off like it was trying its best but barely hanging on. I scoured grant databases until my eyes went fuzzy, searching for anything, any program, foundation, endowment that might keep CIMC alive long enough for real progress to happen.

Every deadline felt like a countdown. Every application felt like a lifeline. Because Rafa had made one thing painfully clear: if I didn't bring in grant money, he would shut the center down.

The pressure sat on my shoulders like something solid and cold. I loved the dolphins, but they weren't captive. They came because they chose to. If CIMC closed, they would probably survive in the wild, but the chance for connection, learning, communication... that would vanish. And the people here, the future, the discoveries, the potential, would disappear with it. Isabel would lose this job she loved. Gabe's soundboard project would be pointless.

Most afternoons, when the office heat became unbearable, I'd haul my computer back to *Windy*. I'd sit at the small table with papers spread everywhere, the boat rocking gently as darkness began to settle over the lagoon. Charlie would curl at my feet, occasionally sighing in the way only a dog who had swum with dolphins all morning could manage. From *Windy's* porthole, I could see the glow of Cozumel's waterfront, bars and clubs lit up like someone had sprinkled neon across the island. I couldn't hear the music from this far, but the lights flickered like distant promises of a life I wasn't living.

Instead, I had grant templates, budget sheets, and a blinking cursor mocking me.

Gabe had a sixth sense for when I needed a break. Even after he started his divemaster job, he still drifted back to CIMC most afternoons, talking excitedly about the morning's dives or the lesson he'd taught or the turtle he'd spotted. Then he'd switch seamlessly into soundboard talk, what parts had arrived, which components he was waterproofing next, the new housing he was building.

Sometimes he brought dinner from town, warm tortillas wrapped in paper, smoky grilled chicken, the scent of lime lingering in the cabin long after he left. I'd set my laptop aside and listen, grateful for a few minutes of easy conversation that didn't involve academic jargon or the fate of an entire research center. Those moments were becoming the quiet edges of my day, unexpected pockets of comfort I found myself looking forward to.

But once he headed back to shore, I'd reopen the laptop. Because the truth was simple: if I didn't write these grants, if I didn't succeed, the CIMC would close. The dolphins would still be out there, living their wild, free lives, but everything we'd begun to build would crumble before it had even started.

So I kept writing. And revising. And hoping.

Because connection was worth fighting for. And I wasn't going to let this place slip away without a damn good fight.

Chapter Sixteen

20° N latitude Cozumel, Mexico

Rafa didn't show up that first morning. In fact, we didn't see him for the next three weeks. He communicated by email and once in a while by text. He expected me to run the center per his instructions and on his new "restricted budget." But he wasn't around to enforce it. Part of me didn't know how to feel about that. Every few days, I'd catch myself wondering: Was it good that he stayed away? Did it mean he didn't care? Or was he planning to shut the center down without saying a word?

The uncertainty sat in my chest like a weight, refusing to budge.

The island didn't make the situation any easier. Almost everywhere Gabe went on his dive boat, he seemed to overhear something.

"That new *dueño* at the dolphin place... *cuidadito.*"

"He's bad news."

"Trouble follows him, always."

Every time he told me, my stomach twisted. Rumors on small islands spread like spilled oil, messy, impossible to contain, and usually rooted in something true.

I talked with Ana about Rafa regularly, asking her if she could find anything on Rafael Calderón. I kept hearing rumors he was bad news, but nothing concrete ever surfaced. Ana hadn't found anything. I felt guilty for not doing enough to find out more about the animal trafficking, but Ana insisted that I needed to worry about funding my center first. I knew she was right, but I wished I had time to do everything.

Still, the dolphins were coming in. Tursi, Solana, Kai, Luma, Jax, Maris, even shy Isla. I had a job to do. So I focused on them.

The soundboard sat perched at the edge of the dock. The buttons were getting sprayed with saltwater, and I was having to replace them every few days. I couldn't wait for Gabe to finish the new waterproof soundboard. I had twelve buttons on this board, and all of the dolphins were using at least some of them. Tursi was using all twelve buttons.

I was crouched by the water, encouraging Luma to come over, when Tursi dove underwater and swam out to the middle of the lagoon. I looked around, but didn't see anything that might have startled her. From the corner of my eye, I saw Charlie. He had been lounging happily in the sun, but now he was standing stiff at attention. Then I heard it. Rafa's voice echoed from the entrance. My stomach sank.

He strolled over, his sunglasses hiding whatever expression was on his face. He stood closer to me than felt comfortable, close enough that I could smell his cologne, and watched me. He made me uneasy, but I didn't want to show it. I tried to continue working with the dolphins.

Tursi surfaced near the dock, clicked, and slapped the water. I tapped PLAY. The board squawked out my robotic voice: PLAY. Isabel tossed her a ball. Tursi nudged it right back to me.

"Dr. Mercer, how is our experiment?" he asked. His tone landed somewhere between amusement and impatience.

"Did you see Tursi?" I asked, trying to keep the defensiveness out of my voice. "She's making connections. She hears the word, links it to the action. It's rudimentary, but it's a start."

Rafa folded his arms, watching for a moment. His lips twitched into what might have been a smile, or a smirk.

"So the animal presses a button, gets a fish." He shook his head. "You think this will bring in grants? Real funding? Tourists don't want science projects; they want tricks. Leaping through hoops. Kisses for the niños."

"It's not just a trick," I said quickly. "It's language. Communication."

But Rafa was already turning back toward the office. "Language, communication..." he waved a hand. "Maybe someday. For now, don't waste too much time on toys. Focus on keeping the lights on."

Tursi clicked again, softer this time, almost like she knew he was dismissing her. I pressed HELLO on the board, and the speaker squawked the word back at her. Tursi whistled, lifting her head high, as if determined to prove herself anyway.

Rafa didn't bother looking back.

I stood there, one hand still resting on the soundboard, my chest tight. Maybe to him it was just a toy. But to me, it was the beginning of something extraordinary.

Later that afternoon, the other dolphins circled the lagoon lazily, their dorsal fins slicing through the turquoise water like slow-moving shadows. Sunlight danced across the ripples, turning everything silver and gold. The air was thick with salt and the faint, sweet rot of seaweed. I worked with Maris on her puzzle, watching her careful precision as she fitted the shapes together with her rostrum.

When Rafa came out of the office, Jax squealed sharply and darted toward the soundboard, shoving Maris out of his way in a blur of white foam. I barely had time to react before he spun at the surface, tail fluke slapping down with a loud crack that sent a wall of water straight over the dock.

Cold seawater hit me full in the face. The soundboard was completely drenched. A couple of the buttons let out tiny squeaks and one even sparked a little. Rafa stood there, soaked, his shirt plastered to his chest. His expression hardened, irritation breaking through whatever mask he'd been wearing.

"Dr. Mercer, you need to get that animal under control. Possibly a shock collar for dolphins?"

I froze, half convinced I'd misheard him. But when I met his eyes, there was no trace of humor there, just anger and something darker, something that made my stomach twist.

I swallowed hard, searching for words that wouldn't come. The laughter of gulls echoed overhead, too loud in the silence that followed. The only thing I could think to do was scoop up the waterlogged soundboard, water running down my arms, and carry it into the lab. I tried to stop my hands from shaking. I'd probably have to replace every single button now.

Inside, the air felt cool and sterile compared to the heat outside. I set the board on the counter, watching small droplets slide off the edge and fall to the floor. I pressed a button. Nothing. Another, a tiny squawk, then dead. My throat tightened. I wanted to cry, but I wouldn't give Rafa the satisfaction.

I thought he might follow me into the lab. Instead, in the silence, I heard the gate swing shut as he left, without another word.

I didn't notice Charlie until he nudged my leg. When I looked down, he was staring up at me with soft, worried brown eyes. His ears were slicked back, and he pressed himself against my shins like he used to do as a puppy, when thunderstorms felt personal.

"Oh, Charlie..." I whispered.

He followed me to a chair, rested his head on my knee, and stayed there, unmoving, offering the quiet, steady comfort only a dog can give.

The sky had started to dim by the time Gabe returned from divemastering. I didn't hear him at first, just the soft footsteps, then his voice, gentle, cautious.

"Marie? Hey, what happened?"

I turned slightly, and something in my expression must have told him everything.

He took one look at the dripping soundboard on the counter and let out a low whistle.

"That bad, huh?"

I shook my head. "Worse."

For a few breaths, he said nothing. Then he stepped closer, bracing his hands on the counter beside the ruined board.

"We'll fix it," he said quietly. "Okay? Together. We'll make the waterproof version work. No more saltwater, no more replacing buttons every day, no more sparks. I promise."

Something inside me eased, just a tiny bit, but enough to breathe again.

I nodded. "Okay."

Outside, the dolphins whistled softly in the fading light, as if reminding me they were still here. Still trusting me. Still waiting.

And I wasn't going to let them down. Not now. Not ever.

Chapter Seventeen

20° N latitude Cozumel, Mexico

I finished feeding the dolphins for the morning. The scent of salt and fish still clung to my hands as I walked into the lab. Sunlight spilled through the open shutters, bright and hazy, turning the floor tiles silver where it caught the reflection of the lagoon.

Gabe was sitting cross-legged on the gray tile floor, surrounded by a small galaxy of buttons, wires, bits of metal, and every kind of tool imaginable. Four laptops were open around him like petals. He had his safety glasses pushed up on his head and a pencil tucked behind one ear. The low hum of fans and the faint static of electronics filled the air.

He was chewing on the corner of his lip, his thinking habit, and so deep in concentration that he didn't notice me at first. I hesitated, not wanting to interrupt, but it was almost 7:30 and he was supposed to be on the dive boat at eight. He needed to leave now to make it in time.

"Gabe, do you need to get going so you're not late for the dives this morning?" I asked softly, not wanting to startle him out of whatever problem he was solving.

Without looking up, he said, "I gave Dan my shift. He needs the money."

His tone was casual, but my stomach tightened. Dan, the new guy in the apartment above the dive shop, definitely needed the money, but so did Gabe. Rafa wasn't paying him for all this work on the soundboard, even though he was rebuilding the entire system from scratch.

I bit back my irritation. I hated how Rafa took advantage of people. He had the funds; he just didn't care to spend them on anyone but himself. I'd brought it up when he visited, and his response had been, "I will not pay your boyfriend a salary to hang around and watch you work."

I hadn't even known what to say. Just, "He's not my boyfriend," and I'd walked away, my face burning. Not paying someone for their work felt unethical to me.

Soon, hopefully in a month or so, when a grant or two came through, I'd be able to pay Gabe what he deserved. For now, all I could do was make sure he had coffee.

"Okay," I said, keeping my voice light. "You need a coffee?"

He looked up then, eyes a little bleary from staring at screens, and smiled. "Coffee would be awesome. Thanks."

That smile always hit me like sunshine through water, unexpected, warming, and slightly disarming.

In the breakroom, the air was thick with the smell of sea salt and fish. I filled the coffee pot and started a brew for Gabe and Isabel, then boiled some water for my tea. The sound of the percolating coffee mingled with the muffled calls of the dolphins outside.

When everything was ready, I carried the mugs back out, careful not to spill. I set them on the floor beside Gabe and sank down to sit near his small ring of controlled chaos. The tiles were cool beneath me, and I felt that same hum of purpose that always filled the lab when Gabe was there.

"Tell me where we're at," I said, handing him his mug.

He smiled again, the kind of smile that made the long mornings worth it, and turned one of the laptops toward me, wires snaking between us.

"I'm still working on the software connections and the recording to the computer," Gabe said, adjusting one of the wires looping out from the soundboard. His fingers were steady, precise, careful. "But I've got the hardware pretty much figured out. Everything's encased in clear plastic to protect the button components from the saltwater. But you and the dolphins can still press the buttons, like this."

He tapped a large button under a clear dome. It glowed soft blue and a warm digital voice said, WANT, in Gabe's own voice. The sound echoed faintly against the tile and glass walls.

"I like the light-up feature," I said, leaning closer. The plastic case was cool against my fingertips. "I can see what was just pressed, even if I don't hear it underwater. That's especially helpful."

He grinned, pleased. "Spacing is based on dolphin rostrum size, so it should be comfortable for them. I measured Tursi's from your data logs."

I felt a rush of affection so sharp it startled me, how he paid attention to details, how much he cared about getting it right.

"That's why I've got the GoPro to record, too," he added, motioning toward the camera setup nearby. "I know you've got videos from your grad school research, but those are just of the soundboard. If a GoPro's running during every session, capturing a wider angle, you can capture more body language, gestures, context. Not just the button presses."

I could almost see it: sunlight shimmering through the water, dolphins circling curiously, the glow of the buttons flickering like underwater fireflies. The thought filled me with a familiar thrill, that spark I always felt when science met possibility. He really understood it. The essence of my research, communication as connection, not control. He wasn't just building a machine; he was building a bridge.

"This is incredible, Gabe," I started to say, but he beat me to it, looking up from the circuit board.

"The one thing I don't quite get," he said, "is how you actually teach them each word, and where the buttons are. I mean, I know Charlie can't read, but he somehow knows if a button's in the wrong spot and gets mad about it. How did he learn that? How will the dolphins know?"

His voice carried genuine curiosity, not skepticism. It made me want to explain everything, the long hours, the first breakthrough with Charlie, the patience it took to see a spark of understanding in another species' eyes.

I smiled, tucking my hair behind my ear. "It's not reading," I said softly. "It's memory, pattern, spatial awareness. They learn the placement of each button, so if one gets moved, that's confusing. It comes down to trust. Charlie trusts that his buttons will be in the right places. That's why they're in a weird order, not alphabetical. They're in the order he learned the words." I was excited now; this was my passion. "That's really the essence of communication, right there!" I said, unable to keep the excitement out of my voice. "If I can teach them that, then we're really communicating, not just doing tricks. I mean, I can teach any animal to press a button to get a treat, but to understand the meaning, that's the real challenge."

I leaned back on my hands, watching the light from the lab's high windows catch in the water and scatter across the walls. The room smelled faintly of salt and coffee.

I started to explain how I'd taught Charlie with his toys and concepts like OUTSIDE and WALK. With Heidi and Callie, my dolphins in grad school, I'd started the same way, with toys, and then moved on to people they knew and daily activities. They already understood most of those words, so the buttons were just a new way to express what they already knew.

"The dolphins here are a little different since they're wild," I said, looking toward the big open garage door that led down to the lagoon. I could hear faint splashes and the rhythmic whoosh of waves brushing against the dock. "I know Donna taught them some words, but I think they might've heard some Spanish before she started using English with them. So I wonder if they're bilingual... well, really trilingual." I smiled. "But I decided on English, mostly because it's so much easier for me."

"Donna was the woman who had the researcher job before you, right?" Gabe asked. He was still crouched near the soundboard, tightening a screw with gentle precision. "Why do you think she didn't tell you about Rafa and his plan to shut down the center?"

I sighed, watching the way his brow furrowed in concentration. "I doubt she knew he would close it. I'm pretty sure he didn't decide until after she left. And I'm sure she had to sign an NDA before the sale went through, so she probably couldn't say much even if she wanted to." I took a sip of my tea, the peppermint warmth grounding me.

He looked up, curious. "You think the dolphins are really trilingual?"

"Well, yeah," I said, smiling at how seriously he asked it. "They obviously have their own language. The clicks and whistles and squeals are their words. It doesn't seem fair that they have to learn ours instead of us learning theirs, does it?"

He met my eyes, and for a moment I forgot about the wires and the work and the coffee cooling between us. He got it. Really got it.

Now he was asking the right questions, the ones that lived in my head at night, humming through me like the rhythm of the sea. I'd wished I could understand dolphin language since I was a kid. In grad school, I had recorded and studied every click, every whistle, every strange hybrid sound. Dr. Thatch had thought it was a dead end, and maybe he was right. But I'd understood a few words Heidi and Callie said. I could never imitate them back though, not in any way that felt real. Still, I couldn't shake the feeling that maybe someday, if I listened hard enough, I might understand their language.

"It's not fair. But it seems easier for another species to learn our language than the other way around. Maybe that means they're smarter than us." I looked around the lab, the cables coiled like sleeping snakes, the faint hum of the water pumps, the gentle whoosh of the filtration system. "Even with all of our stuff," I added, "I sometimes think animals are smarter than us. It's not okay to say that in scientific papers though."

Gabe followed my gaze into the kitchen area, where Isabel was wiping down the stainless steel counter, the sharp scent of disinfectant cutting through the briny air. She'd just finished sealing bags of extra fish for the next morning's feeding, stacking them neatly in a bin. Charlie was sprawled on the cool tile beside her, tail thumping lazily, eyes bright and expectant, waiting for a fish to "accidentally" slip from her hand.

"You know what Charlie's barks mean, right?" Gabe asked.

"Yeah, maybe not the exact word, but the basic meaning."

"Like 'I'm hungry,' or 'Hey, Isabel's here,' or 'Yikes, Rafa's here.' I mean, I can tell most of those too now."

"Yeah, for sure," I said, smiling. "I think I know where you're going."

"Do you think you can learn to do that with the dolphins—"

"Gabe, I'm already starting to," I interrupted, the words tumbling out faster now, excitement bubbling through. "I can distinguish the sounds for each dolphin's name, and I'm starting to get a couple of other words too. Back in grad school, I could understand the words for a red ball they had and the words PLAY and BAD. PLAY and BAD sound pretty much the same with these dolphins, which to me means bottlenose language is at least somewhat universal."

"Yesterday, Tursi came over to the dock while I was rinsing dive gear. She started talking. So I stopped and tried to listen. I'm really starting to get a few words here and there. I got JAX and BAD. It seemed like she was telling on Jax! I'm not exactly sure what he had been doing, but I understood his name, and her tone was somewhere between grumpy old man 'get off my lawn' and gossipy teenager. I just couldn't quite decide which one. Either way, I wanted to laugh, but I didn't; I was afraid I'd offend her."

"She was probably telling on him for going under the docks again. Most of the other dolphins have told him not to go under there too."

I looked at Gabe, my mouth falling open. "How on earth do you know that?" My voice came out higher than I meant it to.

"I pay attention too, Dr. Mercer." He winked at me.

That wink again, quick, playful, and entirely disarming. I felt the flutter in my stomach before I could stop it, a soft rush of warmth against the cool, salt-heavy air of the lab.

"What does that even mean?" I asked, forcing my voice to steady even as my pulse wasn't.

"Last week, I was diving, checking out placements for the soundboard, and I saw Jax swim under the big dock. I thought it was weird, so I followed him. There's all kinds of equipment stored under there, old ropes, tubing, pieces of scaffolding. It didn't look very safe; lots of places for a dolphin to get stuck or tangled. When he came out, Solana read him the riot act."

Gabe's voice took on a mix of amusement and admiration. "I don't know the words she used, like you, Dr. Mercer," he smiled, that small teasing one, "but I could see by her body language she was mad at him. You know that sharp tail flick they do? Yeah, that kind of mad. She was definitely telling him he'd better not go under there again."

I couldn't help smiling. Gabe really did pay attention. He noticed details, not just with his eyes, but with his curiosity. He watched the dolphins the way I did, as if every small motion meant something important. I liked that about him. A lot.

But the bigger issue tugged at the back of my mind. We'd need to do something about that hazard under the dock.

Gabe continued, "I kept watching Jax the next couple of days. He tried to go under the dock at least three more times. And I watched Maris and Tursi both yell at him for doing it." He laughed softly, shaking his head. "It's kind of amazing, you know? They really look out for each other. Like an underwater neighborhood watch."

That made me laugh too, but underneath the humor was a flicker of awe. This feeling I never got tired of. The dolphins weren't just learning our words. They already had their own language, their own rules, their own stories, and we were just beginning to listen.

"Wow, that would be such a cool interaction to be able to document," I said, my brain already switching into scientific mode. My mind spun through possibilities, behavioral data, social learning, maybe even a new kind of dolphin reprimand pattern. But the excitement gave way to concern. "More importantly, we really need to either clean out whatever's under the dock, or make a barrier so no one can swim under there and get stuck or hurt."

"Already on it," Gabe replied, glancing up from his tangle of wires. "Isabel and I talked about it. We didn't want to interrupt you since you've been working so hard on the grants. Isabel's getting some small-mesh netting from her dad's fishing business. We can tack it to the dock all the way down to the sand so no one can swim through. She thinks she'll be able to get it by next week. She's even working on a major discount since we're on a 'restricted budget,'" he said, rolling his eyes and doing exaggerated finger air quotes.

I laughed despite myself, the tension in my shoulders easing a little. Still, I felt terrible that I couldn't pay him for all of his hard work. "About that, I'm really sorry. I'm writing grants like crazy and I hope at least one comes through in the few weeks—”

“Don't give it another thought, Marie,” he interrupted gently but firmly. “It's absolutely not your fault.”

He looked up at me then, his expression soft but steady, the light from the big windows behind me reflecting in his eyes like shards of sea glass. “I love getting to do an ocean engineering project that actually feels good. It's not about the money. You know that.”

The sincerity in his voice caught me off guard. I felt my throat tighten a little.

He smiled, just slightly. “If anything, I think you're working too hard on the grant writing. I wish you'd focus more on the work you love and talk to the dolphins more.”

I sighed. That's what I wanted too. To just be with them more, to listen and learn, and not constantly worry about keeping the lights on. My hair was still drying from the morning session with the dolphins, but I knew I'd spend the rest of the day writing. “I have to bring in money or this all goes away,” I said quietly. The truth of it sat heavy in my chest.

“Then let's quit talking,” he said with a teasing grin, “so I can get back to working on this high-tech, saltwater-proof soundboard that's going to advance your research light-years ahead.”

His grin was contagious. I smiled back, feeling the knot in my chest loosen just a bit. “Deal,” I said, handing him another cable from the pile beside us. For a moment, the hum of the equipment and the faint slap of waves against the dock outside filled the silence between us. A calm, steady rhythm, like the ocean itself was agreeing.

Chapter Eighteen

20° N latitude Cozumel, Mexico

It's crazy how much science depends on paperwork. I got into science to be in the water working with dolphins, but from grad school until today, I've probably spent about sixty percent of my time on paperwork.

You'd think it would be about data and discoveries, about being in the water with dolphins, soaked in salt and sunlight, recording the soft bursts of clicks that might mean PUZZLE or PLAY. But no. Apparently, the key to saving dolphin communication research was writing grant proposals. Endless, soul-crushing, brain-frying, jargon-packed grant proposals.

It's strange, isn't it? That something as alive and electric as what we were doing here—dolphins learning to use words—came down to whether I could convince a panel of reviewers in New York or London that we were worth their money.

By mid-morning, my laptop was already sticky from snacks I'd been stress eating, my peppermint tea long gone cold. Charlie was sprawled out beside my chair, sighing occasionally as if he, too, understood the futility of trying to sound "innovative yet feasible" for the twelfth time in one week.

Outside the window, I could hear the dolphins, that crisp fwooosh of breath when one surfaced, a splash, a burst of high-pitched clicks. Every sound tugged at me like a thread. I wanted to be out there with them, not in here rearranging the same sentences over and over.

"Explain potential outcomes and broader impacts," the form said. Ugh, that question was on every grant form. I knew the answer, but it was so hard to put into words.

I stared at the words. If successful, this project could revolutionize human-dolphin communication. Too dramatic? Probably. But wasn't that the truth? If we could prove that dolphins could use symbolic language, even just a handful of consistent words, we'd be rewriting what humans thought was possible.

And yet, all Rafa cared about was money. No grants, no center. No dolphins. That thought hit like a gut punch. Every time I tried to focus, I saw the lagoon abandoned, the docks empty, Tursi's curious eyes searching for a soundboard that wasn't there anymore.

I rubbed my temples. "Okay, Marie," I muttered to myself, "pretend you're explaining it to someone who's never met a dolphin at all. Why does this matter?"

Charlie lifted his head and blinked at me like he knew the answer.

"Because connection matters," I whispered. "Because communication changes everything."

I typed it down before I could talk myself out of it. Because when another species looks you in the eye and chooses to speak to you, even through a button, the world suddenly feels a little bigger and kinder than it did before. It wasn't "scientific language," but it was honest.

By the time the sun went down, I had three half-finished proposals open, two rejected drafts in the trash, and a dull ache behind my eyes. Isabel brought me leftover tacos for dinner, which I ate without tasting. Gabe came by to test the latest soundboard version, and I tried to sound optimistic when he asked how the grant writing was going.

"Fine," I lied. "Totally fine."

But it wasn't. I was terrified. If the funding didn't come through, this all went away. I couldn't let that happen.

I went to bed that night with my laptop still open on the desk, glowing faintly in the dark. Outside, a dolphin chuffed softly, a quiet exhale that almost sounded like comfort.

***

Two weeks later, I was sitting at the same desk, same sticky keyboard, same dog sighing in the same spot. I wasn't even thinking about the grant when I checked my email. I'd been rejected so many times that the notifications didn't sting anymore; they just numbed.

But then I saw it: Subject: Congratulations—Funding Award Notification

I froze. I blinked. My first reaction was disbelief. Then, a strangled noise came out of my throat that startled

Charlie into barking. I reread it three times, heart pounding so hard it felt like it might crack my ribs.

"Charlie," I said, laughing and crying at the same time, "we did it. We actually did it!"

I sprinted down the dock barefoot, the sun already bright over the lagoon. The dolphins were there, Tursi, Kai, and Maris, circling near the soundboard. I pressed the PLAY button just to hear it echo back at me. Tursi clicked and leapt, her whole body shimmering silver and blue in the light.

"That's right," I said through tears. "We get to keep playing."

Isabel came running, still chewing on breakfast toast. I showed her the email. She screamed, and the dolphins echoed her excitement in a chorus of whistles and jumps. The relief didn't erase the pressure; if anything, it deepened it. The money bought us time, not permanence. But it was enough to breathe again, to keep the dream alive. Maybe John Lilly's dream had gone astray. Maybe mine would too, someday. But for now, in this quiet stretch of ocean, it felt like the universe had whispered back: Keep going.

That afternoon, with the grant win still humming in my chest, I stared down at the new button I'd velcroed onto the soundboard.

FRIEND.

How on earth was I supposed to teach that? FISH was easy. I held one up, pressed the button, handed it over. PUZZLE? I showed them the floating toy, hit the button, and we played. But friend wasn't something I could toss in the water or hold up in my hand.

"Okay, Marie," I muttered to myself, "think, how did I teach Charlie FRIEND?"

Tursi surfaced right on cue, cocking her head at me, eyes sharp and waiting. She was already the star pupil, pressing buttons with a kind of deliberate grace. Maris clicked behind her, probably hoping I'd hand her another puzzle game, but it was Tursi I locked onto.

I tapped the button. FRIEND. Then I pointed to myself and said, "friend."

Tursi blinked at me. Silence.

I tried again, pressing FRIEND, then pointing at Charlie, who was pacing happily at the dock. "Friend."

Charlie gave a sharp bark like he was in on the lesson. Tursi whistled back at him. My heart jumped. Could that possibly be recognition?

I pressed the button again. FRIEND. Then leaned down, touched my hand to the water near Tursi's rostrum. "Friend."

She floated there, watching me. Then, in the slowest, most deliberate way I'd seen yet, Tursi raised her melon out of the water and nudged the button with her rostrum. FRIEND.

My breath caught. She immediately rolled sideways, exposing her belly, a sign of trust, vulnerability, an offering. I laughed, half with relief, half with sheer joy. "Yes! Exactly, Tursi! Friend!"

Behind her, Solana gave a half-hearted whistle and slapped her tail, clearly unimpressed that the lesson wasn't about food. But Tursi clicked again and pressed the button a second time. FRIEND.

This time she looked not at Charlie, not at the puzzle toy, but right at me. It felt like the word had bridged something invisible between us, like she hadn't just learned the button, but claimed the relationship. I wiped at my eyes quickly before anyone, even Isabel, could notice. "Friend," I whispered back, pressing the button myself.

Charlie barked again, and I knew it was his way of saying it too.

It was late afternoon, the kind of hour when the lagoon shimmered bronze and the dolphins got restless. Charlie was stretched out on the dock, half-dozing, while Isabel and I went through the routine checks.

Jax was in one of his moods, darting around the dock where Isabel and Gabe had installed the netting to keep the dolphins out. He splashed deliberately, nudging Maris hard enough to make her squeak.

"Hey, knock it off," I called, waving him back. He circled once and surfaced right next to Charlie, spraying him with a sharp puff of water.

Charlie yelped, startled, and scrambled back, ears flat.

Before I could intervene, Tursi surged up, a flash of silver muscle between Jax and the dock. She pressed her beak down hard on the board mounted at the water's edge. FRIEND. FRIEND.

The word rang out twice, sharp and deliberate.

I froze. My throat went dry.

Jax gave a dismissive whistle, flicked his tail, and swam off. Tursi lingered, turning her head toward Charlie, then back at me, then nudging the button once more. FRIEND.

Charlie barked uncertainly, tail thumping against the planks.

I crouched down, heart hammering. "Yes, Tursi. Friend. Charlie's our friend." My voice cracked, and I didn't care.

Isabel let out a low whistle of her own, almost reverent. "She wasn't just repeating it," she murmured. "She was... protecting him."

Tursi clicked softly, then rolled sideways, eye on Charlie, as if making sure he was alright.

Charlie stretched his nose out over the dock until it brushed her fin.

And in that golden light, I swear the word friend hung between all of us like a bridge, something larger than training, larger than the soundboard. Something that felt alive.

For the first time since arriving in Cozumel, I truly believed: We were on the brink of something extraordinary.

Chapter Nineteen

20° N latitude Cozumel, Mexico

Gabe was making steady progress on the new underwater soundboard. Each button was now sealed inside a clear plastic casing, gleaming like smooth bubbles scattered across his workstation. He still had to make sure the buttons could be pressed easily and that the sound was amplified enough to carry underwater. He was also experimenting with a new lighting system. Each word would pulse in soft color when pressed, a visible shimmer the dolphins and I could follow even in low light.

The whole thing was getting more complex than I'd expected. Wires snaked across the lab floor, the hum of electronics blending with the distant calls of gulls and the rhythmic slap of water against the dock. But if Gabe could pull off what he kept describing to me, it was going to be incredible—more sophisticated, easier for the dolphins to use, fewer malfunctions. And a system that recorded every button press straight to the connected computer.

Even after landing a divemaster job and moving into the little apartment above the dive shop with two other divemasters, he still came to the lab every afternoon. Some mornings, too, when he wasn't scheduled to dive. He worked tirelessly, salt still in his hair, the scent of ocean and solder mingling around him. I knew he was dedicated to the project, thrilled to be doing ocean engineering that actually meant something, but his work ethic still amazed me.

He had to be exhausted, but every afternoon he arrived smiling, tanned and windblown, acting like CIMC was the only place he wanted to be. The moment he settled onto the lab floor with his tools spread around him, he looked completely at home.

Soon he'd be finished. I should've been excited about that, but instead I felt an odd flicker of unease. I wondered how much upkeep the soundboard would need, if I'd be able to add new buttons on my own, or if I'd have to ask Gabe to come back every time I wanted to add a word. I wasn't sure why the thought of him not being here every day made my chest feel tight, like the air in the lab had thickened somehow.

Maybe it was just because I'd gotten used to the quiet rhythm of our afternoons, the whir of his laptop fans, the occasional yelp when a wire shocked, the way he'd glance up and grin when something finally worked. Maybe that was all it was.

Maybe.

***

Gabe slid the new waterproof soundboard into the water for the first time. It splashed down with a heavy thunk, a shimmer of bubbles rising around it, then settled against the dock as he cinched it in place with thick webbing straps. The casing gleamed pale blue under the late-morning sun, LEDs winking faintly as it powered on.

I tugged on my mask and snorkel, my pulse quickening. This was it, the moment I'd been waiting for.

The water was glassy and warm against my skin as I slipped in. Sunlight fractured into shifting silver ribbons, and the muffled underwater world wrapped around me. Tursi was already there, drawn in like a magnet. She glided toward the board, her sleek gray body shimmering in the sunlight, eyes sharp and curious. She tapped the first button with her rostrum. A soft chime rang out, bubbles shimmering from the speaker. BALL, lit up in bright blue. She pressed another button, PLAY glowed blue.

I grinned behind my snorkel. Gabe had even kept the button layout exactly the same as the old board, smart. He knew from Charlie that moving buttons around caused frustration.

I quickly reached into the net bag hanging by the dock and pulled out a ball, holding it out toward Tursi. She glanced at it, but flicked her tail dismissively. No thanks. Her attention was on the new soundboard.

I laughed through my snorkel. "Me too, Tursi. Me too."

She swam tight circles around the board, then returned and pressed: MARIE TALK. The words lit up, casting a pale glow across her rostrum.

Something fluttered in my chest. She was asking for me.

I drifted closer and touched the buttons slowly, deliberately: TURSI TALK MARIE HAPPY. Each press released a burst of light and sound, like tiny underwater fireworks. The GoPro strapped to the dock was recording every second.

This was it. Day one with the underwater soundboard, and Tursi had already initiated communication. Not mimicry. Not a trick. Real, meaningful interaction.

I popped my head out of the water, mask dripping. "Gabe, this is great! Did you hear that? Tursi asked me to talk to her!"

He was crouched on the dock, sunlight glinting on his hair, tools scattered beside him. He raised an eyebrow, but his eyes shone with pride. "How do you know it was a question?"

I froze, my excitement colliding with the weight of his words. How did I know? With Charlie, I'd used a question-mark button. That had made it clearer. I hadn't set up anything like that yet with the dolphins.

"I'll need to introduce a question marker," I said slowly, thinking it through as I tasted salt on my lips. "If I can get a few of them to grasp that concept, the others might follow."

Gabe gave a small smile and a wink. "Always three steps ahead, Dr. Mercer."

I ignored the flutter in my stomach and went back under, jotting mental notes as I watched Tursi circle the board again. Maris might engage later, but she preferred puzzles. Kai would get interested if I wrapped it in a jumping game. And Luma... Luma would only talk about Charlie, but maybe that could be useful too. The trick would be letting each of them talk about what they loved most.

When I finally pulled myself out of the water, dripping and flushed, Gabe was coiling up spare webbing. My hair clung in salty strands to my neck, and I pulled out the freshwater hose for a rinse.

"How do I add new words when I need them?" I asked, trying to sound casual.

"Are you trying to get rid of me, Dr. Mercer?" His voice was mock-serious, but his eyes flicked toward me in that sideways way of his.

"What? No, I just—"

"Kidding." He let the coil drop with a soft thud. "I can add a new button anytime. It's no big deal."

"Tursi's talking really well. I might need to add buttons almost every day." I hesitated, the practical worry creeping in. "I know you have to work. And it'll still be at least two weeks before we actually receive the grant money. I can't... we can't pay you for all your work yet."

"It's okay." His voice was quiet, steady. He didn't look at me right away, just tightened one of the straps on the dock. Then finally he glanced up, and his eyes were warmer than I expected. "I enjoy being here," he said, simply.

Something in my chest shifted. I couldn't name it, didn't want to. I just nodded, suddenly very interested in wringing every last drop from my towel.

"Thank you," I said finally, my voice softer than I intended.

For a moment, only the soft lap of water against the dock filled the space between us. Gabe glanced around the lagoon, then back at me with that half-smile that always carried more weight than it should.

"Marie," he said, hesitating just long enough that I knew he'd been working up to this. "I think we both need a break from work tonight."

I blinked. "Like grilling burgers on *Windy* for dinner?" That was safe. Familiar.

He shook his head, still watching me carefully. "No... I was thinking maybe dinner out. At a restaurant. You know... like a real date."

The word landed with a splash in my chest, ripples of panic and something dangerously close to excitement spreading outward.

"Like a date?" My voice came out too high. What if it didn't go well? I needed Gabe for the research. If we dated and it ended badly, I would lose him completely. This was reckless. And yet, "Yes, that sounds fun," I heard myself say, cringing inwardly at the implications already. "Can Charlie come?"

Brilliant, Marie. Just brilliant. Dogs didn't come on dates. Especially not Charlie, who had a track record of ruining them, with good reason, granted, but still.

Gabe laughed, easy and unbothered. "I'll come by *Windy* to pick you and Charlie up at six. We can head downtown for dinner, cool?"

"Cool," I managed, though my stomach was in full rebellion. This was a terrible idea. A wonderful, terrible idea.

Chapter Twenty

20° N latitude Cozumel, Mexico

The only dress I currently owned was a blue sundress patterned with delicate white coral. It fluttered lightly in the evening breeze as we stepped onto the deck. Since we were going downtown, Charlie wore his collar and leash for once. He danced around my feet, tail wagging, proud to be dressed up, alert to every sound and movement as if he knew something special was happening.

Gabe arrived promptly at six, wearing khaki board shorts and a pale blue aloha shirt splashed with big, white hibiscus flowers. The smell of leather lingered faintly on him, but beneath that was the clean, briny scent of the ocean and the subtle trace of cologne, warm and slightly sweet.

"You look beautiful," Gabe said, his eyes meeting mine as Charlie and I stepped onto the pier.

My cheeks heated. I crouched down and patted Charlie's head. "He's not used to wearing a collar and leash anymore."

"I think he likes it," Gabe said with a small smile. Charlie held his head high, tongue lolling, prancing down the pier like he owned the place. He wasn't nervous at all.

As we walked the mile toward downtown San Miguel, I talked easily about the dolphins while Gabe asked thoughtful questions about the soundboard. The closer we got to town, the more the streets came alive. Shopfronts spilled color into the narrow lanes, vivid textiles draped over racks, hand-painted pottery glinting in the last rays of sun, and small canvases leaning against walls, some depicting the reef, others the streets and plazas. Shopkeepers leaned casually on door frames or waved from porches, calling out with friendly invitations, their voices mingling with the distant hum of traffic and the faint clatter of shoes on cobblestones. The air smelled of fresh tortillas from a nearby stall, salty sea spray drifting in from the harbor, and a hint of sizzling seafood from a corner cantina.

Even Charlie seemed entranced, sniffing at everything, tail wagging, occasionally letting out a soft bark at a particularly colorful sign or a passing cat. I laughed, feeling lighter than I had in weeks. Being here, with him, with Charlie, amidst the warmth and color of San Miguel, it felt like stepping into a little world separate from work, research, and deadlines.

We turned off the busy main street and walked a couple of blocks away from the ocean. The sound of scooters faded behind us, replaced by the soft clink of dishes and low laughter drifting from nearby patios. Casa Mission sat behind an arched gate, glowing with warm light. It was a traditional Mexican restaurant styled like an old Spanish mission, red tile floors, thick clay walls, and high ceilings that held the coolness of the evening air.

Gabe got us a table for "dos personas y un perro." Charlie trotted proudly beside the waiter as if he'd been dining out his whole life. We sat beneath a lazy ceiling fan that stirred the scent of lime, grilled meat, and cilantro. The colorful tablecloths, bright pinks and yellows and turquoise, and hand-painted tiles on the walls made the space feel festive but relaxed, the kind of place where time slowed down a little.

We ordered margaritas, taco plates, and water for Charlie, who flopped at my feet with a sigh, head on his paws.

"I really appreciate you working so hard on the soundboard," I said once the waiter left. "The progress has been amazing."

"I enjoy the work," Gabe said, meeting my eyes over the rim of his drink. "And I enjoy helping you." He hesitated, still holding my gaze. "Can I ask you something? I don't want to ruin our first date, but I really want to know."

"Sure, anything." I smiled, expecting something harmless like dolphins, dogs, soundboards, maybe even sailing. Nothing dangerous.

"Why can't I call you Rie?" he asked, stirring his margarita slowly, the ice clinking against the glass. His tone was gentle but deliberate, and he didn't look away.

My heart lurched. That. I could laugh it off or change the subject, but the air between us had shifted, too intimate, too real. My stomach twisted.

"My parents died," I croaked, voice smaller than I meant it to be.

"Well, I knew that," he said easily, without the slightest trace of surprise.

I stared at him. "How could you possibly know that? I never said anything. I don't have 'orphan' tattooed across my forehead."

He choked on his margarita, face flushing red. "Orphan tattooed on your forehead. That's good," he said between coughs. "Don't be mad. I've known since Panama."

"Panama?!" I sputtered.

He nodded sheepishly. "No one our age talks about their parents with as much reverence as you. When I complained about my mom trying to get paper airline tickets, your face…" He paused, searching for the right word. "You were jealous. I thought it was weird at first, but then I put it together. You own a $200,000 sailboat. Your dad taught you to sail, right? If he were alive, he'd have come with you on that trip."

He wasn't wrong. If Dad had been alive, he'd have insisted on coming. Mom too. They would've loved that trip, every mile of it.

"Yeah," I said softly. "They would have." I pushed black beans around my plate, fighting the sting behind my eyes.

"It's okay to be sad about that," Gabe said quietly. He reached across the table, gently pried the fork from my hand, and squeezed it. His hand was warm and steady against mine.

I looked up into his eyes, the low light catching the flecks of green in them. "Dad always called me Rie," I said, my voice barely above a whisper. "He was the only one who ever did. I loved it." I felt the tears coming. I hadn't said the word Rie out loud in years.

Without a word, Gabe stood, rounded the table, and pulled me up into his arms. His hug was strong, grounding, and unexpectedly safe. I felt tears spill onto his blue and white aloha shirt, smelled the faint salt of the sea still clinging to him, mixed with sun and leather. For a moment, the world went still, just the quiet hum of the fan, the rustle of palm leaves outside, and the steady beat of his heart.

"I really am sorry," he murmured, pulling back slightly but still holding me. "I didn't mean to ruin our first date. Honestly, I thought you were going to tell me some story about a high school boyfriend who called you that."

I laughed through the tears, half-sniffling. "More than you bargained for with the whole orphan thing, huh? Six years ago. Plane crash over the Pacific."

"I didn't ask," he said gently, hands raised.

"But you were curious. Probably since Panama," I said, raising an eyebrow.

"True," he admitted.

"It's why I love *Windy* so much. Probably why I love science too," I said, voice softer now. "I loved sailing and science before, but after... they became my ways to stay connected to my parents. Mom taught chemistry at a community college."

We sat back down and finished our dinner. The restaurant hummed with soft Spanish guitar strumming from a speaker in the corner, mingling with the clink of cutlery and low chatter in both Spanish and English. The faint scent of citrus and grilled meat lingered in the warm, clay-scented air. Candles flickered on the tables, casting soft golden pools of light across our faces. I took a slow breath, letting the warmth of the room and the sound of Gabe's quiet presence anchor me, still carrying a tender ache from thinking of my parents. Charlie lay at my feet, occasionally lifting his head to sniff at the aroma of fresh fish and tortillas, then settling back down with a satisfied huff as the server refilled his water bowl. I smiled at him, grateful for the little anchor of normalcy and for the chance to let the rest of the evening feel light again.

When we finally left the restaurant, the cool night air of San Miguel wrapped around us like a soft blanket. Gabe reached for my free hand, our fingers interlacing as naturally as if we'd done it a million times before. My chest fluttered with exhilaration, and I turned to smile up at him. He winked, and my stomach flipped, butterflies all over again.

We strolled toward the main street, the cobblestones cool beneath our thin shoes. Instead of heading back toward the center, we turned toward the main square. The street thrummed with life: tourists clustered around colorful shops, the scent of roasted nuts and churros mixing with the salty tang from the nearby ocean. Shopkeepers leaned out from the sidewalks, calling to everyone to come inside.

"Honeymooners?" one asked with a sly grin as we passed.

"No—" I began.

"Oh, let them have their fun," Gabe interrupted smoothly. I couldn't help smiling at his quick response.

We arrived at the town square, where street painters were hard at work. Cans of spray paint rattled and hissed, mixing with the buzz of conversation and laughter. Elaborate underwater scenes covered pieces of cardboard propped up on the cobblestones: coral reefs, dancing fish, and dolphins leaping through sparkling water.

We approached one artist whose work caught my breath, dolphins arcing above sunlit waves, reefs teeming with color beneath. He had a short beard and mustache, white pants splattered with paint in every color imaginable, and a t-shirt that looked like it had once been bright but was now a kaleidoscope of layered spray paint.

"If you like, I can make a painting just for you?" he offered, his eyes crinkling in a smile.

"With a sailboat?" Gabe asked.

"And dolphins!" I added automatically, unable to contain myself.

The artist's hands moved like magic. He covered the cardboard in white spray paint, then pressed crumpled newspaper dipped in blue paint to make waves, layering different shades for depth. He dotted coral and sponges across the reef, and carefully created a horizon with another piece of cardboard. Then he painted a golden setting sun, dolphins leaping above, and finally, the sailboat. My breath caught as I watched. It was flawless.

He paused, eyes meeting Charlie's for a few seconds as if to get his approval. Then, delicately, he mixed brown paint on a tiny palette, took a fine knife, and etched Charlie onto the bow of the sailboat, his ears flapping in the wind.

I squealed, unable to contain myself. "Look, Charlie! It's you!"

The artist's face split into a wide, toothy grin. "You like it?"

"I love it!" I said, almost bouncing in my excitement.

"It's perfect," Gabe said softly, awe in his voice.

"You even got Charlie's ears just right," I whispered, leaning down to rub the top of his head. Charlie wagged his tail happily, as if he agreed.

The artist signed the painting, "Rolando," and took out a small blow torch to dry it. When he lit it, Charlie jumped back, ears flicking, tail wagging nervously. "I'm so sorry, my friend, I did not mean to scare you," Rolando said, speaking directly to him.

"We'll go walk around the square for a minute so you can dry it and not scare Charlie," I said.

As we stepped away, Gabe's voice cut through the hum of the crowd. "This might sound crazy, but I think that guy could understand Charlie."

"Yeah," I shook my head, smiling through a small warmth in my chest, still carrying a hint of the ache from earlier. "I certainly can't explain everything I see with animals, and that's one of them."

We went back for the painting, chatted with Rolando for a few minutes, and let him and Charlie linger together, this time without the blow torch. The late evening air was warm and heavy with the scent of fried tortillas and sugar from nearby street stalls, and the sounds of distant guitar strumming mixed with the chatter of tourists and locals alike.

On the walk home, I told Gabe about my first dog, Lilly, and how she had come to me in a dream to show me Charlie. I couldn't explain how or why, it wasn't scientific, but Lilly had brought Charlie to me, and that made him all the more special.

Gabe didn't laugh or look skeptical. He simply nodded, his hand brushing mine briefly, grounding me in the moment. The sincerity in his eyes made my chest tighten with something I couldn't quite name. Even after the tears at dinner, this might be the best date I'd ever been on.

Gabe walked us all the way back to the center and to *Windy Possibilities*, even though we passed his apartment on the way. "It's such a nice night, I'm enjoying the walk, and the company," he said, his voice soft against the gentle hum of the evening breeze and the distant clinking of boat rigging. The salt air carried hints of hibiscus from nearby planters, and the warm glow of street lamps reflected off the water, shimmering across the pier.

I glanced over at the painting we'd just picked up, leaning it against the rail of the boat. The sunset colors glowed in the soft lamplight. Seven dolphins arced above painted waves, the sailboat cutting through a golden sea. It even looked like *Windy*.

Charlie huffed a little, annoyed that we were just standing there. He stood on the deck, tail flicking uncertainly, ears twitching, trying to figure out what was happening.

I looked up at Gabe, my knees suddenly feeling like jello, heart fluttering. "I, uh... had a really nice time tonight," I managed to say.

"Me too," he replied softly, eyes warm, catching the lamplight from the pier.

He reached up, hand resting gently behind my neck, and leaned down. When his lips met mine, it was soft and slow, electric and grounding at the same time, a mix of nerves and thrill twisting in my stomach. The faint smell of leather and ocean clung to him, warm against my senses. I felt Charlie brush past my legs, tail wagging like he approved, or maybe he just wanted attention, but it somehow made the moment sweeter, more real.

"I'd better get going, early boat trip in the morning," Gabe said reluctantly, stepping back, giving me a small, lingering smile. He hopped off *Windy* and walked away, the sound of his footsteps fading along the pier.

"Charlie, I think that was the best date I've ever had, even with the whole crying-during-dinner incident," I murmured, scratching behind his ears. I paused at the cabin, letting the night settle around me. My eyes drifted to the painting again. Seven dolphins jumped above the waves. The boat even looked like *Windy*. Every detail was perfect, every brushstroke capturing a moment of joy—except for Charlie's missing front leg. I frowned, tilting my head, making sure I wasn't imagining it. "Weird..."

Chapter Twenty-One

20° N latitude Cozumel, Mexico

Rafa arrived without warning, just like always. One moment the center was quiet except for the hum of the pumps and the chatter of gulls; the next his truck was roaring onto the street outside. Charlie barked once, low and uncertain. Kai made an odd squeaking sound I hadn't heard before. Gabe and I exchanged a glance that said brace yourself.

I wiped my hands on my shorts, swallowing hard. Rafa hadn't set foot on site in weeks. His texts were always clipped, his emails shorter. Mostly, he left me in charge of everything—budget cuts, repairs, grants, dolphin care. Honestly, I welcomed being in charge. But that didn't ease my nerves. If anything, it made them worse.

People who disappear like that rarely come back with good news.

"Dr. Mercer!" he called as he strolled through the gate. Strolled wasn't even the right word. He swaggered in, like someone entering a party he fully expected to be about him. His sunglasses reflected the whole scene: Gabe crouched by the soundboard, Isabel tossing fish, and Tursi hovering at the edge of the lagoon like she'd been waiting.

"Rafa," I said, forcing warmth into my voice. "You picked a good day. Tursi's been... well, see for yourself." He stood close to me, too close. I cringed involuntarily.

Tursi pressed her rostrum to the glowing buttons. A sharp chirp came from the speaker: FISH. Isabel laughed and tossed her one. Then another button: PLAY. Tursi gave a bubbling whistle and dove, surfacing a heartbeat later with a powerful spray that splashed us all, Rafa included.

Rafa froze, blinking as salt water splattered his immaculate linen shirt. For once, he didn't look skeptical, didn't mutter about tricks or wasted time. His mouth actually opened, wordless, as he stepped closer to the board.

I guided Rafa back to the water's edge. The lagoon glinted blue-green in the sun, turning his sunglasses into dark mirrors. "All of the dolphins are using the buttons now. Tursi knows over twenty words. She's extraordinary." As much as I didn't trust him, I needed Rafa to see our progress. The CIMC depended on it.

"She's choosing buttons consistently," Gabe said, trying not to smile as Tursi gave another triumphant whistle and rolled onto her side, clearly pleased with herself.

I led Rafa closer to the soundboard, sunlight flickering off the water and reflecting in silver shards across his face. "They all understand at least some of the words. Tursi is our star communicator," I said proudly.

As if on cue, Tursi leapt high into the air, slicing through sunlight and mist before splashing back down.

Then she darted to the soundboard, nudging the JUMP button with decisive enthusiasm. Isabel laughed. "Yes, Tursi, you can jump just as well as Kai."

Rafa watched, but not like someone appreciating magic. More like someone checking the weight of a gold coin. His gaze tracked Tursi's every move, calculating in a way that made the back of my neck prickle.

Rafa took a step closer to the water, then angled slightly toward me, lowering his voice.

"Walk with me," he said casually, already moving.

I hesitated, then followed him a few paces down the dock, just far enough that the others blurred into background noise. The lagoon lapped softly against the wood beneath our feet.

"You've done impressive work," he said, not looking at me. His gaze stayed on Tursi, who hovered just beneath the surface. "More than I expected."

"Thank you," I said, unsure where this was going.

He nodded once. "Centers like this fail all the time, you know. Passion projects. Too much heart, not enough structure."

My stomach tightened.

"But this," he continued, gesturing vaguely at the soundboard, the dolphins, the whole fragile ecosystem of my life, "this could be positioned differently."

"Positioned how?" I asked.

He finally turned to me, smiling. "Carefully."

There was a pause. Long enough to feel deliberate.

"You're very good at the science here," he said. "With the animals. That's rare. But you're not the only marine biologist in the world."

The words landed lightly. Too lightly.

"I'm not planning on going anywhere," I said, keeping my voice even.

Rafa's smile didn't change. "Of course not. I just believe in contingency."

Behind us, Charlie shifted, nails clicking softly on the dock.

Rafa patted my shoulder—too familiar, too brief to pull away from—and stepped back toward the others as if nothing had happened.

"Let's see what else they can do," he said brightly.

Tursi was intent on Isabel and the soundboard. She pressed the ISABEL button, and Isabel laughed. "Yes, you know who I am!"

"Why doesn't she give the dolphin a reward?" Rafa asked, frowning slightly as water dripped from his sleeve. His tone wasn't hostile, just uneasy, like he was trying to fit this into a world he understood.

Charlie, who had been lounging in the shade nearby, lifted his head and gave a low, quiet rumble. His tail stayed still, ears slightly back as he watched Rafa. I reached down to pat his head, hoping Rafa wouldn't notice. But Tursi did. She paused mid-circle and emitted a short, sharp chirp, not playful, not angry, just alert. Watching.

"It's different," I explained, pretending not to notice the tension. "We're not teaching them tricks. We're giving them the option to communicate. At first, it's teaching for a reward, but as it progresses, the rewards go away, and it's completely the dolphin's choice to communicate."

Rafa made a small noise in his throat, something between disapproval and confusion. Charlie lifted his head at the sound, ears tipped back, a soft growl ghosting through his chest. He inched closer to me, as if trying to place himself between us.

Tursi noticed too. She halted mid-circle, giving a sharp, decisive chirp in Rafa's direction.

The faint smell of brine and fish hung in the warm air, and he wiped at a drop that had landed on his cheek as if it burned.

"What they say is really up to them," I continued, my voice growing steadier as I spoke. "They can lead the conversation. I'm adding more words almost every day, and it's beginning to get interesting. Tursi's talking about friends and things she likes and wants now. We're learning about her personality. Even Maris, Solana, and Kai are talking about things they like to do."

I knew I was rambling, but I couldn't help it. Pride swelled in my chest. Even with the tension prickling in the air, I wanted Rafa to see what I saw, how extraordinary this was. "I'm writing research papers about it now, and soon I'll start more grant proposals based on my findings."

I studied Rafa's face. Something dangerous flickered behind the charm. Not anger, but ambition.

"You've built something promising," he said, looking up at me with a smile that didn't reach his eyes. "Maybe

I judged too quickly. Maybe this could become... something profitable. After all, that is why this center exists."

There it was. Not wonder. Not connection. Profit. The word clung to him like a shadow.

Still, I forced a smile. "If we keep going, we can bring in more grants. Maybe even partnerships."

Rafa stood, wiping sweat from his forehead. "Yes... perhaps we can make this work."

Behind him, Charlie gave another soft huff, almost like a sigh of warning.

"Maybe I was too quick to think of closing. Maybe..." He trailed off, shaking his head with a grin I'd never seen on him before. "Maybe this is the start of something... more sustainable."

Rafa patted my shoulder again, letting his hand rest a beat too long, and walked back toward the gate, whistling to himself.

I stood still long after he was gone.

Hope flickered... but caution stayed.

Tursi surfaced again, her eye locked not on me, but on the path Rafa had taken as he disappeared through the gate. She hesitated, then swam back to the soundboard, pressing two buttons with slow, deliberate precision.

NO FRIEND, the soundboard squawked.

The words punched the air out of my lungs. Isabel froze. Gabe looked up sharply from the power cables. Even Charlie stiffened beside me, ears pricking, gaze flicking from Tursi to the empty walkway.

I crouched at the edge of the dock, my hand brushing the warm wood, the salt-sticky air thick around us. "You...

you don't like him?" I whispered, even though I knew Tursi hadn't just meant dislike. She meant something deeper. A warning.

Tursi surfaced again, slower this time, her head tipping toward me with something that felt like concern. She clicked softly, almost apologetically, then nudged the board again, this time touching nothing, as if emphasizing the silence.

My throat tightened. This wasn't anthropomorphism. She'd learned the word friend joyfully, proudly, offering belly and trust. She had used the opposite now with purpose.

I drew in a breath. "Thank you," I whispered, because it was all I could think to say.

Behind me, Charlie pressed his head against my hip, leaning his whole weight into me in that grounding way only he ever could.

Gabe walked over, wiping his hands on a rag. "Everything okay?" he asked quietly.

I didn't look away from Tursi's dark, steady eye. "I think," I said, voice soft but sure, "she's telling us to be careful."

Tursi dipped beneath the surface, her dorsal fin slicing cleanly through the water as she moved to join Kai and Maris. The lagoon shimmered gold around her, but something inside me felt newly shadowed.

Hope hadn't disappeared completely, but it had company now...caution. Real caution with a reason.

Chapter Twenty-Two

20° N latitude Cozumel, Mexico

I stood on the dock thinking about the conversation I'd just had with Tursi. Even a week later, her NO FRIEND still echoed in the back of my mind, a quiet pulse of warning I kept trying to ignore. I'd talked with Ana about it too. She agreed with Gabe, Isabel, and me that it was a warning to be heeded. She still hadn't found any evidence of Rafa doing anything illegal, but we all believed he was capable of it.

I listened to the splat of fresh water hitting the Cordura fabric of my buoyancy control device (BCD). The hose hissed, and little beads of water caught the sunlight, sparkling for an instant before soaking into the black fabric. The faint smell of rubber and salt hung in the air, and somewhere behind me a gull screamed, circling for scraps.

I jumped a mile when I felt water hit my ankle and saw it splash onto my BCD and regulator from the side. The shock was sharp and cool, raising goosebumps on my leg. I turned just in time to see Jax finish shooting a stream of water out of his mouth, his jaw curved in what I swear was a smirk.

"Jax, the whole point of rinsing my gear is to get the salt off. Now I'm going to have to do it again."

He laughed at me. Wait. He actually laughed at me. Not just a squeaky whistle or a random burst of clicks, but he unmistakably laughed. It was a series of short squeaks strung together, pitched and patterned just enough to sound like a real human chuckle. It had rhythm, a tone, the rise and fall of an actual laugh. I froze, heart pounding. I'm sure he'd heard me laugh, and probably a few other humans, but to replicate the sound so well was impressive.

John C. Lilly had documented dolphins making all kinds of different human sounds, but seeing it and hearing it, directed at me? This was huge.

I turned the hose and sprayed at him, a weak stream barely reaching across the dock. "That's what you get," I said, laughing.

Not to be outdone, Jax gave me a flick of his tail fluke and launched a wall of water at me. It smacked me in the chest like a wet slap, drenching my hair, my shirt, and, of course, all of my freshly rinsed scuba gear.

I sputtered, half laughing, half annoyed, and plopped down on the edge of the dock. The wood was hot under my legs, the contrast of the sun-warmed boards and the cool, clear water lapping against my feet felt good in the moment. My legs dangled, and Jax hovered just below, tilting one eye up at me.

"Okay, you win, you silly dolphin. That was a funny trick, Jax."

He laughed again, this time higher-pitched, almost shrill. It sounded eerily like a little girl's giggle, and I wondered for a moment: was that what my laugh sounded like to him?

"You're a very smart boy, Jax," I said, leaning down toward him. "We like to assume you're just a jerk, but I think maybe there's more to you than that. Maybe I just need to figure out what really motivates you." I wanted so badly for him to prove me wrong, for him to be more than the troublemaker everyone warned me about.

I couldn't believe what had just happened. This was such clear communication—the entire interaction—and Jax had initiated it. If I could just figure out how to motivate him to talk to me on my terms, he might even become one of my star communicators. The thought thrilled me, but it also unsettled me. Jax didn't wait for permission the way Tursi did. He didn't seem interested in rules at all.

***

The water was warm, a pale turquoise that shimmered with broken sunlight. I floated face down, snorkel in my mouth, fins making lazy swishes to keep me hovering at the surface. I loved talking with Tursi, and we were making great progress with the new soundboard. Now came the real challenge. I was going to try to motivate Jax to use the new soundboard and communicate with me.

If I could get him to play a game of splashing, that might motivate him.

He circled just outside my field of vision, a flash of gray sliding behind my shoulder, then disappearing again. He knew it was his turn, and he was making me wait, typical Jax.

I tapped the board myself: PLAY. The speaker's synthetic voice carried through the water, loud and clear. PLAY. I looked up, scanning the blur of my mask until Jax appeared. "Come on Jax. You love to play and splash. Show me."

For a moment, it looked like he might. He glided closer, tilting one eye toward me, rostrum angled toward the glowing button. Then, at the last possible second, he veered away and rammed the side of the platform so hard the whole thing shuddered, sending a vibration straight up my arms.

I jerked back, bubbles spilling from my snorkel. "Jax!" My voice was muffled in the snorkel, but the anger was unmistakable.

He rolled onto his back and let out a screechy burst of squeals that sounded almost like a laugh—mocking, sharp. Then he shot to the surface, slapped his fluke, and dove again, scattering a cloud of bubbles right in my face.

"Great," I muttered, clearing my mask. My pulse was up, not from the exertion, but from sheer irritation.

I tried again, pressing: FISH. The word buzzed through the water. "Fish," I said, holding up a pouch of sardines clipped to my swimsuit. "All you have to do is ask, Jax. Just press it."

He hovered. Looked at the board. Looked at me. Then, with deliberate slowness, he opened his mouth, grabbed the corner of the board, and yanked it sideways until the anchors creaked against the dock.

"JAX!" I lunged forward, pushing the board back into place. He let go, swam a lazy circle around me, then came in fast, headbutting me square in the ribs. Hard enough to knock the snorkel from my mouth. The hit knocked the breath from my chest. Dolphins were powerful, whether they meant to be or not. This wasn't play. This was control, and I'd just handed it to him.

I gasped, choking on a mouthful of salt water. My chest burned as I spat the snorkel, surfaced for a breath, then ducked back down, furious. "That is enough!"

Charlie, watching from the dock as always, saw what had happened and leapt from the dock with a splash, paddling straight toward me. Of course he came. Of course he did. Even terrified, he chose me. His paws churned against the water, his ears plastered back. Jax darted over to intercept, circling him like a shark. For one heart-stopping second, I thought Jax might ram him too.

"Charlie, no! Stay!" My words were garbled underwater, useless, but my panic bled through every motion as I shoved myself between them.

Charlie barked, high and frantic, bubbles exploding from his muzzle. Jax gave a short, sharp burst of sound, something between a bark and a squeal, that sounded uncomfortably close to the word no. Then he swung back to the soundboard and slapped the surface above it with his fluke, churning up bubbles so the buttons disappeared in a cloud.

I broke the surface again, ripping my mask off, gulping air. Charlie scrabbled against my side, trying to climb onto me, whining. I wrapped an arm around him, chest heaving, hair plastered to my face.

"Fine!" I shouted into the lagoon, not caring who heard. "You win, Jax! No game, no fish, no anything!" My voice cracked, sharp with rage I didn't want to feel.

Jax surfaced a few yards away, eyeing me with that sly, unreadable look. Then he gave one short burst through his blowhole, like a dismissive snort, and dove. Gone, just like that.

Charlie whimpered, leaning heavy against me. I kissed the top of his wet head, but my hands were trembling.

I'd come into the water hoping to bridge a gap. Instead, Jax had widened it into a chasm, and for the first time, I wasn't sure if I should try to cross it.

Chapter Twenty-Three

20° N latitude Cozumel, Mexico

"Your parents have never seen the center?" I blinked at Isabel, genuinely stunned. She had worked here for over a year. Her dad supplied nearly all our fish. Her parents had fed us—Gabe, Charlie, and me—five or six times since we'd arrived almost three months ago. "How is that possible?"

She shrugged, twisting a loose thread on her sleeve. "Well, they work a lot. And it's not like we're really open to the public. And before..." She hesitated, eyes darting away. "Before, I didn't feel like I could ask if they could visit."

My heart squeezed. "They're so proud of you, Iz. They adore you. I want them to see where you work." I leaned against the railing, looking toward the lagoon where the water sparkled like broken glass. "When could they come by?"

"I don't know... Mom can't close the shop before five, and Dad isn't done cleaning up after fishing until four or later."

"That makes it a little tricky, doesn't it?" I sighed. "The dolphins usually don't hang around that late." I imagined Mr. and Mrs. Gutierrez peering into an empty lagoon, missing out on all the wonder their daughter helped create every day. "I mean, they can certainly still see everything, but it'd be so much more fun if they met the dolphins."

I loved her parents almost as much as she did. They were warm, steady, and kind in that way that made my heart long for what I didn't have anymore. And honestly, I wanted to show off the dolphins, and Isabel's part in caring for them.

"Maybe..." I brightened. "Maybe we host dinner here. On the pier. We can watch the sunset after we show them around. They can even take a little tour of *Windy*."

Isabel's whole face lit up, her smile bright and effortless. "They'd love that." She gave a little bounce on her toes. "Let's do it this Friday!"

"Done," I said, already picturing lantern light on the pier. "It'll be perfect."

***

Friday arrived warm and golden. The kind of day that smelled like salt, grilled corn from the food carts down the road, and possibility. Gabe had tidied up his tool disaster area in the lab so well I barely recognized it. I'd organized the chaotic mountain of papers on my desk until it looked almost respectable. Isabel had scrubbed the break room until it smelled faintly of lemon and elbow grease.

Around two o'clock, the usual time the dolphins drifted off for the day, I floated in the lagoon with Tursi circling near me. Sunlight shimmered along her back like liquid silver.

"Tursi," I murmured, brushing water away from my eyes, "I'd love it if you and some of your friends came back tonight. It would mean so much to Iz and me if Mr. and Mrs. G got to meet you."

Tursi clicked softly, then dipped her rostrum beneath my palm, a gentle nudge that sent warmth straight through my chest. Maybe she understood all of it. Maybe she understood none of it. Either way, I felt heard.

She rolled once, a graceful silver arc, then vanished into deeper green water. I hoped maybe that was a yes.

Climbing out of the lagoon, the hot wooden boards warmed my legs as I toweled off. I glanced around. Isabel was chopping vegetables in the break room. Charlie was sprawled in the shade of the pier chewing happily on a stick. My heart swelled.

Tonight had to be special. I wanted it to be perfect.

I was still rinsing gear and scrubbing salt off my fins when Gabe came strolling back from his dive shift, a giant bag of charcoal slung over one shoulder and whistling like he didn't have a care in the world. His skin was still damp, hair dripping little trails onto his shirt, and he smelled like ocean and sunscreen, my new favorite combination.

"That's a lot of charcoal for *Windy's* little grill," I laughed, pushing wet hair out of my face.

"I found a bigger grill in one of the storerooms," he said proudly, hoisting the bag higher. "Cleaned it up yesterday.

This way we don't have to cook the steak and shrimp in batches."

"How did I miss that?" I shook my head. "A bigger grill is a game changer."

"Game changed." He grinned.

Inside, Isabel was already chopping bell peppers, onions, and zucchini on the little breakroom counter, her braid bouncing as she worked. The whole place was fresh and bright, like excitement in the air.

The menu was a Gutierrez-family favorite: steak and shrimp fajitas. Perfect for cooking here at the center on the new grill and the small stovetops. The tiny oven on *Windy* could barely fit a baking sheet, so this was our best option. Isabel had brought her rice cooker from home and had jasmine rice steaming away, filling the break room with a soft, sweet aroma. I had black beans bubbling in the slow cooker on *Windy*, their earthy scent drifting through the open cabin windows.

I headed into the storeroom and pulled out the folding table and chairs. The metal legs clanged softly against each other as I carried them out onto the pier. We'd chosen the end of the pier because nothing beat the sunset from there: an open sweep of sky, the water turning from green to gold to fire as the sun dipped lower.

The chance of the dolphins hanging around at 6 p.m. was slim, but if they happened to be here, even just for a minute, it would be unforgettable.

I unfolded the table, smoothed out the cloth, and set out plates and napkins. The breeze tugged at the corners, so I placed forks on top of each napkin to keep them from blowing into the lagoon. Pelicans drifted by in lazy formation, their wings casting shadows that skimmed across the water like quiet brushstrokes.

As I arranged everything, I couldn't help smiling. I had real friends here. Not just coworkers. Not just boat neighbors. Friends.

Gabe with his easy warmth. Isabel with her fierce loyalty and bright energy. Her parents who fed us, worried about us, and somehow treated me like family from the moment I stepped through their door, something I hadn't had in almost six years. Even Dan and the guys at Aqua Safari, who had adopted me as if I'd always belonged.

I'd built more of a community in three months on Cozumel than I had in years anywhere else. That wasn't like me. I'd always been the quiet, keep-to-myself scientist on the edges of things. Maybe it had something to do with Gabe and his effortless way with people. Or maybe Cozumel itself held some strange gravity that pulled lonely souls together.

After our first date, Gabe had told me that Isabel and her parents knew I had lost my parents. Mrs. G had pulled him aside after that first dinner and asked what had happened to them. At the time, he had assumed they'd died but hadn't known for sure. And she, sharp-eyed, intuitive, impossible-to-fool, had simply nodded and said she knew they were gone. She could see it in me—she'd told him later. She was an astute woman; nothing got past her. Of course, I hadn't realized that yet.

I could smell the steak and shrimp grilling long before I reached the pier. The warm, smoky scent drifted across the lagoon on a lazy breeze, mingling with the sweetness of roasting bell peppers and the sharp citrus bite of lime. My stomach growled loudly enough that Charlie's ears perked. It was definitely time to start warming tortillas and make sure the beans hadn't turned to paste in the slow cooker.

The Gutierrezes would be here any minute. A flutter of nerves mixed with excitement stirred in my chest. I couldn't wait to show them the center, to show them Isabel's world, our world, but I kept reminding myself to hang back and let her lead. She was their daughter. This was her moment. But that didn't stop the spark of pride that kept flaring inside me; I wanted them to love this place as much as I did.

When Mr. and Mrs. G finally arrived, they walked down the path toward the dock with matching bright smiles, the evening sun gilding the edges of their hair. I wrapped them both in big hugs. Mr. G immediately slipped Charlie a treat from his pocket, and I pretended not to notice. Charlie had him wrapped around his paw.

I followed behind as Isabel took over, guiding her parents through the lab, then out onto the docks, her voice animated and warm. The pride radiating off her was enough to make my heart ache. She showed them the lagoon, explained feeding schedules, and pointed out the soundboard with the same excitement she'd had the very first day I met her.

"Do the dolphins really use those buttons to talk to you?" Mrs. G asked, eyes wide and soft with wonder.

"Oh yes! Marie has won grant money because they do it so well—tell them, Marie!" Isabel beamed.

I stepped forward, trying not to sound like an overexcited kid. I explained the research, the grants, the new waterproof soundboard Gabe had built, and how quickly Tursi had taken to learning new words. I got halfway through describing Charlie and Luma's unlikely friendship before I caught myself. "Sorry, I could talk about this all night. We should probably eat."

"No, no, first we want a tour of this sailboat we keep hearing about before it gets dark!" Mrs. G insisted.

So I led them onto *Windy*. The cabin lights glowed softly, bouncing off the warm wood and little brass fixtures. The space smelled faintly of cedar and salt and a hint of whatever soap I'd used when I last scrubbed the floor.

"This is an awfully small space to live," Mrs. G said, though her tone suggested fascination more than judgment.

"Oh, I'm used to it. I've lived on *Windy* since I started grad school almost six years ago."

Mrs. G gave me a sideways smile. "And you and Gabe both lived here when you traveled from Panama to Cozumel?"

I choked on my own breath. "Yes. Well...yes. There are two cabins," I said quickly, gesturing. "The main one up front, and a smaller one off the galley."

"I see." Her smile turned sly. "I hear you two are dating now."

If my face got any hotter, I would combust. "I... um..."

She took my flustered silence as confirmation. "You two are a good match. You shouldn't let him go. Someone like Gabe doesn't always come along. Back in my day—"

"Marisol," Mr. G cut in, "leave her alone. Can't you see you're embarrassing her? Let's go eat dinner."

I was very grateful, though I still felt my cheeks glowing like the setting sun as we stepped off *Windy*.

Before we left the cabin, Mrs. G paused at the spray painting Rolando had made on our date. She traced her fingers lightly over the colorful swirls.

"Rolando did this?" she asked. "It's beautiful... Charlie only has three legs... curious."

"Why do you think—"

She waved a hand. "Rolando has his ways, dear. I wouldn't worry about it. Now come on, let's go eat. It smells delicious."

We sat down at the little table at the end of the pier. The sky was already dipping into that soft pre-sunset gold, the kind that made everything, food, water, people, look warmer, more alive.

We passed dishes around, piling warm tortillas with strips of charred steak and pink curls of shrimp still sizzling from the grill. There were caramelized onions and peppers that glistened with olive oil, a pot of black beans fragrant with cumin and garlic, and fluffy rice that smelled of lime. The air around us was thick with smoke, salt, and spice; every few minutes the wind would shift and send a wave of grilled-steak aroma rolling across the pier, making my stomach do a happy somersault.

Mr. G thought he was being very stealthy, slipping Charlie bites under the table, but the rhythmic thump-thump of Charlie's tail on the pier gave him away every single time. I pretended not to notice, mostly because it made both of them so happy.

We were mid-conversation, something about Isabel learning to cook shrimp correctly, when the light shifted. Not gradually, but like someone dimmed the world by half a shade. Without a word, every one of us turned toward the horizon.

The sun had begun its descent.

It melted into the Caribbean like a drop of molten gold, spreading ripples of orange and rose across the sky. Clouds caught the colors, turning cotton-candy pink and lavender. The ocean mirrored it all, a shimmering sheet of molten metal broken only by tiny waves licking at the reef.

It was too beautiful to speak through. Too beautiful to breathe through. We sat in reverent silence.

And then, like the universe wanted to add its own exclamation mark, a sleek gray body shot out of the water directly across the sunset. Kai arced in a perfect crescent, sun glowing through his spray, droplets catching fire in the last light of day.

Mrs. G gasped. I felt the sound in my chest.

Another dolphin followed, Tursi, leaping with even more height, her whole body outlined in a halo of sunlit mist. Then Solana. Then Maris. Even shy little Isla darted in with a small, sweet half-jump, barely clearing the surface but shimmering all the same. They played like that for several minutes, jumping, spinning, surfacing in trios and pairs, a sunset ballet just for us. Even though I saw the dolphins every day, something about this moment felt different. As if they knew this night mattered. When they finally turned toward the pier and swam in, the water around them glowed bronze, swirling with reflected colors.

"Go say hi," I whispered, nudging Mr. and Mrs. G forward.

Tursi was the first to reach them, lifting her head high enough for her rostrum to clear the surface. She clicked softly, a greeting as gentle as a handshake. Her eyes were bright with curiosity.

"What's she saying to us?" Mrs. G whispered, voice trembling with awe.

"She's just saying hi, Mom," Isabel said, eyes shining.

One by one, the others approached. Solana hovered close enough that Mr. G reached out and let his hand skim her back, just a whisper of a touch. Maris bobbed under the pier, popping up on Mrs. G's other side with a squeaky whistle that made her laugh through her tears. Even Isla swam tight circles near Isabel's ankles, letting herself be seen without demanding attention.

The air hummed with joy, quiet, warm, living joy that settled on my skin and sank right into my heart.

I crouched down beside Tursi, my feet hanging over the edge of the pier, the water licking at my toes. "Thanks so much for coming tonight," I told her softly. "It means so much that they got to meet you."

She gave a soft, almost musical chirp and nudged her rostrum against the wooden beam, like she understood exactly what I'd said.

My eyes stung. I blinked the emotion back, but only barely.

The dolphins lingered for another minute, one last glide by, one last curious look, before turning as a group and slipping back into deeper water, their dorsal fins fading into the darkening sea like shadows. The world felt impossibly gentle in their wake.

As we gathered up plates and leftovers, Mr. G touched my elbow. "Walk with me a second?"

We stepped a few paces down the pier toward the lab. The breeze lifted the smell of grilled shrimp from the plates we'd just cleared. A pale wash of moonlight had begun to rise over the lagoon.

He looked out at the water for a long, quiet beat before speaking. "Marie," he said, voice low. "Thank you."

"For dinner?" I teased softly.

He shook his head with a smile that didn't quite reach his eyes. "For bringing my daughter back to life."

My breath hitched.

"She was lost for a while," he continued. "Drifting. Feeling like she wasn't good enough, or smart enough, or... enough of anything." He swallowed. "Since you came, she wakes up excited. She comes home talking about dolphins and research and things I don't fully understand." He chuckled. "But she's glowing again. Like she used to when she was little."

Emotion tightened my throat, warm and unexpected.

"You gave her purpose," he said. "You gave her a future. You gave her joy." He cleared his throat softly. "I can never thank you enough for that."

I didn't trust my voice, so I squeezed his hand instead. The gesture said everything.

As we walked back toward the table, toward the lantern glow, and laughter, and the last wisps of dinner smoke curling into the night, it hit me with quiet certainty: I wasn't just building a research program here. I was building a life. A real home.

Chapter Twenty-Four

20° N latitude Cozumel, Mexico

The next week, I was feeling confident. I wanted to work on something more complicated with Tursi. I chose the words Trust and Love.

Two words that sounded so simple. But the more I thought about them, the more impossible they felt to explain.

The two words felt connected, almost inseparable, but I didn't think I could explain love to a dolphin without first helping her understand trust. And honestly, I wasn't sure I understood it myself.

I looked up the definition online: "Trust, at its core, is confident belief in the reliability, truth, ability, or strength of someone or something." That sounded clinical, too polished to mean anything. Another description said, "It's about feeling secure in another's intentions and actions, based on their past behavior and demonstrated character."

That one landed a little closer. Still, it wasn't something you could just... teach through words.

I never taught Charlie the word trust, but he knew it. I knew it. I trusted him completely, his judgment of people, his instincts about weather, the way he somehow knew when I needed him close. I trusted that he was good, and that he cared.

Then it hit me. Trust is about giving up control and believing the other won't hurt you. I'd never put it into words like that before.

That might be the hardest thing to explain to any creature, especially one who's had to rely on humans for food and care. Still, Tursi was different. She already seemed to sense things I couldn't even define. And these dolphins were still wild. They chose to be in the lagoon; they didn't completely rely on us for food like most dolphins used in research did.

Trust, I realized, was all about vulnerability. It's what happens when you give someone the power to hurt you, but believe, deeply, that they won't. Like a dolphin choosing to swim into a lagoon every morning to talk to some humans, maybe do some exercises and tricks in exchange for some food.

And suddenly, I understood trust at its core. But it didn't feel any easier to teach.

Next on my list was love. Even saying the word out loud felt risky, like I was about to overstep some invisible boundary between science and soul.

I looked up the definition anyway, because that's what I do when I'm trying to make sense of something too big. "A complex emotion characterized by strong affection, attraction, and deep attachment toward another person, animal, or thing."

Completely unhelpful. Just a string of human words stacked like driftwood, sturdy maybe, but hollow. Another said, "Intense affection; great interest or pleasure in someone or something." That one was... closer, I guess. But still too tidy for what love really feels like.

When I taught Charlie the word love, it wasn't philosophical. It was simple and small, just one button: LOVE YOU. It was really just him and me then, and I thought of it like a closing phrase. A soft period at the end of our conversations.

But Charlie made it his own. He used it like please after he'd ask for a walk or a toy, his version of saying I'm trying to be good, see? He also used it in moments that stopped me cold: when I came home crying, when thunder rolled in and I tried to pretend I wasn't scared, when he curled up beside me after I'd yelled at myself for some stupid mistake.

That's when I realized he understood more than I'd ever given him credit for. Maybe Love You wasn't just affection...it was recognition. I see you. I choose you. You matter to me. That was his understanding of love. And maybe, in its simplicity, it was purer than mine.

When I thought about teaching love to Tursi, I wondered what it could mean to a dolphin. Would it be about her family, the way she protects Jax even when he drives her crazy, or the way she presses close to me when she senses I'm tired? Would love, to her, be the safety of belonging to the pod, the comfort of knowing no one swims alone. Or could it be something even deeper? An emotional current running between species, wordless and ancient, that says: we are connected.

The more I thought about it, the more I realized I didn't just want to teach Tursi the word for love. I wanted to understand her version of it. Because maybe dolphins already know things about love that we humans forgot a long time ago.

This was not going to be easy. But it was certainly going to be interesting.

***

The next morning, the dolphins came gliding into the pier at 6 a.m. like clockwork. The water was smooth as glass, painted in soft pinks and golds from the rising sun. I fed them their breakfast and said my good mornings. Charlie barked his in return, tail wagging so hard he nearly slipped off the dock.

Gabe checked on the soundboard before heading out for his dives, setting up the new TRUST and LOVE buttons, then adjusted the underwater cameras for me. The buttons gleamed wetly in the morning light.

Tursi stuck close, her sleek gray body tracing lazy figure eights in the shallows, clicking softly like she was humming to herself. She was excited to talk today. I pulled on a mask and snorkel and slid into the water. The coolness enveloped me. Tursi surfaced beside me with a sharp exhale, close enough that I could feel the vibration of her breath through the water.

"Good morning, Tursi. I'm happy to see you this morning," I said.

She darted straight to the soundboard. Her rostrum tapped the buttons with precision: TALK MARIE.

Wow. Okay.

"Yes," I replied, pressing: YES and TALK on the board. "Good."

I grinned. "Tursi want new word?"

YES, came out of the soundboard immediately.

I took a deep breath, both nervous and thrilled. "New word trust. Trust means good, safe, know." I hit the TRUST button each time I said the word.

There was barely a pause. She pressed: TURSI TRUST MARIE.

Just like that. My throat tightened. I blinked hard against the saltwater already stinging my eyes.

Was it really that easy for her?

I looked at Tursi, her intelligent eyes meeting mine through the rippling water, steady and open. The late-morning light shimmered across her gray skin, each movement turning her into liquid silver. A warmth bloomed in my chest that I hadn't expected, a mix of awe and something deeper, something like hope.

I spoke as I pressed a few buttons: MARIE TRUST TURSI.

She circled me slowly, brushing my arm with her flank—a soft, deliberate touch, like a question answered without words. The water was cool against my skin, her movement sent gentle currents swirling around my legs.

I swallowed hard, my voice catching a little as I pressed the next buttons: TURSI TRUST JAX?

She clicked softly, a thoughtful trill that vibrated through the water. Her gaze shifted toward the deeper lagoon where Jax and Kai darted through the sunbeams, carefree. Then, after a long pause, she returned to the soundboard and pressed: JAX YOUNG NO SAFE.

I nodded, smiling through the ache in my chest. "Yes, that's fair," I said softly.

The lagoon felt still for a moment, as if the whole world were listening. I hesitated before asking the next question. One I thought I already knew the answer to, but somehow I needed to hear it from her.

I pressed the buttons slowly: TURSI TRUST RAFA? I had only added the RAFA button a week ago, but I knew she understood it.

Tursi froze. Her sleek body tensed, and she backed away from the soundboard, eyes wide. For a moment she hovered, suspended in the water, staring at me like she couldn't believe I'd even said his name. Then, in a sudden burst of motion, she returned to the board and pressed furiously: NO NO TRUST RAFA NO SAFE NO GOOD.

The words hit me harder than I expected. I felt a chill despite the warm sun on my shoulders. Tursi's clicks echoed in the lagoon, sharp and insistent. She dove once, fast, then resurfaced beside me, exhaling a spray into my face like punctuation.

"I know," I whispered. "I don't trust him either."

She lingered there, watching me, her eye so close I could see my reflection in it, small and uncertain.

I'd need to remember to erase this footage later today. I was pretty sure Rafa never looked at any of my research data, but he had access to the files and videos as the facility owner, and I certainly didn't need him seeing this.

Now to introduce love. The word felt fragile and huge at once. I wondered what Tursi's understanding of it might be. Could a dolphin grasp love the way humans do? Or would she interpret it through trust, play, and belonging?

Here goes nothing. I cleared my throat, feeling the salt-sticky breeze on my cheeks. "New word," I said softly, fingers moving over the button: LOVE. "Love means trust, like, friend, fun, happy." It was the best I could come up with using the words I knew she understood. I looked at her, half-grinning. "Let's see where that gets us."

Tursi circled me slowly, her sleek body flashing silver and slate beneath the surface. She made a low series of clicks and chirps, the sound carrying through the water like a question. I waited, nervous I'd tangled her up. Then she turned back, eyes bright and curious, and pressed the buttons: CHARLIE LOVE LUMA?

A laugh bubbled out of me before I could stop it: YES CHARLIE LOVE LUMA. I spoke it as I pressed the buttons, my voice coming out softer than I expected. If I had to define pure, uncomplicated love, that would be it. Charlie and Luma, my sweet dog and the little dolphin who adored each other without words.

I pressed a few more buttons: MARIE LOVE TUR-SI. I wondered if Tursi would understand I adored her as much as Charlie adored Luma, even though I didn't follow her around or swim after her.

Tursi glided closer until her flank brushed my arm. Her skin was cool and smooth, the faint vibration of her breath rippling through the water. She lingered there, then pressed: TURSI LOVE MARIE.

A warmth spread through me, light and quick as sunlight through water. I smiled, throat tightening just a little. "I love you too," I whispered.

She paused, eyes narrowing slightly as if she was studying me. Then, with deliberate precision, she pressed: MARIE LOVE CHARLIE?

I chuckled and nodded, pressing back: YES MARIE LOVE CHARLIE.

Tursi clicked softly, thinking again. Then, with a tilt of her head, she pressed another sequence: MARIE LOVE GABE?

The question hit me like a wave. I froze. My hands hovered above the buttons, my heart thudding in my chest. Love Gabe? My mind spun, replaying his laugh, his quiet eyes, the warmth of his hand brushing mine under the stars. Could you love someone after just one real date?

But it wasn't really just one date, was it? We'd been working together for months now. He'd lived aboard *Windy* with me for weeks at sea. The memory of his easy laughter drifted through my mind like sunlight over water.

I loved that he appreciated my research, that he cared so deeply about the dolphins and Charlie. I loved that he had a technical mind, the kind that found solutions instead of problems, and that he could explain circuitry with the same calm he used to name stars. I loved that he knew the constellations, could point out Orion's Belt even through the sea haze. I loved that he knew the names of the fish and corals and would tap my shoulder underwater to show me something rare. I loved that he talked to Charlie like he was a person, with respect, humor, and gentleness.

The word love echoed in my mind like a ripple expanding through still water.

I thought about Tursi's question. She waited for me, floating just beneath the surface, eyes fixed on mine. Her gaze felt ancient, almost knowing. The sun caught her skin in silver flashes, and for a second, I felt as if she could see everything inside me, the confusion, the ache, the truth I hadn't dared to name.

I took a slow breath, then moved toward the soundboard. My hands trembled. I couldn't believe I was about to say this out loud, even in this strange, secret language between species. But I would never lie to Tursi.

YES, I pressed. The word floated between us.

Tears welled and flooded my mask. My breath hitched. Through the blur, Tursi let out a soft series of approving clicks, the kind she used when Isla, the youngest dolphin, got something right.

This had been a real breakthrough lesson in communication, but my heart was a mess. I wiped my mask, blinking back the sting of salt and sunlight. The video. I couldn't delete it; it was too important. But if Gabe or, worse, Rafa ever saw it… I grimaced. It would be incriminating, embarrassing, or both. I'd just move the file to my own computer, tucked safely away from the shared drive.

I climbed out of the lagoon, the air warm and heavy around me. Isabel was waiting near the dock, clipboard in hand. "How'd it go with Tursi? Looked like she was talkative today."

"Yes," I said, forcing a small smile. "She was great. She's a model student."

As I rinsed the salt from my hair, the dolphins called to one another in the distance, high, clear whistles that shimmered through the air like laughter. I glanced back at Tursi, who lingered near the dock, watching me. I wondered if she understood what she'd done to me.

Chapter Twenty-Five

20° N latitude Cozumel, Mexico

Charlie, Gabe, and I were sitting on *Windy's* deck having grilled burgers for dinner, watching the sky deepen into that golden-orange glow that always made the water look like molten glass. I had my feet propped on the railing, my plate balanced on my knees. Gabe was telling us about his dives that morning with a group from Ohio.

"They were brand new divers," he said, grinning. "Some needed help putting their gear together. Two of them even forgot to add weight until they were bobbing around on the surface." He laughed. "But once they got going, they did all right. No kicking the corals, no touching turtles. They loved the splendid toadfish I showed them, hiding in his little crevice like a grumpy old man."

Charlie's head was on Gabe's foot. A few months ago, that would have bothered me, but now it felt natural when he cuddled up to Gabe. The air smelled like salt and grilled onions. The waves tapped gently at the hull, that slow, steady heartbeat of the pier.

Then, a sudden splash. Sharp, close. The sound cut straight through Gabe's story.

I stood, shading my eyes. A sleek gray back broke the surface beside us. Tursi. She chirped and squealed, circling tight, her movements jerky and frantic.

"Whoa, Tursi, what's up?" I called, surprised by her behavior. Her squeals grew sharper, almost like cries.

Gabe set down his plate. "That doesn't sound playful."

I could feel it too, a buzzing tension that had nothing to do with the warm air or the fading sun. "Gabe," I said, "get the old soundboard in the water, quick. She's talking about Jax."

He didn't hesitate. We'd kept the small, older board strapped to the rail for when the dolphins came by. He dropped it over the edge, water sloshing against the hull.

Tursi was on it instantly. She pressed her rostrum hard to the buttons, clicking and squeaking in between.

JAX TROUBLE DEEP BAD. She rammed each button hard with her rostrum.

"Is he stuck under the dock?" It was my first thought, even though Gabe and Isabel had put netting up to keep the dolphins from going under there and getting caught up.

NO DOCK DEEP. The board echoed as Tursi's whistles overlapped, high and urgent. She circled back, pushing at a spot where there weren't any buttons. Water sprayed up in frustrated bursts.

"Easy, Tursi, show me again," I said, heart pounding.

But she rammed the same place again and again. It was the spot where, on the big board at the lagoon, the word FISHING LINE was positioned.

"Oh no." My throat went dry. "She's trying to say Jax is tangled in fishing line, deep."

Tursi let out a long, mournful whistle that made my skin prickle. Charlie was up now, pacing and whining at the sound, ears flattened. Gabe's eyes met mine, wide, steady, and already shifting into action mode.

"Gabe, go grab tanks, trimix if it's available, air if not, and go fast. Meet me on the dock."

"Trimix, not nitrox?" he asked, already on his feet.

"Right. We might need to go deep, I'm not sure how deep. I think Jax is caught in fishing line somewhere, hopefully close to the lagoon. We won't have much time to get to him."

"Whoa, okay. I'll meet you on the dock," he called, already running down the pier.

I was right behind him, heart hammering, feet pounding against the wood. The evening air was thick and heavy, our dinner forgotten. Charlie barked once from the boat, sharp and anxious, then fell silent as I sprinted toward the lab to get our dive gear.

The lights inside flickered when I flipped the switch. I threw open the door to the gear room. My hands shook as I grabbed my gear and a spare set Gabe used here: regulators, BCs, masks, fins, weights, lights. The familiar routine helped me focus, kept me breathing and moving.

By the time I reached the dock again, Gabe was fast-walking toward the lagoon, arms loaded down with two heavy air tanks. No trimix. We'd have to be careful.

He set one tank down beside me, catching his breath. "No trimix."

I nodded. "Air it is."

I tried to push away the creeping worry about depth. What exactly did "deep" mean to Tursi? With trimix, a blend of oxygen, nitrogen, and helium, we could have gone to 300 feet safely, maybe more. The helium helps prevent the toxic buildup of nitrogen and oxygen under pressure, but without it... we were limited. 130 feet, maybe less, depending on conditions.

And I knew my limit. Around 110 feet, I started to feel it, that weird, dreamy haze of nitrogen narcosis. It was like being just a little drunk, warm, fuzzy, confident, maybe too confident, and dangerously slow to think. I couldn't afford that now. Not if Jax was tangled and running out of oxygen.

Tursi surfaced again beside the dock, squealing and clicking so fast the sounds overlapped into one long, trembling note. Her urgency buzzed through me like static.

"I know, sweetheart, we're hurrying," I said softly, crouching near the edge. "We're coming. Show us where."

She whistled once, a short, high note that I knew meant follow. Then she dove, leaving a small whirlpool where she'd been.

The last of the sunset was almost gone now, and the lagoon was turning to inky glass. But as we clipped our lights to our BCs, the faint shimmer of bioluminescence began to ripple in the water where Tursi had been, like stardust swirling in liquid form.

Gabe looked at me, mask in hand. "You ready?"

I nodded, swallowing the tight lump in my throat. "Let's go find him."

We slipped into the water together, the world instantly colder and quieter, except for the soft hum of the sea and, somewhere below, Tursi's fading clicks, leading us into the dark.

We descended to twenty feet, following Tursi as she darted toward the south end of the lagoon where the seafloor dropped away quickly into deeper water. My heartbeat echoed in my ears louder than the hiss of my regulator. The last of the sunset filtered down through the water in thin ribbons of gold and green, fading fast into blue shadow.

Tursi dove straight down, a streak of silver vanishing into the dark. Gabe followed immediately, his fins slicing the water in long, powerful kicks. I had to take it slower, pausing to equalize the pressure in my ears, swallowing hard, exhaling through my nose, but I pushed myself as fast as I could. The water was cooler now, heavier. The faint glow of our dive lights cut narrow tunnels through the black.

At eighty feet, there was still no sign of Jax. Only the reef wall rising beside us, covered in waving sea fans and dark crevices where the light couldn't reach. My chest tightened, both from depth and worry.

Tursi slowed, circling a massive coral head that loomed out of the darkness like a boulder from another world. When I shone my light across it, my stomach dropped. The coral was wrapped in a thick snarl of fishing line. It glinted silver in the beam of my light.

Then I saw him. Jax.

He was thrashing weakly against the reef, rolling his body in tight circles, his movements frantic but fading. His sleek gray skin was marred with deep, angry cuts where the line had bitten into him, across his flanks, around his rostrum, even across his pectoral fins. My throat ached seeing him like that, this strong, stubborn dolphin who had spent months testing every boundary, now caught and helpless.

Gabe was already there, working fast with his dive knife. Bubbles streamed from his regulator as he sawed through the line, methodical but desperate. Jax stilled a little when he saw Gabe, his dark eye caught the light, and I could swear there was relief in it, maybe even trust.

I pulled my knife free and joined in, sawing through strand after strand of that thin, invisible death trap. The current had carried more line around the coral, making it almost impossible to see where it started or ended. My fingers brushed Jax's skin and came away slick, not blood exactly, but the rubbery smoothness of dolphin flesh torn raw.

We were already at 120 feet. My dive computer beeped a warning, its sharp electronic chirp muffled in the deep water. Not much time left, not on our air, not before we hit our no-decompression limit. And Jax... he had even less.

I didn't know how long he'd been trapped. Dolphins usually breathe every five to seven minutes, sometimes ten if they're resting, but not while panicking. He must have been holding his breath to exhaustion.

We worked like our lives depended on it. Jax's life did.

The line loosened around his body, and I felt him start to move again, small, jerky pulls at first, then stronger, urgent. He was fighting to get to the surface now, instinct taking over. I cut through another tangle, the plastic line snapping with a sharp twang that I could feel more than hear.

And, in a rush of motion, he was free.

Jax shot upward, a blur of motion disappearing into the black. The surge of water rocked me backward. Tursi whistled, a high, piercing note of pure relief that vibrated in my bones even through the regulator.

Then Solana, Isla, and Luma appeared out of nowhere, rising from the shadows like ghosts. The rest of the pod had come to help. They circled around Jax, escorting him upward in a protective formation, their sleek bodies flashing through the beams of our lights like streaks of quicksilver.

I turned to look at Gabe. He gave me a quick OK sign, the faint edge of a grin showing through his regulator. The water above shimmered faintly with bioluminescence stirred by the dolphins' movements, glowing green-blue trails that looked like constellations swirling to life.

Gabe and I had been at 120 feet for about seven minutes, breathing hard, our bubbles streaming upward in a constant hiss. My dive computer beeped its reminder, time to ascend. We followed the glow of our lights back toward the faint silver shimmer above us. The water pressed heavy against my body, cool and thick, the taste of salt sharp in my mouth.

We stopped at fifteen feet for a three-minute safety stop, hanging weightless in the dark, our bubbles spiraling up through the blue-black water like tiny stars. My heart was still hammering from the adrenaline, from the image of Jax struggling in that tangle of fishing line. I tried to slow my breathing, but each exhale sounded too loud in my own ears; the rush of air and the faint crackle of distant snapping shrimp along the reef were the only sounds in that suspended silence.

When we finally broke the surface, it was full night. The lagoon shimmered with faint trails of bioluminescence where the dolphins moved, glowing arcs of turquoise that rippled outward in slow, mesmerizing rings. All of them were there, circling Jax, their sleek backs breaking the surface one after another. The air smelled like salt and rain and the faint diesel tang from *Windy* on the pier.

I floated closer, pulling my mask up onto my forehead. "That was really scary, buddy," I said softly, my voice shaky in the warm night air. "You okay?"

Jax was drifting in the middle of the pod, breathing fast but steady, his dorsal fin slicing through the water with each exhale. He looked exhausted, dazed. In the dive light's glow, I could see the thin red lines of his cuts, raw against his gray skin, still oozing.

Tursi swam up behind me, her movements slow and deliberate. She nudged my arm with her rostrum once, twice, then pushed harder until I stumbled slightly in the water.

"I don't want to hurt him," I protested, my voice catching.

She pushed again, more insistent this time, guiding me forward until I was within inches of Jax. It was unmistakable. She was pushing me toward a hug.

I hesitated, then let myself drift into him. Jax's skin was warm and slick, the muscles beneath it twitching faintly as he rested his rostrum on my shoulder. He exhaled hard through his blowhole, letting out a wet raspberry that splashed my cheek, half sigh, half apology.

"You'll be okay," I murmured. "And I'm not mad at you. I really never was."

His breath came slower now, steadier, and when I looked up, the other dolphins had drawn in closer, forming a loose circle around us. Their clicks and low whistles echoed softly in the night, harmonizing under the stars like the sea's own lullaby.

For a long time, none of us moved. Gabe floating nearby, silent, the dolphins keeping watch, and me holding Jax as if sheer will and love could keep him breathing.

***

The lagoon was glassy and still the next morning, the kind of quiet that feels like a held breath. I hadn't slept much. Every time I closed my eyes, I saw the fishing line cutting into Jax's skin, the frantic look in his eye as he struggled for air.

Isabel and I walked onto the dock, the early light painting silver ripples across the water. Jax surfaced a few yards away, his dorsal fin breaking the surface in a slow, tired arc. The other dolphins hovered close. Tursi, Solana, even shy little Isla, all keeping a respectful distance, like they knew he needed space.

"Hey, handsome," I said softly, crouching at the edge of the dock. "Let's take a look at you."

He turned on his side, letting me see the worst of the damage. Thin, angry red lines crisscrossed his flank where the fishing line had bitten into his skin. Some had already begun to seal over; dolphin skin heals fast, but the deeper cuts still looked raw.

Isabel knelt beside me, scanning the wounds. "He's lucky," she murmured. "If you hadn't found him when you did..." She trailed off, shaking her head.

I ran a gloved hand gently over his side, avoiding the open wounds. His skin felt warm and smooth under the water, like wet silk. He stayed still. No tail slap, no indignant click, no attempt to pull away. Just stillness.

It was the first time he'd ever let me touch him like that.

"Looks like you're finally letting me in," I whispered, half to myself.

Jax blinked, then turned and glided toward the sound-board. I exchanged a puzzled glance with Isabel.

"Is he...?"

Before she could finish, Jax pressed his rostrum against a series of buttons: MARIE HELP LOVE.

I felt my throat tighten. "Did he—" I couldn't even finish the question.

Isabel's eyes were wide. "He said your name, Marie. And... the rest. That's incredible."

"I didn't even think he knew the placement of any buttons other than PLAY, SPLASH, and FISH. You're a surprising dolphin, Jax."

Jax surfaced again, meeting my gaze. His eyes, dark, steady, intelligent, held none of the defiance I was used to. Just something deeper. Vulnerable.

I slid into the water without thinking, letting the cool lagoon close around me. Jax floated beside me, and for a long, quiet moment, we just stayed there, human and dolphin, breathing the same air, floating in the same fragile peace.

"I love you too," I whispered.

He let out a soft, bubbling whistle and brushed his rostrum against my shoulder.

Chapter Twenty-Six

20° N latitude Cozumel, Mexico

I'd been in the lab since sunrise, the hum of the equipment and the rhythmic clicking of the dolphins echoing through the open windows. My peppermint tea had gone cold hours ago, but I was too focused to care. I was drafting another grant proposal, my third this month, trying to secure another year of funding before the current one ran dry. I was ecstatic about the first two grants I'd been awarded, but I didn't want to give Rafa any reason to put us back on "restricted budget." Between Jax's rescue, late-night observations, and the emotional weight of teaching concepts like trust and love to another species, I hadn't taken a day off in weeks.

But it was worth it. Tursi was using the TRUST and LOVE buttons in ways that felt meaningful. When she pressed LOVE while resting her head against Kai's side, I'd nearly cried. Jax, the young dolphin we'd rescued tangled in fishing line, was healing faster than I expected. The lagoon felt alive with hope and happiness.

I was mid-sentence, something about "interdisciplinary collaboration," when Gabe leaned against the doorway, his hair damp from a dive, a crooked smile on his face.

"Let's take a day and really go exploring," he said. "Check out Punta Sur and the other side of the island."

I blinked at him, my brain still half in scientific jargon. "We don't have a car."

He grinned. "Always practical, aren't you? Dan's going to let me borrow his Jeep. I've been giving him so many of my dive shifts, he says he owes me."

"That sounds fun," I said, surprised at the lightness in my voice. "Is this a real date too?"

He raised an eyebrow. "Do you want it to be a real date?"

I hesitated for only a second. "I think I do," I said, and immediately felt my cheeks warm.

On Friday, we packed a cooler with drinks and snacks and took the day off to explore the less-traveled parts of Cozumel. The sun was already hot by the time we left the lagoon, glinting off the turquoise water. We headed south from the center, toward Punta Sur, the island's wild edge. The Jeep rattled and bumped even on the newly paved road, its open sides letting the warm wind whip through my hair. Salt clung to my skin, and the air smelled of seaweed and hibiscus.

Charlie sat in the cramped backseat, tail thumping against the cooler, his tongue lolling in the wind. Every time we hit a bump, he let out a delighted bark, his head hanging out the side like he'd been waiting his whole life for this moment. I couldn't help but laugh.

For the first time in weeks, I wasn't thinking about data, deadlines, or dolphin politics. Just the road, the sea, and the easy rhythm of Gabe's hand resting near mine on the gearshift.

Our first stop was the Celarain Lighthouse at Punta Sur. The white tower rose above the mangroves like a sentinel, elegant and solitary, with its lantern room glinting in the midmorning sun. A narrow spiral staircase wound its way up through the cool interior, the air smelling like rusted metal. The walls were thick, painted the soft ivory of seashells. As we climbed, the view through the narrow windows widened, first mangroves and lagoons, then the pale sweep of dunes, and finally the endless blue of the sea.

By the time we reached the top, the wind was wild and exhilarating. My hair whipped across my face as I stepped out onto the narrow platform. The ocean stretched in every direction, layers of turquoise fading into deep indigo at the horizon. White foam curled along the reefs like lace. To the west, the calm lagoon shimmered under the sunlight, while to the east, waves crashed against the rocky shoreline in rhythmic bursts.

Gabe leaned against the railing beside me, his hand steady on the small of my back, not possessive, just grounding. "Hard to believe this is the same island," he said, his voice nearly lost in the wind.

"It's beautiful," I said. "I've always loved lighthouses. There's something romantic about them, standing guard over the sea, keeping people safe."

He smiled. "You'd like to think you're the lighthouse, wouldn't you? Keeping dolphins safe."

I laughed, a real, unguarded laugh that startled me. Gabe wasn't usually so cheesy, but he wasn't wrong. "Maybe I would."

Inside, the small museum was quiet, the air cool with stone and faintly musty with age. Old maritime charts and faded photographs lined the walls. We lingered over the exhibits, stories of shipwrecks and storm rescues. I traced the edge of an old brass compass in a display case and imagined what it must have been like to light that lamp every night, watching the sea alone but never really lonely.

From there we drove around to the east side of the island, where the landscape changed completely. The road narrowed and twisted through low dunes and sea grapes until suddenly, the open Caribbean filled the windshield. The water here was wilder, electric turquoise near the shore, shifting to sapphire blue where the reef dropped off. Wind whipped the waves into white froth that crashed against the rocks. The sound was constant, alive, almost joyful.

Charlie bolted out of the Jeep the moment Gabe parked. He tore across the beach in great looping circles, ears flapping, tongue lolling, stopping only to bark at the waves like he thought he could chase them back into the sea. Every so often he'd dive into the shallows, then emerge dripping, sand already clinging to his wet fur, tail wagging furiously.

Gabe grinned, watching Charlie dart along the edge of the waves, nose in the foam. "You know," he said, "I think the dolphins aren't the only ones who'd follow you anywhere. You've got that... steady pull, like the tide. Charlie feels it too; I can see it."

I tilted my head, studying the way his eyes crinkled when he smiled. "Steady pull, huh?" I said, laughing. "So I'm like some sort of... dog-and-dolphin magnet?"

"Exactly," he said, reaching out to tuck a strand of hair behind my ear that had come loose in the wind. He looked right into my eyes. "I'd follow you anywhere too, honestly."

I felt my chest warm, a little flutter in my stomach. The ocean stretched endless and turquoise behind him, waves crashing and white foam scattering across the sand, the wind tugging at my shirt and hair. I couldn't remember the last time I felt this relaxed, this... happy.

Charlie barked, leapt, and spun around in the surf, looking between us like he approved. I laughed, throwing my hands up. "Charlie, you really know how to ruin a moment!" It was far from the first time he had broken into a moment with a guy, but this time no one was annoyed with him. Gabe loved Charlie almost as much as I did.

Gabe laughed too, and for a moment we just stood there, watching Charlie chase the foam, listening to the wind and waves, and sharing that quiet, perfectly messy little moment together.

We walked along the shoreline, our bare feet sinking into the soft, sun-warmed sand. The air smelled of salt and seaweed and something wild, like freedom. Gabe reached down, picked up a tiny, pink conch shell, and handed it to me. "For your collection," he said with a grin.

"For the record," I said, "I don't actually have a collection."

"You do now."

We stopped for a late lunch at Mezcalito's, a tiny, tucked-away spot where hammocks were slung between the swaying palm trees. The soft rustle of the fronds mixed with the gentle lapping of the turquoise water against the shore. There were only five people in the entire restaurant, and the quiet made it feel like we had the whole island to ourselves. The salty breeze carried the scent of grilled fish and the tang of citrus from the ceviche being prepared in the open kitchen.

Charlie curled at our feet, one paw stretched toward the sand, ears twitching at every sound. The distant call of seabirds, the low rumble of the ocean, a scooter rattling somewhere far off. When our ceviche arrived, the bright reds and greens popped against the simple clay plate, and the tangy aroma made my stomach rumble. We dug in, the citrusy tang of lime and fresh fish mingling with the warm, earthy flavors of the locally made tortillas.

"This has been really fun... and relaxing," I said, leaning back in my hammock, letting it sway gently. "I can't remember feeling so comfortable."

"You've been working hard. You deserve to relax, Marie. Everyone needs a break," Gabe said, tilting his head in the dappled sunlight that filtered through the palm leaves, a soft smile tugging at his lips.

I knew he was right. I pushed myself hard, always setting high expectations for my research, my communication work with the dolphins. But right now, swaying gently in a hammock, the ocean glittering beyond the trees, and Charlie snoring softly at our feet, I realized it wasn't about accomplishing something today. It was about feeling... light. Content. Connected. Wow. Was I actually happy? Not because of accolades or breakthroughs, but just like this, sitting here, with someone I cared about, and a dog who made every moment better.

A gust of wind ruffled my hair, and I laughed softly, tucking a strand behind my ear. Gabe's eyes met mine, and in that quiet instant, everything else, the deadlines, the worry about Jax and the pod, the work that never ended... fell away.

We drove back toward town, but instead of heading straight to the center, Gabe turned into the streets of town. He parked the Jeep near his apartment, and we walked to the Reef Monument, a copper sculpture of scuba divers and a reef encircling the ocean. The metal shimmered faintly in the golden light, catching the last glints of sun.

We waited for just the right moment. As the sun dipped closer to the horizon, it slid perfectly into the circle of the monument, making the copper glow as if it were on fire. The ocean beyond reflected the colors, molten gold spilling across gentle waves. Isabel had told me I needed to see it, but I hadn't made the time. Standing there now, I felt a lump in my throat, a mixture of awe and regret at waiting so long. I wanted to cry at the sheer beauty, and the quiet gift of being here with him.

Charlie trotted around us, sniffing the concrete benches and nudging my ankle with his wet nose. He barked softly, his tail wagging, as if urging me to soak it all in, reminding me that moments like this were meant to be savored. I bent down and scratched behind his ears, feeling his warmth and joy spill into me, grounding me even as my heart raced.

I loved that Gabe helped me slow down, that he reminded me to notice life's small, fleeting miracles. I loved being here with him.

"I loved when my dad called me Rie. I miss hearing it," I admitted, my voice soft, almost swallowed by the breeze. I looked up at him, heart racing. I couldn't believe I was asking this, but I wanted it. "Maybe you could call me that sometimes?" My voice faltered, betraying my vulnerability.

Gabe hugged me close, the warmth of him grounding me. He didn't make me say any more words. "I'll test it out when the time feels right. But if it doesn't feel right to you, let me know...maybe more nicely than in Panama," he added with a playful wink.

"Shut up," I whispered, laughing through my tears, feeling light and unsteady all at once.

Charlie nudged my hand one last time, then plopped down at our feet, tail thumping softly against the cement, a contented little weight in the moment.

Gabe leaned in and kissed me as the sun finally slipped behind the horizon, the fiery glow of the Reef Monument fading to a gentle, lingering shimmer. The salty scent of the sea wrapped around us, the distant waves crashing softly against the shore, and I felt, completely, unreservedly, at home.

"Can we go to the square and check out the street painters?"

"Sure. You want to find Rolando?"

"Yeah." I gave him a sheepish smile. Gabe already knew I'd been a little obsessed with why Rolando had painted Charlie with one front leg missing. Every other detail in the painting had been perfect. The curve of *Windy's* sail, the shimmer of the dolphins, even the way the sea seemed to breathe with light. It was an incredible painting, especially for quick-drying spray paint on cardboard. That single missing leg had stuck with me like an itch I couldn't quite scratch.

We found Rolando in the plaza just after sunset. The air was warm and sweet, heavy with the scent of roasted corn and sugar from the churro stand. Lights strung between the palm trees blinked on one by one as musicians tuned guitars and children darted between the vendor stalls. Rolando was setting up his booth beneath a flickering lamppost, his array of spray cans lined neatly in rows like a rainbow of possibility.

He recognized Charlie first. "¡Ah, mi perrito favorito!" he exclaimed, spreading his arms wide. Charlie's tail wagged so hard his whole body wriggled. I smiled as the two of them greeted each other like old friends. Rolando crouched down, cupping Charlie's face in his hands, whispering something low and affectionate in Spanish that I didn't catch. Charlie licked his cheek and gave a happy snort before settling beside me, tail still swishing across the tiles.

"Can I ask you something?" I said.

"Of course, señorita."

"Do you remember the painting you made for me? It had my sailboat, the dolphins, and Charlie?"

"Yes, of course! One of my best, I think." His grin was genuine, proud, a flash of white teeth beneath the yellow light.

"Yes, it's a wonderful painting. It's... almost perfect."

He tilted his head, curious. "Almost?"

"Charlie only has three legs in it. One of his front legs is missing." I tried to sound casual, light, though something about saying it out loud made my chest tighten.

Rolando looked at Charlie, then back at me. His expression softened. "Ah, sí. That painting, I painted what Charlie showed me. He showed me a happy moment in his life. That is all I know." He placed a hand on his chest, earnest. "Sometimes, when I touch an animal, I have a connection. I see what they see. Dogs do not always see what is. Sometimes they see what will be. But do not worry." His smile returned, gentle and sure. "In that time, Charlie is very happy. Maybe it is his happiest memory of all."

The air around us felt suddenly still. I looked into Rolando's eyes. He absolutely believed what he was saying. There was no trick, no smirk, just quiet certainty and kindness. And Charlie adored him too. He leaned against Rolando's leg as if to prove it. Maybe Rolando was just a sweet, eccentric painter. Or maybe he really did have some gift, some bridge into the hearts of animals. Who was I to question it, when I spent my days doing the same thing beneath the sea?

Later, as Gabe and I walked home along the waterfront, the waves whispered against the rocks, and a salt breeze curled around us. The sound of the plaza music drifted faintly behind us, soft guitar chords, laughter, the rhythm of feet on cobblestones.

"Do you believe him?" Gabe asked quietly. "Do you think he can really see what Charlie sees?"

"I don't know..." I said, staring out toward the dark line of the horizon. "But I don't think I can completely refute it when I'm teaching dolphins about trust and love."

He smiled at that, a quiet, knowing smile.

"I should tell you something," I said, stopping to face him. The lamplight caught in his eyes, warm and gold. "Tursi asked me if I loved you the other day."

"Oh yeah? She's a perceptive dolphin. What did you say?"

I took a breath, heart racing. "I said yes. I love you, Gabe."

For a moment, the world went still, just the surf, the soft sound of Charlie's tail brushing the sand, and the pulse in my ears.

Gabe smiled, slow and certain. "I love you too, Marie."

Charlie barked once, as if to punctuate the moment, tail sweeping happily through the sand. Gabe laughed, and I joined him, leaning into the warmth of him as the sea shimmered under the starlight.

Chapter Twenty-Seven

20° N latitude Cozumel, Mexico

I woke before sunrise, warm and loose-limbed, still wrapped in the afterglow of my date with Gabe, our second date, our second kiss, our ridiculous "I love you" that tumbled out so unexpectedly and felt so right it made my cheeks heat just thinking about it. I lay in my bunk for an extra minute, cocooned in the soft hum of *Windy Possibilities*. The air was still cool from the night, smelling faintly of cedar, salt, and Gabe's shampoo—because I'd borrowed his hoodie, and it lay in a heap near the foot of my bed.

Life suddenly felt bright, like the sun hadn't risen yet, but somehow everything was already glowing. I had work I loved, dolphins who were choosing to speak to me, friends who felt more like family, and now... Gabe.

Then I picked up my phone.

Two missed calls from Ann Whitestone.

The glow shattered. My stomach flipped hard, like *Windy* had just hit an unexpected swell.

Why would Aunt Ann be calling me? I hadn't spoken to her in over a year. Technically, she was my only living family, but I never thought of her that way. Family was supposed to feel soft, warm, familiar. Ann felt like... static. Abrasive. Always one comment away from a migraine.

Growing up, I'd heard Mom mutter about her more than once. "Why can't Ann understand that I love my career and I love my child?" "If Ann had ever left our hometown, ever tried anything new, she might not cling so tightly to her old ideas," Mom said it with exasperation, but also pity.

When my parents died, Ann suddenly stepped in as executor of the estate, worrier, unwanted adviser. She'd insisted I take the rest of the semester off; I refused. She wanted me to keep the house and sell *Windy*; I did the opposite. She nagged me endlessly about finding a husband, settling down, and moving back home. I knew she cared about me, but she never understood me.

She started a huge lawsuit on my behalf against the airline. "To give you a chance at a good life," she said, shaking her head as though I hadn't already been building one. I'd signed papers, nodded politely, and pushed it out of my mind. Lawsuits took years, and I'd had much more important things to do.

When I accepted my grad school position at UC Santa Cruz and moved *Windy* out west, she'd exploded.

"So I'll never see you again, is that it?"

"With that kind of attitude? Probably," I'd snapped back.

We'd only spoken once or twice since, always stilted and awkward. Every Christmas, I sent her the same card, a picture of me and Charlie on the bow of *Windy*, wind in my hair, Charlie grinning. I thought it was sweet. I wondered if she considered it a personal attack. I could practically hear her opening it each year, clucking her tongue, muttering, "Still living that wild life. No husband, no stability…"

Now: two missed calls.

I felt the boat sway gently beneath me, water lapping against the hull in slow rhythmic taps. Charlie's soft snores drifted up from the foot of the bed. The sky outside the tiny cabin window was still indigo. Everything was peaceful. Except me.

Bad news. It had to be bad news. Instead of calling, I tried the coward's route. I texted her: Just checking in. The reply came instantly, like she'd been staring at her phone waiting for me.

Please call me, Dear, we need to talk.

Ugh. Dear. She knew I hated that. Fine. Better to rip the Band-Aid off. I hit call. My pulse thudded in my ears as it rang.

"Hello, Dear," she answered on the first ring, bright, almost musical. I froze. Aunt Ann had never sounded musical in her entire life.

"Um… hi. What's up? I'm pretty busy here," I said, not bothering to match her cheer.

"The lawsuit has come through," she trilled.

My brain stalled. "Come through? What does that mean?"

"It means you've got enough money to live comfortably for the rest of your life, Marie! It means you can leave that silly job and come home and settle down for good."

There it was. The old Ann flickering through. But her voice still had an edge of delight I'd never heard before.

"I love my job. I don't want to leave. I love it here—wait. The lawsuit is finished? We... we got money? Like, how much?"

"Just over two million dollars."

"Holy—"

"Marie, Dear, you knew that was the amount we were after. It's been on all the paperwork."

"Yeah, but I didn't think it would actually happen. So... what's your cut?"

"My cut?" She gave a soft, rueful laugh. "Marie, I'm an old woman now. I have no use for this money. It's yours to make a good life for yourself. Settle down, have a family."

"I have a good life now, Aunt Ann," I said softly. *Windy Possibilities* creaked around me as if agreeing. "I'm happy here. I think... this might be my home now."

Home. The word drifted through the cabin like warm air. For years, it had been meaningless, a place I'd lost, a place I carried with me instead of lived in. But now? I had Gabe. I had dolphins who chose to speak to me. I had Isabel and her parents. Charlie. Even the guys at the dive shop, who always saved me the last churro. Home had snuck up on me and made itself comfortable.

"For now," she said, but her voice wasn't sharp. More... wistful. "I just don't want you to end up alone like me."

The retort rose automatically, you were married once, and that didn't exactly work out, but I swallowed it. Last time I went there, it hurt her. And I didn't want to hurt her now. I wondered if all of her talk about settling down over the years had always been her own loneliness, instead of about my sense of adventure.

"Do whatever makes you happy, Dear. That's all I really want for you."

I froze, hand still pressed against the side of the cabin wall. Whatever makes you happy. I'd never heard her say anything like that.

"I'm happy here," I repeated. "And... I have a boyfriend."

A stunned pause. Then: "You have a boyfriend! Oh, Marie, why didn't you tell me sooner? What's his name? Will you bring him here for a visit?" Her excitement was so abrupt that I couldn't help but roll my eyes.

"His name is Gabe. Maybe we'll visit someday, but we're both really busy right now. I'm working on grant proposals. I'm hoping a few more come through soon."

There was a long shift of silence, the soft kind, like snow settling. I found myself thinking, if the grants didn't come through, could I use some of that settlement to support the center? Would I? The thought sat quietly in the back of my mind.

"Well..." Aunt Ann said, almost shyly, "Maybe I could come visit you sometime. If you're not too busy. I'd love to meet this Gabe."

She giggled. My aunt, Ann Whitestone, actually giggled. I stared at the teak ceiling panels over my bunk, utterly stunned.

"What?" I asked. "You'd... come to Cozumel?" Ann had never left Illinois in her life. She barely crossed county lines.

"You sound truly happy, Marie," she said, voice softening. "That's all I've ever wanted for you. I realize now my idea of happiness isn't the same as yours. You're a free spirit, like your mother. She and your father were always traveling... always laughing. They were so happy." Her voice broke. "I wish my marriage could have worked out like theirs."

A lump formed in my throat. I'd never heard her talk like this, not with honesty, not with vulnerability. For years, I'd painted her as rigid, judgmental, immovable. But maybe I'd misjudged her. Maybe something had softened in her too.

"Aunt Ann," I whispered, "I'd love for you to come visit. Really. I'd love for you to meet Gabe and Isabel, and the dolphins. And Charlie, he's such a gentleman now. Last time you saw him, he was still a puppy." My voice wavered. I wasn't sure why. "Maybe early in the new year?"

"Oh, Charlie," she said warmly, "he does look so dignified in your Christmas card pictures."

When we finally hung up, I sat in the dim cabin for a long time, the phone still warm in my hand.

Windy Possibilities rocked gently beneath me, the early morning light shifting to gold around the curtains. I felt... tilted. Like someone had reached into my life and rearranged all the furniture.

I didn't know what stunned me more: the two-million-dollar settlement or Aunt Ann telling me she was happy for me, and wanting to come visit.

Maybe both.

I curled under my blanket, Charlie shifting to press his weight against my feet, and decided to keep the settlement to myself for now. I didn't want anyone's opinions about me to change. I didn't even know my own opinion yet.

I just needed time. Time to breathe. Time to let all the pieces settle into place.

Chapter Twenty-Eight

20° N latitude Cozumel, Mexico

I should have been asleep hours ago.

Everything was finally going right, the kind of right that almost scared me. I was a freaking millionaire now. I had family and friends who loved me. Even Aunt Ann, for the first time in my life, was supportive. The dolphins were talking to us, actually talking. The recordings were clear, the syntax patterns were emerging. And Gabe...I could still feel the warmth of his hand on my back, his voice telling me he loved me.

Even Charlie knew everything was perfect. He'd curled up with a sigh like the world had clicked into place. And yet, as I lay in my bunk that night, staring at the faint shadows sliding across the low cabin ceiling, I couldn't sleep.

The air felt too still. A stillness that presses just a little too hard on your chest. The kind that hums with something unspoken. Charlie snored softly at the foot of the bed, his paws twitching in some happy dream. I envied him, his certainty, his peace.

Eventually I exhaled, long and shaky, and swung my legs over the side. The floor was cool under my bare feet.

I climbed the companionway ladder with the soft, instinctual quiet of someone trying not to wake their own doubts.

The night was dark and still.

The bay was glass, no wind, no ripple, only the reflection of stars, perfect and endless. The research center was a dark silhouette onshore, a faint glow from the security light bleeding gold into the water. Somewhere far away, a frog croaked, then silence again.

I wrapped my arms around myself, breathing in the soft salt and diesel and mangrove. And then I heard it. A single, crisp click through the hull, faint, unmistakable. My heart jumped. Another click. A higher whistle, distant but growing nearer.

"No way," I whispered.

I leaned over the rail, eyes scanning the inky water. At first, there was nothing. Then, light. A faint shimmer under the surface, like moonlight caught in motion. It pulsed once, then spread, a soft blue-green ribbon curling outward.

Bioluminescence.

I smiled without meaning to. "You show-offs."

The glow thickened, spreading until the whole area beneath the boat shimmered in pale turquoise. Then a shape darted through it. Sleek, fast, trailing a glowing contrail of light. Another followed, smaller, weaving behind.

"Kai?" I whispered. "Isla?"

A burst of air broke the surface, a quick whoosh and spray of mist that glittered in the moonlight. I laughed, startled, delighted. Kai circled back, slicing through the water, his dorsal fin leaving a comet's tail of light. Isla surfaced next, slower, her round head emerging just enough for one dark, glinting eye to meet mine.

"Hey, sweetheart," I said softly. "Couldn't sleep either?"

Charlie appeared beside me, toenails clicking on the deck, tail wagging sleepily. He gave one deep woof toward the water and looked up at me as if to say, They're here.

The dolphins stayed close, circling *Windy* like a dance. Every movement stirred glowing clouds in the water. It looked like the ocean itself was alive. A shifting galaxy of blue fire blooming and fading.

I knelt at the rail and dipped one hand into the glowing surface. The cool water tingled against my skin. The plankton flared brighter where I moved my fingers, like trailing constellations.

Kai rose again, exhaling sharply, the spray catching moonlight like glass dust. "You're painting in the ocean," I whispered.

A soft whistle echoed back, short, bright, rising in pitch. Laughter. The sound vibrated through the hull, through the air, through me.

For once, I didn't want to measure or record or label anything. I just wanted to be there.

I hummed a note, low, steady. Kai responded almost instantly, a short sequence of clicks and trills, like conversation. Isla added a gentle rising whistle, tentative but warm. The sounds wrapped around me, echoing through the still night air.

Something inside me opened. That's the only way I can describe it. Like my chest loosened, my heart remembering something ancient and wordless.

We know you. I didn't hear the words exactly, but I felt them, a shared understanding so complete it left me dizzy.

Tears stung my eyes. "I know you too," I whispered.

They circled once more, closer this time. Kai breached halfway out of the water, twisting, sending a shower of glowing droplets into the air before vanishing below in a blaze of light. Isla surfaced beside the boat, her eye level with mine. For a long, quiet moment, neither of us moved. Just breathing. Watching. Knowing.

Then she slipped away, the glow fading as she joined the others beyond the dock. One by one, the lights dimmed, the blue fire dissolving back into black.

The sea went still again.

I stayed there, hands resting on the cool rail, the night wrapping around me like a secret. Charlie leaned against my leg, tail brushing once, twice, before he settled with a sigh.

"Maybe they came to say goodnight," I said softly.

But it felt bigger than that. It felt like a promise, like a reminder of everything I'd ever believed about connection, and everything I still didn't understand.

When I finally went below, the air inside *Windy* felt different. Charged somehow. As I drifted toward sleep, I could have sworn I heard one last click, faint through the hull. A sound that felt like good night, sleep tight.

Chapter Twenty-Nine

20° N latitude Cozumel, Mexico

I rubbed my eyes and blinked at the laptop screen, the cursor pulsing like it was taunting me from the half-finished grant application. My third cup of peppermint tea had gone cold beside my elbow, the sharp scent still curling faintly from the mug. The morning sun pressed hot against the tin roof of the lab, warming the air until it smelled like salt, thawing fish, and sun baked plywood.

Charlie sprawled across the floor beside me, paws twitching, sighing dramatically every few minutes as if to remind me that fetch, not funding, was the true priority in life.

"Just one more section," I muttered, scrolling through the budget template. "We have a good chance at this one. If I can get it in by Friday, maybe we'll have funding for the entire next year."

But the words swam. I wasn't tired, not exactly. I just couldn't shake the strange hum under my skin, the left-over electricity from last night on *Windy*. The bioluminescent glow, the dolphins circling me like they knew something, the way Isla's eye had stared into mine as if trying to tell me...something.

The unease had followed me into the day like a shadow.

My inbox pinged. A welcome distraction, I thought. Probably another grant portal update. Or Isabel forwarding me another ridiculous meme involving a dolphin threatening to unionize.

I clicked over.

Subject: Private Transfer Window—Cozumel Cetaceans

I frowned. It wasn't addressed to me the "To:" field was blank, but my address sat in the CC line like a warning flare.

A mis-send?

Rafa's name hovered below in the thread, unmistakable. My stomach tightened. The room felt suddenly too warm, the air too still. Outside, a gull screamed, sharp, jarring, and Charlie's ears flicked, but he didn't get up.

I hesitated, fingers frozen above the trackpad. I should delete it. I should pretend I never saw it. This wasn't meant for me.

But something in the phrasing—"Private Transfer," "Cozumel Cetaceans" that awful clinical coldness made my pulse climb.

Curiosity or dread, or both, tipped the balance.

I clicked. I scrolled a bit to Rafa's reply.

And the words hit me like a punch to the chest.

I can guarantee private access to the facility. The researcher remains unaware of any arrangements and has no authority or suspicion that would interfere with your team.

The animals can be prepared for transport within the timeline you set.

I stared, unblinking, pulse pounding in my ears. For a second I thought it was a scam, some bizarre phishing attempt. Maybe I had misread. I looked back at the word transport. It felt wrong, like it had to mean something else.

But Rafa's name was in the signature, clear as day. The dates matched. The response was waiting right there, bold and businesslike, as if we were talking about crates of fruit instead of living beings I loved like family.

My mouth went dry. My hands went cold. The dolphins weren't research subjects anymore, they were product.

Charlie stirred, sensing something wrong, and rested his head against my knee. I kept reading even though I didn't want to.

And when I reached the final line, I slammed the laptop shut, my heart hammering.

The emails had been meant for Rafa. Somehow they'd landed in my inbox. And now I knew. I paced around the lab, Charlie following, confused. I opened the laptop.

I read the email again. This time reading the entire chain, but I still couldn't believe my eyes. I knew it wasn't legal to capture wild dolphins without permits. Even if it was legal, it was so far from ethical that I couldn't even fathom how anyone could do it. But as I reread the email, that's most definitely what it said.

Subject: Private Transfer Window—Cozumel Cetaceans

Mr. Duarte,

As discussed, the dolphins are fully conditioned and accessible. Their communication abilities continue to advance. The lead female responds consistently to English vocabulary words.

I can guarantee private access to the facility. The researcher remains unaware of any arrangements and has no authority or suspicion that would interfere with your team.

The animals can be prepared for transport within the timeline you set.

Awaiting final confirmation.

—Rafael Calderon

Subject: Re: Private Transfer Window—Cozumel Cetaceans

Rafael,

Your previous delays have already cost me time and resources. The CIMC has produced no profit and no progress toward repaying the funds I invested in your acquisition of the property.

You have offered these dolphins as repayment. I accept that arrangement.

Here are the terms:

• My extraction team will arrive at night.

• You are responsible for ensuring the dolphins are secured and restrained without incident.

• There will be no paperwork and no permits.

• You will remain onsite and compliant throughout the transfer.

Do not attempt to renegotiate. Your debt is outstanding and overdue.And, Rafael, if you fail again, remember that you are not the only one who is replaceable.

Confirm readiness.

—Marcelo Duarte Duarte Marine Holdings

Marcelo Duarte.

The name slid into place with a sickening click. I'd seen it before—on the list Ana handed me in Turtle Bay. Probable animal traffickers.

Subject: Re: Re: Private Transfer Window—Cozumel Cetaceans

Mr. Duarte,

Confirmed. The animals will be ready within the window you specified. The staff here are young and easily managed. The researcher suspects nothing and does not pose a threat.

You will have the demonstration footage by tomorrow. I understand my obligations.

—Rafael

Subject: Cetacean Transfer Proposal

Mr. Duarte,

The dolphins' cognitive and communicative abilities far exceed typical wild populations. Their facility with communication could be of significant value to your new Mexico City Aquarium.

They are habituated to human presence, healthy, and accustomed to daily training routines.

As repayment for the funds you loaned me to purchase the CIMC, I propose transferring the entire group and the communication device used in training.

I can provide footage verifying their capabilities and ensure they are ready within days.

Awaiting your approval.

—Rafael Calderon

I read the emails again, slower this time, as if maybe I'd misread them. Each word cut deeper.

My throat tightened until it hurt to swallow. The edges of the screen blurred, but I couldn't look away. This was because of me.

I'd taught the dolphins to speak, to trust, to reach across the impossible gap between our worlds, and now those same gifts had turned them into something to be taken advantage of. A hot wave of shame rolled through me. My hands went cold against the laptop keys, the metal edge biting into my wrist. I wanted to slam it shut, to erase the words, to rewind time by a single impossible day.

But I couldn't. Rafa was serious. He was going to capture the dolphins and take them away. The dolphins were in real danger.

The lab felt suddenly too small, too bright, too hot. I pressed my palms hard against my eyes, trying to block everything out, but the darkness only made the words burn louder in my mind:

ready for transport... the researcher remains unaware... private night extraction... repayment...

Repayment. He was using them as repayment, for some kind of debt.

My chest ached with that same hollow, collapsing pressure I'd felt the day Lilly couldn't stand up. The same ice-cold shock that had swallowed me whole when Mr. C told me my parents' plane had gone down.

But this time it wasn't just grief.

It was guilt—sharp and splintered, like stepping barefoot on coral.

I'd opened this door. I'd shown the world what the dolphins could do. And now I was the reason they'd be stolen, crated, silenced somewhere far from the sea.

I shoved back from the desk so hard the chair screeched across the floor. Charlie jumped, ears pinned. I couldn't even look at him. I stormed out of the lab, the air thick and hot in my lungs, and stumbled toward *Windy*.

I didn't even remember climbing aboard, just that I ended up face-up on the bed, staring at the ceiling fan slicing the air in lazy, useless circles. Charlie padded in quietly, tail low, and curled beside the bed. His eyes tracked me with that deep, dog knowing, like he sensed my whole world had tilted off its axis.

I couldn't cry. Not yet. The grief sat in my throat like a stone, too solid to move.

I'd ruined everything.

Now the dolphins, my brilliant, trusting, curious friends, Jax with his mischievous clicks, Solana's gentle certainty, Tursi's bold, fearless questions...

All of them would spend their lives in concrete tanks, circling endlessly under fluorescent lights until they gave up. Until they stopped breathing.

And it would be my fault.

I'd wanted to communicate with them. To bridge our worlds. To teach, to learn, to help others see what I saw when I looked into their eyes, intelligence, wonder...connection. And I'd done it. It was working.

But I hadn't accounted for greed. For the human hunger to possess anything beautiful. How could I have been so naïve? So stupid?

The dam finally broke. I pressed my face into the pillow and finally let the tears come, hot, unstoppable, and useless.

Charlie climbed up beside me, pressing his whole warm body against mine like he was trying to anchor me in place. I clutched fistfuls of his fur and sobbed until I couldn't breathe.

"Hey, buddy," I whispered. My voice cracked. "I ruined everything. I'm so sorry. I can't believe this."

Charlie nudged my cheek with his nose and let out a soft, worried whine. I held onto him like he was the only solid thing left in the world.

Then I heard footsteps on the dock.

"Hey, Marie? You in here?" Gabe's voice floated in, casual, unaware.

Something inside me thin and fragile as glass, snapped.

This was his fault too. If he hadn't recorded every interaction, every button press, every breakthrough, then Rafa wouldn't have had the proof, the data, the evidence that made the dolphins so valuable and vulnerable. He must have known someone could misuse it. Maybe he'd even known Rafa would. Maybe he'd been working with him all along. I knew it made no sense, yet it wouldn't leave.

The thought made my skin go hot.

"Hey, Marie," Gabe called again, closer now. "I need to order more buttons and casing and wiring. I wanted to check before I placed the order. I assume with the funding coming in now, it's no big deal?"

His tone was light, casual, like nothing had happened. Like we were just two colleagues talking logistics.

I saw red.

I stormed up the companionway and onto the deck. The sunlight felt sharp, too bright. "I can't believe you!" The words tore out of me before I even reached him. "You ruined everything! This is all your fault!"

He froze. "What? Marie, what are you talking about?" His voice was small, caught between confusion and fear.

"Rafa is going to capture the dolphins and take them to Mexico City." My voice shook with the effort of holding myself together. "He arranged a nighttime transfer. Crates. A plane. He's been planning it."

Gabe stared at me, eyes wide. Then he exhaled sharply. "Motherfucker," he muttered low and venomous. He looked back at me, eyes wide with something like horror. "You think I knew? Marie, how could I possibly–"

"You recorded everything," I snapped, slicing right through his protest. "You sent him the data, the footage, everything he needed!"

"I...Marie, I was trying to help you," he stammered. His voice cracked like he couldn't believe what I was saying. "I sent those updates to Rafa because I thought he was the one keeping the center running, because you told me he needed to know. I was trying to support your work."

"Help?" I spat. "You handed him everything. And now they're going to die, Gabe. The dolphins. My dolphins. Maybe not on the way there, but soon after. They'll give up. They'll lose hope. You don't come back from that."

He took one slow step toward me, palms slightly raised like he was approaching a wounded animal.

"Marie...please. You can't believe I'd ever—"

"Don't." I flinched backward, the movement sharp enough to make Charlie bark from below deck. "Just don't. Go."

It landed like a physical blow. Gabe's mouth opened, closed, opened again—no sound coming out. His eyes shone with something raw, devastated. He scrubbed a hand over his face, once, hard.

"Okay," he whispered. "Okay."

He turned and walked down the pier, his steps uneven, shoulders slumped like the whole world had just dropped onto his back. I stood there shaking, gripping the rail until my fingers ached.

I didn't go inside until he was a distant blur. When I finally stumbled below deck, the cabin felt too small, too suffocating.

I dropped into the chair at the table and buried my face in my hands.

Charlie climbed up beside me, pressing his warm head against my leg. His big brown eyes held that quiet, gentle knowing, like he understood heartbreak in a way only dogs do.

"I never should have trusted him," I whispered into his fur. "I should have known better."

Chapter Thirty

20° N latitude Cozumel, Mexico

I didn't sleep. Not really.

Every time I closed my eyes, I saw the dolphins, my dolphins, crated like cargo, their sleek bodies bruised from transport, their eyes dull with fear. The nightmare replayed, jagged and merciless.

Windy pitched violently in black water, lightning splitting the sky wide open. The dolphins cried out through the storm, raw, panicked whistles that shook something ancient inside me. Charlie stood on the bow, wind whipping through his fur, staring at me with Rolando's painted three-legged silhouette. A warning. A prophecy. Something I didn't want to understand.

Then the dream dissolved... sudden, brutal, and the memory that followed wasn't a dream at all.

It was the worst day of my life.

The day my parents died.

I was twenty. Second semester of junior year. Organic Chemistry, the class I hated most. I was taking notes when the door creaked open and the counselor, Mr. Cunningham, stepped inside. A strange hush fell over the room. He never interrupted class. Not ever. He bent to whisper in Dr. Chung's ear, and Dr. Chung, stone-faced, terrifying Dr. Chung, actually frowned.

Then they both looked at me. My stomach dropped.

"Marie," Mr. C said gently, "will you come with me, please?"

It felt like getting called to the principal's office in high school, which I'd never experienced, but suddenly understood. Everyone stared as I followed him out, my heart beating too fast for reasons I couldn't name.

Outside, the March air was crisp, hovering between winter and spring. The kind of day where the sun pretends to be warm, but your breath still fogs the air. I could already see the Mississippi through the trees, still frozen in wide gray plates. In a couple weeks, we'd get the Lasers out. Six weeks of sailing before summer. Something to look forward to.

"Would you mind joining me in my office for a few minutes?" he asked.

His voice was soft. Too soft.

"Sure," I said, confused. Why pull me out of O-chem to talk in his office? Maybe he needed volunteers for an event. Or maybe something with the sailing club.

His office smelled like lemon cleaner and old books. He gestured for me to sit in the big, overstuffed chair opposite his own. I sank into it, hands curled in my lap.

I'd known Mr. C almost my whole life. He and Dad went to college together, so every time my parents visited campus, we all went out to dinner with him and his wife. He was practically an uncle. I'd never seen him look nervous.

But now... his eyes were red. He took a deep breath. *Oh no.*

"Marie," he began, "your parents—"

"They're good," I interrupted, smiling. "They should be getting back from the Pacific tonight or tomorrow. They wanted to be home in time for my spring break so we can do a three-day sail on *Windy*. Dad wants to test the new gear before our big graduation trip down the river next year."

His face... crumpled. Just slightly.

"Marie," he whispered, "their plane went down."

The room fell away.

"They've been pronounced..." He stopped. The silence stretched, cruel and infinite. Finally he said the word. It was so quiet I could almost pretend I didn't hear it. "Dead."

"No." I said it instantly, automatically. A reflex. "No. It's a mistake. They always check in. They always..."

"I will drive you home," he said gently. "Your Aunt Ann will meet us there."

Aunt Ann? Really? That was the moment my denial started to crack. Not all at once. Just a hairline fracture.

"But I have O-chem lab tomorrow." My voice sounded wrong, thin, far away.

"Dr. Chung will allow you to make it up."

Dr. Chung never, never allowed makeups. He said it at least twice every lecture. Maybe it wasn't a joke. Maybe it wasn't a mistake.

He drove. I stared out the window at the bare cornfields and skeletal trees flashing past. Cows huddled in muddy pastures. The sky was too blue. Offensively blue.

I kept waiting for my phone to buzz, for Mom to text, *Honey, they mixed up the manifest! We're fine!*

But the phone stayed silent.

I shut my eyes and imagined I was on the bow of *Windy Possibilities*, wind in my hair, spray on my cheeks. Dad laughing as he trimmed the main, Mom calling out for someone to put on sunscreen.

If I stayed in that place long enough, maybe I wouldn't have to open my eyes.

When we reached my house, Lilly was at the door. She barreled into my arms, whining softly, tail thumping, so happy to see me. I collapsed to my knees. Hugged her. Buried my face in her warm neck.

And that's when the truth finally hit. Mom and Dad were gone. Really gone.

The sound that tore out of me didn't feel human. I clutched Lilly tighter as if I could hold myself together by holding her.

"We'll be okay," I whispered into her fur. "I'll take care of you."

But I didn't believe it. Not then.

I don't know how long I sat on the floor with Lilly before Aunt Ann appeared in the kitchen. I heard her talking to Mr. C about funerals and wills and arrangements I couldn't think about.

Eventually, he left. I went upstairs and lay in bed with Lilly curled against me. I stroked her fur over and over until my hand cramped. I didn't sleep. I didn't think. I just... existed.

Morning came anyway.

I found Aunt Ann at the table, drinking coffee and crunching cereal like it was any other day.

"Morning, dear," she said. "Have a seat."

I walked to the cupboard, grabbed the mug with the dolphin on it, filled the kettle, and set it on the stove. The normalcy of the motions felt absurd.

"I made coffee," she offered.

"I don't drink coffee." My voice was flat. "I prefer tea."

"Right." She cleared her throat. "Well. First things first. You'll take the rest of the semester off and come live with me. You can't stay in this house alone. In the fall, maybe you'll meet a nice young man—"

"No." The word came out sharp, surprising even me. "I'm finishing the semester. I'm going back to campus. I need to think about grad school."

She blinked. "Grad school? What nonsense. Your mother went to grad school, and what did it get her?"

"My mom loves her job," I shot back, louder than I meant to. Too loud. Talking about her like she was still alive. "She helps people. She makes a difference. What have you ever done?" I wanted to hurt her. I wanted to bring up her divorce.

But Lilly nudged my leg, sensing the shake in my voice, and I stopped before I could really hurt her.

"We can talk about your... plans... later," she said stiffly. "Your parents named me executor. You'll inherit everything. I'll begin sorting their documents today."

Everything?

Windy Possibilities.

My throat tightened. The thought of stepping onto the bow again was both relief and agony tangled together. But suddenly I knew. I needed to go sailing. Needed to feel the wind and the water. Needed to be somewhere that still held their echo.

"I... I need to run an errand," I said.

Before she could respond, I ran upstairs, changed, grabbed the keys to Mom's car, and Lilly and I headed for the marina.

Anything was better than that kitchen. Anything was better than feeling the grief crash over me in slow, unbearable waves.

And now, even years later, even after healing, even after finding a new home in Cozumel, a new purpose, love... the memory hit like the plane crash all over again.

Because tonight, lying on *Windy* with the taste of salt still clinging to my skin, I realized: I was losing family again. Not by accident. Not by fate. But because of greed. Because someone chose it.

The dolphins weren't just animals I worked with. They were my world. My second chance at connection. My everything.

And Rafa was going to take them away. My chest tightened until I couldn't draw breath. *Windy* creaked against the dock, the sound hollow, mournful. Charlie shifted beside me, sensing the old wound tearing open.

I curled onto my side, pressed my face into the pillow, and let the grief swallow me whole. The old grief of Mom and Dad, the fresh grief of betrayal, and the fear that I was about to lose another family I loved.

The room blurred. The memory faded. The ache stayed.

Chapter Thirty-One

20° N latitude Cozumel, Mexico

I woke with my heart pounding, sheets twisted tight around my legs, the echo of those screams still vibrating in my chest. For a moment, I wasn't sure if I was still dreaming, the grief, the water, the dolphins' calls, my parents—all of it still clung to me like humidity.

The cabin felt too small, too warm, too still. I pushed myself out of bed and padded barefoot into the galley. The painting hung just where I'd left it, its colors muted in the dim early light. I ran my fingers along the frame, tracing the outline of *Windy's* hull, the arch of the dolphins. Seven of them. Exactly seven.

And there... Charlie. With one front leg missing. A detail Rolando should never have known. A detail I hadn't been able to stop thinking about. It didn't feel like a mistake. And yet Charlie had stood right there in the town square with all four legs solid and strong. The artist's precision everywhere else, the shimmer of the sea, the curve of *Windy's* bow, made the single imperfection feel deliberate. Beautiful. And eerie.

I stared until the lines blurred and realized I was shaking. I wrapped my arms around myself and forced a breath in. And out.

If I couldn't sleep, I could at least think. I sat at the small table, opened my notebook, and started scribbling ideas. I needed a plan. Any plan. Because Rafa wasn't going to wait, and neither could I.

I could close off the lagoon to keep the dolphins out. Maybe block the inlet with nets? It might buy time, but he'd just capture them in open water. I could sabotage the crates or the transport tanks. But how long could I stall him? I could tell the dolphins to go far away and never return. The idea of it made my heart hurt. I still couldn't believe I'd put them in so much danger. My mind felt sluggish, heavy, like moving through wet sand. I pressed my palms to my temples, trying to force the fog away.

Nothing I came up with was enough. A tremor of fear worked its way through me, cold and sharp. Every sound outside made me flinch, the wind rattling the mast, a line slapping against the hull, Charlie's nails clicking on the floor. He kept pacing, ears flicking toward the door, whining under his breath.

"I know, boy," I whispered. "I miss them too."

He rested his chin on my knee, eyes full of worry. It hit me then how jumpy he was, how much he mirrored me. I wondered if he sensed that something deeper was wrong, that I'd lost faith not just in the work, but in the people I trusted.

Gabe.

Even thinking his name made my stomach twist. I wanted to stay angry. It was easier than admitting I might have been wrong. But the more I turned it over in my mind, the less it made sense that he'd ever meant harm. He loved this project. He loved them. And... he loved me. I knew that, didn't I?

I pushed the thought away. It was too raw. Too late to take back what I'd said.

Rain started drumming against the deck, sudden and heavy. I glanced out the porthole. Sheets of water streaked down the glass, the wind pushing waves into the lagoon. Must be an early-season Norte blowing through. The sky had that strange, bruised color, and the air carried that electric tang of salt and ozone.

Windy groaned against her mooring lines, rocking harder now. I set down my pen and wrapped both hands around my mug of peppermint tea, letting the steam warm my face.

The dolphins were out there in the early morning dark. I pictured them churning through the waves, confused and afraid, calling for me. And I had no idea how to save them.

"Dr. Mercer, permission to come aboard?"

Gabe's voice carried over the wind, startling me so much I nearly dropped the mug I was holding. I turned, heart hammering. The storm had dulled the morning light until the world looked bruised and gray, waves slapping against *Windy's* hull, rain falling in steady sheets that blurred the pier.

For a second, I thought I was imagining him.

"Gabe?" My voice came out smaller than I meant it to. I was shocked to hear him, and even more shocked at the wave of relief that hit me. I'd convinced myself he was gone for good after the way I'd lashed out.

He stood on the pier, soaked already, his dark hair plastered to his forehead, jacket half unzipped. "Permission to come aboard," he repeated, softer this time, a crooked smile flickering across his face.

I nodded quickly and stepped up onto the deck to meet him. My throat tightened. "Gabe, I... I didn't mean what I said yesterday. I know you care about the dolphins, and my research, and that you'd never do anything to hurt them. I'm sorry." I stared at my feet, the rain splattering against the deck around us, my words nearly lost to the wind.

He took a slow step toward me. "Rie," he said gently, "I accept your apology. I care about you. And we're going to fix this."

And then he wrapped his arms around me. His jacket was cold and wet against my cheek, but his body was warm, solid, grounding. For a moment, the storm faded away, the wind, the fear, the endless guilt, and all I felt was the thud of his heart under my ear.

He'd called me Rie.

The nickname I hadn't heard since before everything fell apart. Except for the last time I'd yelled at him. My breath caught in my chest. I had treated him like a traitor, accused him of the worst, and here he was, back, forgiving me, still ready to fight beside me.

I swallowed hard. "How can you still... after what I said?"

"Hey," he said quietly, brushing rain from my hair. "We don't have time for guilt right now. The weather's getting bad; there's a tropical system forming out there. It probably won't hit, but we need to be ready just in case. And, Marie..." he paused, meeting my eyes, "I talked with Isabel yesterday. I told her about Rafa and Mexico City. We came up with a plan."

"A plan?" My voice cracked. I'd been up half the night chasing every dead-end idea I could think of, and he just had one?

He nodded, that spark of confidence back in his expression. "Let's go out to the docks. I want Isabel to help me tell you."

The rain thickened as we climbed off *Windy*, fat drops soaking through my shirt and running down my spine. The lagoon churned with wind-driven ripples, the dolphins circling lazily, restless under the storm-dark sky. The air smelled like electricity.

Isabel was already there, her yellow rain slicker bright against the gray. She was laughing softly as Kai launched himself through a hoop, his body cutting through the water like liquid silver. When she saw us, her smile faded a little. She must have sensed the tension still hanging between Gabe and me. But then she lifted the hoop again for Kai, who squeaked happily.

"Iz," Gabe called over the rain, "let's tell Marie what we were talking about."

Isabel dropped the hoop, her face suddenly serious. "Right," she said, wiping rain from her cheek. "I've got coffee and peppermint tea ready in the lab. Marie, I can't believe this."

We hurried across the dock through the downpour, rain pelting our faces, the wind tugging at our clothes. The lab lights glowed warm against the gray sky, a fragile pocket of safety in the storm. My hair dripped onto the floor as I stepped in, shivering slightly from the temperature change. Isabel was already moving, her hands trembling as she poured steaming coffee into mugs for herself and Gabe, then added hot water to a chipped ceramic cup and dunked in a peppermint tea bag for me. The smell hit me instantly, sharp and comforting, like a lifeline. She slid the mug toward me and met my eyes.

"I knew Rafa was bad," she said quietly, "but I never suspected anything like this. This is next level."

Her usual spark was gone. She looked older, worn, and steady in a way that didn't fit her nineteen years. Her voice trembled just slightly when she continued. "Gabe and I talked. We think you should take the dolphins and go away. Like... really far away."

I blinked at her. "How can I do that? They live here." My voice cracked halfway through, part disbelief, part heartbreak.

"Marie," Gabe said, his tone steady but his jaw tight, "they trust you. They'll follow you anywhere. And you don't have to do it alone. I'll be with you."

Isabel wrapped her hands around her coffee cup, steam curling up around her face. "And for the record," she said,

"I want to go too. But Gabe talked me out of it. He's right, my parents would never let me, and if I disappear, Rafa will find us because my parents would send search teams. If I thought he was wrong, I'd be arguing right now." She tried to smile, but it came out crooked and sad.

I stared between them, my brain spinning. The rain beat against the lab windows, drumming like a pulse. Take the dolphins and go. The idea was insane. Taking a pod of dolphins away from their home, across hundreds of miles of open sea. It sounded impossible. But it also sounded like the only chance they had.

"Where could we go?" I finally asked, my voice barely a whisper.

"I've been thinking," Gabe said, rubbing the back of his neck, "Puerto Rico might be our best shot. Coral reefs, warm protected waters, far from anyone trying to capture them."

"Puerto Rico?" I repeated. The words felt heavy, foreign in my mouth. "That's... over two thousand miles. How do I know they'll follow? What if they just..." I swallowed hard. "What if they turn back?"

Isabel leaned forward. "They love you, Marie. They won't turn back."

Gabe nodded, his voice soft but firm. "You'll explain it to them, Marie, just tell them. They trust you."

I looked down into my tea, watching the steam swirl up like the fog in my chest. Puerto Rico. The words still sounded impossible. Dangerous. Unreal. And yet, deep inside, something flickered. Something wild and desperate that whispered maybe.

I took a breath and looked up at them both. "Okay," I said, my voice trembling but resolute. "Puerto Rico."

Chapter Thirty-Two

20° N latitude Cozumel, Mexico

We went down the checklist. Freshwater tanks filled. Extra fish packed. Old soundboard tested. I moved methodically, my mind spinning through backup plans, cross-checks, and what-ifs. Each motion felt mechanical, but my pulse thudded too fast, echoing the wind's rising rhythm outside. Isabel was on deck loading supplies, her hair plastered to her cheeks, her rain slicker snapping like a flag in the gusts as she ferried crates back and forth from the dock. The air smelled of metal and tension.

Down in the lab, Gabe was a steady hum of focus, surrounded by the faint clatter of metal and plastic as he packed up computers, cameras, wires, and casings, anything that might help rebuild a soundboard if we needed to. He was dismantling his world piece by piece, sealing it into waterproof crates so I could keep speaking to the dolphins once we were gone. The smaller soundboard only had thirty buttons, enough for simple communication, but not the rich, complex conversations needed for my research.

I paused for a moment, listening to the storm pulse through the lab walls, the creak of *Windy's* ropes straining against the dock, and the quiet efficiency of the man below. I couldn't believe I had ever doubted him. Here he was, giving up everything to help me run away with a pod of dolphins, and still making sure I'd never lose their voices.

We weren't leaving immediately, at least, that was the plan. Maybe a day or two more to prepare. That would give us time to make sure everything was right, that we didn't leave anything to chance. But tension hung heavy in the air. Even Charlie seemed anxious, pacing the deck and whining at the wind. The dolphins were jumpy too, clicking and chattering in short bursts, swimming tight circles in the lagoon instead of their usual graceful arcs.

The sky had that strange metallic cast that always comes before a tropical storm, greenish-gray and low. The rain hadn't stopped since dawn, sometimes a mist, sometimes heavy sheets that rattled against the water's surface like handfuls of thrown sand. The air felt thick, buzzing, electric, like the whole world was holding its breath.

"They just issued a hurricane warning for Cozumel and the eastern Yucatán peninsula," Isabel said, coming out from the office, her voice barely audible over the rising wind. Rain streaked her t-shirt, and her black hair was plastered to her forehead. "It's heading this way before turning north. They're saying it probably won't be a direct hit, but there'll be damage. They're calling for full evacuation, everyone's heading south toward Punta Allen."

The words landed like stones in my stomach.

Gabe and I were loading boxes of supplies onto *Windy*, food, medical kits, waterproof logs, when he froze, eyes wide. "A hurricane hasn't hit Cozumel in years."

"Not since I was a kid," Isabel agreed softly. Her voice trembled, barely audible over the rain drumming on the deck.

I tightened the strap around a crate, trying to sound steadier than I felt. "Iz, you should go home and help your parents prep the house."

She shook her head, her wet hair sticking to her cheeks. "But what about you? What about the dolphins?"

"We can manage," I told her. "We've been packing all day, we're almost ready anyway. We can leave early tomorrow morning."

The wind gusted hard enough to rock *Windy* against the dock. Charlie barked once, startled, and the dolphins let out a burst of whistles that echoed across the lagoon.

"The hurricane might actually be a good cover story," Gabe said, shouting slightly to be heard over the wind. "With everyone leaving, we leave too... and just keep going." He shrugged, a crooked, cautious smile breaking through.

Isabel and I both turned to him. The rain was coming sideways now, needling our faces.

"It could work. We just need something to tell other boats when we don't turn to head home with them," he added, almost to himself this time.

I looked past him toward the dark horizon. The sea was already roughening, short, sharp swells breaking white where the reef began. The rain had stopped for now, but the storm was coming, and fast. Maybe it was madness to even think of leaving now. But maybe madness was the only way to save them.

***

Less than twelve hours had passed, but the air was different now.

Heavy, charged, restless. Even before the first bands of the hurricane reached us, I could feel it in my skin, like the island itself was holding its breath. The palm trees along the shoreline bent and rustled with an edge of violence in the wind, their fronds clattering together like chattering teeth.

Charlie pressed close against my leg, alert, the hair along his back standing straight up. His ears twitched at every shifting gust, and I could feel the low rumble in his chest before he barked once, sharp and uncertain.

I rubbed his head with a trembling hand, more for my comfort than his. "It's okay, Buddy. We'll be okay."

The ocean told a different story. Swells rolled in harder, darker, as if they knew what was coming. The reef out beyond the lagoon was hidden under a thick gray chop. I thought of the dolphins and the way their clicks had sounded different that morning. Quicker, sharper, anxious. They knew, too.

How in the world did I come to be in this situation? A city girl from Chicago, about as far from the ocean as you can get, standing on a dock in Cozumel with a Category 4 hurricane bearing down on us. The forecasters still swore it would turn north into the Gulf of Mexico, just missing us, but likely still causing major damage. Everyone was preparing to evacuate to the south, including us. After that, we'd figure out our plan to head toward Puerto Rico instead of coming home. First, we had to escape the hurricane, then we'd figure out what to tell everyone.

I glanced at Charlie again, his brown eyes fixed on the horizon. Normally, he was perfectly happy to follow me anywhere, content to trust my lead. But today, with the first breath of the hurricane blowing in around us, I wasn't sure either of us was ready for where I was leading him. Charlie was pacing the deck, whining, his nails clicking against the wood. He kept darting toward the dolphin dock, then circling back to me, as if trying to drag me by sheer force of will.

"Charlie, the dolphins are fine," I murmured, though my voice was thin. "They know how to handle hurricanes better than we ever could. They can dive deep, ride it out, swim out past the worst of it. I just hope they'll follow us." I had told Tursi and the others yesterday that I wanted them to follow *Windy Possibilities*. It wasn't safe here. Tursi had replied that she understood and would follow. But I was a nervous wreck, afraid she didn't really understand.

But Charlie didn't calm down. His whining rose to sharp barks, insistent, unrelenting. Against my better judgment, I followed him to the lagoon.

The air stung with salt and tension as we approached the dock, the first real gusts of the storm bending the palms and rattling the rigging nearby. And then I froze.

Tursi's sleek head broke the surface of the lagoon. She fixed me with one dark, intelligent eye and clicked sharply, the sound so pointed it felt like a reprimand. I had expected them all to be out near the pier waiting for us, or at least safe in open water.

I fumbled turning on the soundboard, then dropped into the water with my mask and snorkel, heart pounding. "Tursi, there's a hurricane coming. The lagoon isn't safe. Why are you here?" I asked as I pressed: LAGOON NO SAFE.

She hovered, steady despite the chop, and answered: HUMANS GO SOUTH. STORM GO SOUTH. NORTH SAFE. MARIE, CHARLIE, GABE, ISABEL, DOLPHINS GO NORTH.

I treaded water, stunned. Every weather forecast said the hurricane would hook north toward Texas. Everyone on Cozumel, hell, the whole Yucatán, was preparing to flee south. Hurricanes almost never curved the other way. That wasn't how storms worked here.

But Tursi said north. And I trusted her. I trusted all of them. This was the real test: did I trust them with my life? My answer came before the question even finished forming.

"Wait for us outside the lagoon. We'll meet you soon and go north," I said as I pressed: GO NORTH TRUST TURSI. Tursi clicked, then slipped back under the surface.

I hauled myself onto the dock, dripping, my chest tight with adrenaline. Charlie trotted at my side, calmer now, as if satisfied he'd delivered the message.

In the lab, I found Gabe stuffing the last of our gear into waterproof bags. I blurted, "Tursi says we have to go north, the hurricane is going to turn south."

He froze, then turned slowly. "North?"

"Yes. Against the forecasts. Against everyone. She says it's the only safe way."

For a long second, silence pressed between us, broken only by the howl of the wind through the shutters. Then Gabe muttered, "We're going to look insane!"

My throat was dry. "Does that mean you're coming with us, even though we might be insane?"

"Of course I am, Rie. I trust you and the dolphins completely."

I smiled, small but real, and felt a rush of warmth that had nothing to do with the Caribbean heat. "Good."

He picked up the last two heavy bags, carrying them toward *Windy*, his movements quick, decisive.

I followed him. "We need to think about others, warn them. Isabel, Mr. Gutiérrez, the guys at Aqua Safari."

He shook his head. "They'd never believe us. Not over every forecast. Even Mr. Gutiérrez wouldn't. And Isabel can't leave her parents."

I opened my mouth to argue, but I knew he was right. It hurt to know we were going to leave them, especially Isabel. But I knew I was the only person who would believe a dolphin over all the weather forecasts. Even Gabe was following my lead. No pressure.

As he tied down the final load, Gabe glanced at me, his expression sparking with something fierce.

"This is our chance."

I frowned. "What do you mean?"

"With everyone else heading south, we'll be alone going north. After the storm... we just keep going. Detour to Puerto Rico. We don't come back. No explanations, no lies. No one will even see us leave."

My breath caught. "Oh my god. You're right. We wouldn't need a cover story at all. We could just... go." I actually laughed, shaky but real. "I never thought I'd be grateful for a hurricane."

The thought of the dolphins shadowing us across open ocean made my stomach clench. "But what if they don't follow us? It's hundreds of miles. They don't know distance like we do."

Gabe reached for the line, his gaze steady on mine. "Rie, they'll follow you anywhere. You trust them enough to take their word over every human forecast on this island. Don't you think they trust you just as much?"

His words sank deep, as heavy and undeniable as the storm clouds rolling over the horizon.

"What do we do after Puerto Rico?" I asked softly.

"We don't need all the answers today," he said. "We ride out the hurricane. We stop in Puerto Rico. Resupply. Then we figure it out together. We'll have options."

I exhaled, a slow, shaky breath, and nodded. For the first time since the storm warnings, hope flickered beneath the fear.

Palm fronds were ripping loose and cartwheeling down the shoreline, skittering across the lagoon like broken wings. The air itself seemed charged, thick with salt and static, heavy with the promise of what was about to hit. It was time to go.

I stood at the wheel, heart pounding, and turned the key. The engine coughed, then roared to life. Gabe moved quickly and silently on deck, hands steady as he cast off the last mooring line. *Windy Possibilities* drifted free.

I gripped the wheel, steering us into the restless gray chop. The waves weren't huge yet, but they smacked against the hull with a sharp, impatient slap, like the sea was warning us to hurry. My jaw was tight, eyes fixed ahead. Then I caught the flicker of silver through the water.

Dorsal fins. They were following.

Chapter Thirty-Three

21° N latitude 60 miles north of Cozumel, Mexico

The storm had chased us through the night.

Even now, hours after escaping the worst of it, my body still felt the phantom sway of *Windy* heeling under too much canvas, the sting of salt spray on my lips, the ache in my shoulders from gripping the wheel while Gabe shouted adjustments over the howl of the wind.

But the only sound this morning was *Windy's* halyard tapping gently against the mast.

We sat in the cockpit eating eggs, real, hot eggs, while the marine radio crackled with news from shore.

"...Cozumel... major structural damage..."

"...storm surge unprecedented..."

"...the hurricane did not turn north as forecast..."

I felt the words in my bones. "They all went south," I whispered. "Every boat. Every diver and fisherman. The entire island."

Gabe stared at the little speaker, jaw tight. "Everybody followed the forecast."

He didn't say the rest: We followed a dolphin.

Windy rocked gently under us, the swell softening each hour, as if the ocean itself was settling after a fistfight.

"I just hope people are okay," I said softly. "And that no boats sank."

Before Gabe could answer, the marine radio chirped, a different tone, local, faint, slightly garbled.

"...CIMC... *Windy*, do you copy?"

My heart lurched. "Isabel?"

Gabe lunged for the handset and handed it to me.

"This is *Windy*, go ahead."

There was a burst of static, then Isabel's voice, thin, shaking. "Marie? Gabe? Oh thank goodness. Are you safe?"

"Yes, we're safe. We went north. We avoided the worst of it." I swallowed hard. "Are you okay?"

Another burst of static. I imagined her clutching the handset with white knuckles. "We're alive. My parents and I, we're on the fishing boat. It's mostly ok... Marie, it was awful. Boats sank. So many boats. People were in the water, and the current was crazy. But everyone helped each other; fishermen jumped in to grab people. A dive boat picked up five swimmers from a capsized dive boat. It's a mess down here." Her breath hitched. She was trying not to cry.

I squeezed my eyes shut. "Iz... I'm so sorry. I wish—"

"I know," she cut in, voice trembling, "I know, Marie. But you saved yourselves. That storm wasn't natural. It didn't behave like any storm I've seen. Even Dad has never seen anything like it. And after what happened with Tursi..." A choked sound. "I wouldn't have believed it before. But now... I think she really did know."

Another voice entered, Mr. Gutierrez, steadier but heavy with exhaustion. "Marie," he said, "I don't know how your dolphin told you, but she did. We all went south. Everyone. If there's ever a next time, I'll follow that dolphin anywhere."

I pressed the radio to my forehead, tears burning behind my eyes. "I'm glad you're all safe," I whispered.

"We'll check in again soon," Isabel said. "Utilities are out, and the marina is... not good. But we'll manage. Just... stay safe. Wherever you are."

The radio clicked to silence. For a long moment, neither Gabe nor I spoke. The grief in Isabel's voice sat between us like a weight. And the relief, shaking, exhausted relief, made my knees weak.

"They're alive," I said. "That's enough. That's everything."

Gabe nodded softly. "Yeah."

The quiet that followed felt different now. Not peaceful. Not guilty. Just... raw.

We ate the last of our eggs in silence, *Windy* creaking gently beneath us. And that's when a sharp, excited squeal split the morning air. I jumped up and hurried to the rail.

"Tursi?" I called. She surfaced, eyes shining, two silver fish flashing in her mouth. She swam with a bounce in her movement, a proud, buoyant energy. She tossed the fish onto *Windy's* deck with a triumphant flick.

I laughed despite the heaviness in my chest. "Are these for us?" A warm feeling bubbled up in my chest. The dolphins had never offered us food. We'd been feeding them for months. The reversal hit me like a small miracle.

Gabe grinned. "They think we're helpless."

"Maybe we are," I said softly.

I grabbed the portable soundboard and slipped it over the rail. It hung just above the waterline. I slipped into the water too.

Tursi swam before me, her presence grounding, familiar.

I tapped: FOOD THANK YOU.

She replied instantly: FOOD MARIE GABE CHARLIE GOOD.

I coughed around the sudden knot in my throat. "We love you," I whispered, my voice cracking.

Her response was a soft whistle, tender and low.

The dolphins weren't just helping us; they were taking responsibility for us. A shift. A change in the balance. A promise.

When I climbed back aboard, the sun was rising warm and golden. We grilled the fish on the deck, the scent of lime and char and sea salt filling the air. I wrapped the fish in warm tortillas with salsa and avocado we'd grabbed at the last moment from the center's fridge.

They were the best tacos of my life. Maybe because we were safe. Maybe because Tursi had given them to us.

Charlie sat politely beside me, tail thumping, giving me his best I never beg but I definitely deserve fish face. I slipped him a piece. He delicately accepted it like it was a priceless artifact.

The swell rolled gently under us, *Windy* rocking like she was tired too. The air had that strange, electric clarity storms leave behind, as though the world had been scrubbed of something gritty and unseen.

The dolphins were still close, circling lazily, Kai rolling on his side, Maris thwacking the water with her fluke, Solana peeking up with her crooked little grin. They stayed with us all afternoon. We watched clouds drift by. Made jokes about becoming a roving research vessel. Let Charlie nap on our feet. Checked the damage reports, then checked them again.

Everything Tursi predicted was true. Every fear, every warning. We were safe because she'd saved us.

Charlie sat beside me, tail sweeping lazy arcs across the deck, soaking up the warmth and the safety like a lizard on a rock.

"I think we're gonna be okay," I said aloud, mostly to myself.

But a quiet dread still nestled under my ribs. The dolphins had saved us. But somewhere beyond that wreckage was Rafa. And Marcelo. And their plans, their resources. Men who didn't give up. Men who didn't forget debts. Men who saw dolphins not as souls, but as inventory.

I stared at the line where the blue water met the paler blue sky. "We're safe for now," I whispered.

But it felt like the quiet breath before the next storm.

Chapter Thirty-Four

18° N latitude about 30 miles west of Puerto Rico

The days after the hurricane blurred into a strange rhythm, steady, almost peaceful in a way that made my nerves itch. *Windy* creaked and sighed as we sailed south and then east, the Yucatán shrinking behind us until it was nothing but memory and worry. The sea stretched out in endless shades of blue, calm and glassy one hour, choppy and white-flecked the next.

The dolphins stayed close. Sometimes they swam in lazy arcs beside the bow, glowing turquoise at night like living lanterns. Other times they disappeared for hours at a time, hunting, resting, only to reappear with a chirp or a splash that made Charlie stand up and wag his entire backside.

On our fifth night at sea, I sat with my back against the mast, watching the moon paint a silver path across the water. Gabe leaned beside me, his shoulder brushing mine in a way that made the loneliness of the open ocean feel smaller.

"We'll make Puerto Rico in another couple days," he murmured. "Plenty of time to figure out our next steps."

I nodded, but unease tugged at the edges of my thoughts.

There was something unnatural about the calm. Too much quiet. Too much time to think.

The dolphins sensed it too. They didn't whistle as much. They stayed closer to *Windy*, surfacing more often, heads popping up like they were checking the horizon for us. For danger. Maybe it was Marcelo's shadow stretching over the water even from hundreds of miles away.

Every night I dreamed of nets. Every morning I woke before dawn, heart pounding, listening to the low groan of *Windy's* rigging like it was trying to warn me.

We made good time, *Windy* slicing cleanly through the steady trade winds. Charlie adapted easily, eating, sleeping, sticking close to me whenever I moved around the deck. His fur smelled like salt and sun. His presence kept me grounded.

And every day, I checked the horizon more often.

On the eighth morning, the air tasted different. Heavier. Metallic. Wrong. The dolphins surfaced together, seven sleek heads in a perfect line, something they almost never did. Their whistles were sharp, urgent.

"What's going on?" Gabe muttered, stepping beside me as I adjusted the jib.

I didn't get the chance to answer. The dolphins whistled and scattered suddenly, breaking their easy rhythm. My stomach tightened. I followed their line of sight and felt ice settle in my chest.

A yacht, huge, gleaming white, with black windows glinting like sunglasses, was bearing down on us, cutting across the waves with terrifying speed.

For a beat, I couldn't even process what I was seeing, because the image didn't make sense here, out in the deep blue, miles from anything. But the hulking shape knifing through the water had purpose. Not coincidence.

Before I could speak, *Windy's* radio crackled to life. Rafa's smug voice filled the cockpit.

"Dr. Mercer... you've got something that belongs to me."

My throat went dry. Gabe froze beside me. The dolphins drew tight circles near the bow, restless and alarmed.

"Hand over the dolphins," Rafa continued, "and maybe I let you sail away. Otherwise..."

He paused. The silence buzzed like a wasp nest. "Otherwise, you won't like how this ends."

I froze, my hand still on the wheel. My heart hammered, but I forced my voice steady. "They don't belong to you, Rafa. Leave us alone."

And then the world lurched into motion.

A dark RIB—one of those rigid inflatable speedboats—dropped from the stern of the yacht, engines screaming as it gunned straight toward us.

Gabe swore under his breath. "He must have used our last satellite ping. I didn't think..."

The sea foamed white as *Windy* surged forward, engine at full throttle.

Rafa's sleek yacht loomed behind us like a predator closing in. But it was the RIB I feared, the black shape cutting through the chop, fast and low, carrying Rafa and two men with nets piled at their feet, closing in on us.

The dolphins shrieked, sharp whistles, frantic and high. The first net sailed through the air and slapped into the water. Weighted edges sank.

Luma's panicked squeal split the air. She thrashed wildly, caught.

"Luma!" Her name ripped out of me, raw and instinctive.

Before my brain could catch up, Charlie barked, a deep, furious sound I had never heard from him, and launched himself over the rail.

"Charlie, NO!"

Time fractured. I saw his brown body arc above the water, paws tucked tight, ears flattened. He hit the sea with a heavy splash and began churning toward Luma, determined, fearless, stupidly loyal.

My stomach bottomed out.

The loose edge of the net drifted wide in the churn, snaking back toward *Windy's* stern. It was too close. Then came the sound I will never forget, a grinding, choking shriek of metal on rope, a violent jolt through the hull, the propeller seizing in an instant. The net had fouled it, and Charlie was right there.

"CHARLIE!" My scream tore my throat raw.

I lunged for the rail, ready to dive in, ready to claw my way through rope and water and death, ready to drown trying. But pain exploded across my ribs as arms clamped around my waist.

"Marie—NO!"

Gabe dragged me backward, feet skidding on the deck.

"Let go! He needs me! CHARLIE!"

I kicked, twisted, clawed at his forearms, but he held on with everything he had. The wind stung my eyes. Salt spray slapped my face. Panic roared so loudly I could barely hear my own voice.

"I have to get him!" My voice cracked like it was shattering in my chest. "LET ME GO!"

"You can't!" Gabe shouted, breathless. "The prop is locked, *Windy* can't maneuver! We're dead in the water. Marie, look!" He jerked his chin toward the starboard side.

Only then did I see it. The RIB was swinging around for another pass, nets coiled in the men's hands, engines screaming like demons.

If I jumped in, the boat would roll right over me. Or the nets would. Or Rafa's men would grab me instead. My lungs seized, like someone had shoved a fist between my ribs.

Gabe softened his grip but didn't release me. "Marie... if you jump, we lose everyone. Not only Charlie."

His voice was raw, pleading. Not commanding. Begging. I met his eyes. They weren't cold or calculating. They were terrified. For me.

The world tilted. My face was hot, wet, my tears or the sea? Both? I didn't know. "I can't lose him," I whispered. "I can't lose him too."

"I know. I know." His voice broke. "We'll come back for him. I swear."

A wave slammed the hull. The RIB roared even closer. Rafa shouted something in Spanish, harsh, ugly, triumphant. The dolphins answered in sounds I had never heard from them. Not fear. Rage.

High-pitched, shrill whistles. Rapid-fire clicks. A warning. A threat. Then Tursi shot forward, slicing through the water like a silver blade. She hit the RIB full broadside, a bone-cracking, water-exploding collision.

The little boat lurched sideways. One of Rafa's men stumbled, windmilling his arms, barely saving himself from plunging into the sea. Jax surged up next, tail slamming the water with such force it boomed like a gunshot. The shockwave struck the RIB's outboard motor, making it sputter, cough, choke. Another dolphin dove beneath the bow, heaving upward with raw strength. The RIB rose, wobbling, then slammed back down, sending a spray of saltwater exploding into the air.

The dolphins were no longer fleeing. They were fighting. Protecting Charlie. Protecting each other. Protecting us.

And all I could do, all I could do was watch, shaking so violently my teeth chattered, my hands crushed in Gabe's.

"Please," I whispered into the wind. "Please be okay. Just let him be okay."

Luma shrieked, high, piercing. I saw her twist, half-wrapped in the sinking net. Tursi darted in from below, slamming the mesh with her head. Jax rammed the weighted edge from the other side. For a second, the net ballooned upward, loosening just enough, and Luma exploded free in a silver flash. If Luma was okay, maybe Charlie was too.

Something inside me ignited. Not calm. Not logic. Something primal. A survivor's instinct, the same one that had gotten me through the plane crash, that had kept me alive seven years ago when everything fell apart. I grabbed the rail to steady myself as *Windy* bucked in the chop.

"We can outrun them, we can do this," I whispered through clenched teeth.

I bolted for the helm. My bare feet slapped the deck, breath burning in my throat. "We're not done yet," I told her, voice shaking. "We're not done."

I slammed a hand onto the throttle, neutral, before the prop could shred itself. *Windy* shuddered, her fouled prop useless, but her sails still full and waiting. They were our only chance now. The wheel jerked under my grip as I hauled the mainsheet free, letting it snap into the wind. Canvas boomed overhead. The boom swung dangerously, but I ducked just in time. *Windy* responded instantly, bow knifing into the open sea.

Adrenaline flooded me so hard my fingers tingled. "Come on, *Windy*," I breathed. "Fly."

Windy heeled sharply as the wind hit just right, the ocean spraying up in glittering arcs. Behind us, dolphins shrieked, and the RIB sputtered, its engine coughing.

I didn't look back. I couldn't look. I aimed us into the strongest gust I could find, let the boat lean into it, let speed and instinct swallow the terror trying to claw its way up my throat.

"Hang on!" I shouted, the words half to Gabe, half to myself. And then we were flying.

Spray drenched my face as we shot ahead, leaving Rafa's boat struggling in the churn of dolphin-made chaos behind us.

The dolphins surged alongside us in perfect formation, Tursi, Jax, Maris, Kai, moving like living shields. They slammed the RIB again and again, whitewater exploding around their bodies.

The sound of it was violent and beautiful, the wet thud of dolphin bodies hitting fiberglass, the engine roaring and choking, men shouting in panic, the wind howling in the rigging.

Rafa's voice cracked through the radio, oily and furious: "Dr. Mercer, you can run, but they always come home! You cannot keep what belongs to Cozumel!"

I gripped the wheel harder, my knuckles white. Saltwater streaked down my face, sea spray or tears, I couldn't tell.

"They don't belong to you," I screamed through clenched teeth. "They choose."

I knew he probably couldn't hear me over the wind, but the dolphins seemed to. Their clicks sharpened, fierce, echoing off the hull like snapping bones.

The RIB skidded wildly through the waves, men fighting to stay upright. When one tried to throw another net, Jax cut in front of *Windy's* bow, forcing the boat to twist in a spray of foam. Luma's high, furious squeal cut through the air, and she lunged at the RIB, sending water cascading up in an explosion. Jax followed. His tail came down with a whipcrack that struck the motor squarely.

A spark. A cough. A sputter. The engine choked. The men shouted, nets tangling around their legs.

Rafa cursed, an ugly, guttural sound, and swung an oar at Tursi, hitting only foam as she darted just out of reach. The dolphins answered with sharper whistles, warnings layered with fury I had never heard from them.

It was terrifying. And breathtaking. Like witnessing a storm explode from inside its eye. And underneath all of it, threaded like a needle through my heart, was Charlie. His absence was a gaping wound. My chest felt split open, each breath like glass.

But *Windy* kept cutting forward through the waves, sails humming, dolphins defending us on all sides. We were sailing, fast, angled, unstoppable. *Windy* slicing the sea, the dolphins a silver phalanx, the RIB falling behind.

We were fleeing for our lives. And for the lives of the dolphins.

Behind the chaos, Rafa's enormous yacht throttled down, unable to come any closer without running over its own men. It loomed uselessly on the horizon, too big, too slow. I caught a glimpse of Rafa standing in the bow of the RIB, soaked, furious, screaming at the yacht's crew to haul them aboard.

They'd lost their only chase craft. And we were still moving.

I was still crying, trying to steer *Windy* through a blur of tears and salt spray, when Gabe's voice softened beside me.

"Would you look at that. Marie... look."

I turned, and the world seemed to stop, despite our speed.

The dolphins were moving in a strange, purposeful formation, swimming in a perfect square. In the center, Luma nudged gently at a sodden, trembling shape. She clicked softly, a low, soothing rhythm.

My heart stopped. Then soared. Charlie. He was alive.

Blood drifted off him in thin red ribbons, but the dolphins surrounded him like guardians, close and protective, their bodies forming a living shield between him and the chaos left behind us. And then I saw Jax beneath him, steady as stone, carrying Charlie on his back to keep his head above the water, my wild, reckless dog riding the dolphin he had once tried to protect me from.

My throat closed. My knees buckled.

"Gabe, help me get him onboard. And grab the first aid kit."

We scrambled to the stern. Jax surfaced again, lifting Charlie just high enough for us to reach. I leaned over, hands shaking, tears blurring my vision. Charlie looked up at me, eyes glassy but aware, and his tail gave the smallest, weakest thump.

Relief broke over me like a wave.

With Gabe's help, we hauled him onto the deck. His body was limp and slick with seawater. His front leg was torn and bleeding—probably broken. Cuts striped his side. But he was breathing. He was warm. He was alive.

I pressed both hands into his fur, sobbing, whispering, "Good boy... you're okay... I've got you... I've got you..." The dolphins had saved him. They had saved my heart with him.

I forced my shaking fingers to grab the radio mic.

"Puerto Rico Harbor, this is sailing vessel *Windy Possibilities*. We have an injured dog, repeat, we need emergency veterinary assistance on arrival."

Static crackled. My pulse hammered.

Then Rafa's voice cut through, sharp, venomous, desperate.

"You think you've won? You haven't! They'll come back! You can't keep them forever, they belong to me!"

His words blew past me like exhaust, hot, meaningless.

I looked out at the pod instead, at the shimmering, spinning, joyous shapes of my friends in the water.

At Tursi circling close, clicking softly toward Charlie. At Luma diving and breaching in tight loops, her joy fierce and bright. At Jax rolling once, exhausted but proud.

Awe flooded my chest so full it hurt.

"They're with us," I whispered, first to Gabe, then to Charlie, then to the sea itself. "They're choosing us. All of us."

Gabe slid his hand over mine on the wheel. *Windy* surged forward as if she understood, bow cutting cleanly through the swell, sails snapping with new life. The dolphins tucked in beside us, escorting us away from danger, their bodies streaking silver through the blue.

Behind us, Rafa's RIB shrank into a speck on the horizon, broken, powerless, irrelevant.

Windy carried us eastward, toward Puerto Rico, toward whatever came next. Gabe at my side, Charlie breathing softly at my feet, and the dolphins leaping in our wake like sparks of living light. Still together. As the sun broke through the clouds and spilled gold across the sea, I knew one thing with absolute certainty: We were going to fight for each other. All of us. To the very end.

Chapter Thirty-Five

18° N latitude Puerto Rico

Puerto Rico appeared through a veil of morning haze, the mountains rising soft and blue above the harbor. *Windy* slid between the breakwaters with her sails furled, engine coughing, but mercifully still working, after Gabe had cut the netting away from the prop. My hands were numb on the wheel, not from cold, but from everything inside me shaking loose.

Charlie lay in the cockpit beside me, wrapped in a towel, his breathing shallow but steady. The dolphins peeled away before we reached the marina, three slow arcs, three whistles, then they vanished beneath the surface, like they knew they couldn't follow us any farther.

I felt their absence like a hollow in my chest.

A dockhand sprinted toward us shouting for the emergency vet team. People moved around us in a blur, voices I couldn't distinguish, hands lifting Charlie gently onto a stretcher, clips snapping, wheels rattling down the dock toward a waiting van.

Someone asked me questions. I think I answered them. My voice felt like it belonged to someone else.

Gabe stayed at my side the whole time, not touching me, just radiating his steady presence like he was afraid one wrong word would shatter me. He wasn't wrong.

Windy was secured. Papers signed. Charlie driven away with the vet techs. I watched the taillights disappear down the marina road until they became pinpricks, then nothing.

Only then did my legs stop holding me. I sank onto a bench by the harbor office and buried my face in my hands. I didn't cry. There was nothing left in me to spill. Just this raw ache behind my ribs.

Gabe lowered himself onto the bench beside me, elbows on his knees, staring at the water.

"I talked to the vet," he said quietly. "They're prepping for surgery right now. The... the leg is bad, but they think they can save him."

My breath hitched, a small crack in the numbness.

"They said he was lucky," Gabe continued. "The dolphins kept him afloat long enough. If they hadn't..."

"I know." My voice rasped. "I know."

A sailboat ghosted into the harbor, its hull slicing the water like a blade. A gull shrieked overhead. Someone laughed near the fuel dock. Normal things. Ordinary things. It all felt wrong.

I wrapped my arms around myself and shivered, even though the sun was warm. "I keep seeing it," I whispered. "The net. The propeller. Him going under. I thought I lost him, Gabe."

He nodded, jaw tight. "I know."

I couldn't pretend everything else was fine, we were still in danger.

"We need to talk about CIMC," he said gently.

I flinched. "Yeah. We do."

The marina had finally gone quiet, boats rocking softly, halyards tapping like quiet chimes, when Gabe and I found a place to sit on the seawall. I wrapped my arms around myself, more from exhaustion than cold. My eyes felt gritty and swollen from crying.

Gabe watched Charlie's stretcher disappear into the vet's building again, then sat beside me with a soft exhale.

"They said they'll call as soon as he's out of surgery," he murmured.

I nodded, staring out at the dark water. It didn't feel real yet. None of it did.

After a long silence, Gabe said again, "So... about CIMC."

I almost flinched. "I know."

"I'm not sure we can ever go back. Not while Rafa's in charge. That place isn't safe, for the dolphins, or for us."

He wasn't wrong. The idea of Rafa walking through the dolphin lagoon made bile rise in my throat.

"I've been thinking," I whispered. "If I could buy the center..."

Gabe blinked, startled. "Buy it? With what?"

I swallowed.

"The settlement."

His eyes widened. "Marie... how much was it?"

"Two million."

He inhaled sharply, almost a laugh, almost disbelief. "Two million dollars." He let out a soft whistle.

"Yeah," I whispered. "It never felt real. But after everything he's done, after chasing us to Puerto Rico, Rafa will never sell CIMC to me. Not in a thousand years."

Gabe nodded slowly. "No. He won't."

I stared down at my hands. They were shaking. "But... what if he didn't know it was me?"

Gabe turned his head, curious but quiet.

"What if someone else bought the center?" I went on. "Someone he wouldn't see as a threat. Someone far away. Someone he believes is harmless—my Aunt Ann." I wasn't certain I even meant it.

Gabe's eyebrows rose, but he didn't say anything. He was waiting for me to decide if I really meant it.

"She's... timid," I said softly. "She's never left Illinois in her life. The idea of owning anything in Mexico would probably terrify her." But my voice caught. "But she was so kind on the phone. More than she's ever been. She... actually listened. She said she wanted me to be happy."

"And she doesn't need to go there," Gabe said gently. "She wouldn't need to run it. She'd just be the owner on paper."

"Isabel could run it," I murmured, a spark of hope cutting through the dread. "She knows the center. She knows the dolphins. And she'd keep it safe until... until we could come home."

Gabe nodded. "That could work."

I rubbed my palms over my face. "Would Aunt Ann even consider it? I mean, buying a whole research center in another country? She's never even flown overseas, Gabe."

"Marie," he said softly, "she loves you. She fought for that settlement for you. If you told her this is what you want, really want, she'd try. Even if she had to hold her breath the whole time."

A laugh barked out of me, wet and broken. "She probably would hold her breath the whole time."

"But she'd do it," he said again, more certain now. "For you."

I looked out over the marina, at *Windy's* mast silhouetted against the golden harbor lights. At the direction the dolphins had vanished.

Home was behind us—wrecked by a hurricane and a betrayal, I still didn't know how to process. But it was home. I wanted to go back. And maybe... maybe there was a path back.

"I'll call her tomorrow," I whispered.

"Yeah," Gabe said. "Tomorrow."

The waves slapped gently against the wall, rhythmic and steady. For the first time in hours, I let myself believe we hadn't lost everything.

Chapter Thirty-Six

18° N latitude Puerto Rico

The little veterinary clinic near the harbor was warm and too bright. The tiles were scrubbed to a shine, and the air smelled of antiseptic and lavender detergents, too clean, too sterile. Nothing like the raw, salty chaos we'd escaped earlier—yesterday now. It was after midnight.

A tech with soft brown eyes led us to a small waiting room. A fish tank burbled in the corner, casting jittery light across the walls. It made everything feel surreal, underwater, suspended. I sat. My legs didn't stop shaking.

Gabe didn't sit. He paced. Back and forth. Hands on his hips, shirt torn from who knows what, hair stiff with salt. Every now and then he glanced at the door to the surgical wing as if he could will it open.

Minutes blurred into each other. My throat was tight. My heartbeat too fast. All I could see was Charlie disappearing beneath *Windy's* stern. All I could hear was the prop grinding. All I could feel was Gabe's arms dragging me back before I jumped and drowned and made everything worse.

"This is my fault," I whispered. My voice cracked on the last word.

Gabe froze. "Don't," he said softly. "Marie... no."

"If I'd been smarter, faster, if I'd done anything differently..."

"You kept us alive," he said. "And the dolphins saved Charlie. They saved him because of you."

I didn't answer. Couldn't. The fear was still too close, chewing at the edges of my sanity.

The door finally opened. Dr. Ruiz stepped out, her hair tucked into a cap, mask pulled down around her neck. Her eyes were tired, but kind.

"Marie?" she asked gently.

I stood so fast the chair tipped. "Yes. Yes, please..."

She approached slowly, like someone approaching a wild animal that might break apart with one wrong movement. "He made it through surgery."

My knees buckled. A sob tore from my chest before I could stop it. Gabe caught me, steadying me with one arm.

"But..." she continued softly, "we had to amputate the leg. We removed the entire front leg, at the shoulder. The propeller tore through the bone and the brachial artery. There was no viable way to save it."

I nodded, tears blurring everything.

"It was the right choice," she said. "It saved his life. He lost a lot of blood, but we transfused. He's stable now. He's resting."

"Three legs?" I tried not to wail. "How will he swim? How will he talk? I ruined his life. He'll never be happy again. If I hadn't tied the tourniquet so tight..."

"Marie," Dr. Ruiz said gently, "if you hadn't tied the tourniquet so tight, Charlie would have died. You did exactly the right thing, the only thing to keep him alive. Dogs do very well on three legs. He'll adapt to walking and swimming.... I'm not sure about talking." She eyed Gabe as she said it.

"Can I... can I see him?" My voice was barely a whisper.

"Just for a moment. He's very groggy."

She led us into the recovery room. Machines beeped softly, steady and reassuring. The air was cool, smelling faintly of rubbing alcohol and warm fur. My heart twisted painfully when I saw him.

Charlie lay curled on a blanket, his bandaged shoulder rising and falling in slow breaths. His fur was damp from cleaning. His good front paw twitched faintly, as if dreaming. His missing leg looked wrong, unfinished, like a sentence cut short.

But he was alive.

I knelt beside him, my hand trembling as I touched his head. "Hey, sweet boy," I whispered. "You did so good. I'm so proud of you."

His eyelids fluttered. He didn't fully wake, but he leaned, just barely, into my hand.

That small motion nearly broke me.

Gabe stood behind me, silent, one large hand resting on my shoulder. His thumb brushed a single slow arc, grounding me, anchoring me to the moment instead of the terror still thrashing inside me.

"Tomorrow," Dr. Ruiz said gently, "we'll talk long-term care, pain management, mobility. He's going to need rest. But, as I said, dogs do very well on three legs. He's strong and healthy. He should adapt beautifully."

I swallowed hard. "Thank you. Thank you so much."

She nodded and slipped out, leaving us alone with the quiet joy of survival and the jagged edges of everything we'd almost lost.

I stayed there until my legs went numb. Until the clinic lights flickered. Until exhaustion dragged at my bones like lead.

Finally, Gabe helped me stand, and we walked back to *Windy* under a sky as black and wide as the open ocean. I crawled into my bed fully clothed, salt still crusted on my skin.

I didn't cry again. But I didn't sleep either.

I just lay there, listening to the faint hum of the marina, the distant call of night birds, and the steady, ghostlike memory of dolphins circling us in the moonlit water.

Alive. We were all alive.

Chapter Thirty-Seven

18° N latitude Puerto Rico

The next morning came too early.

Gray light leaked through the small cabin window, turning the edges of *Windy's* cabin soft and blurred, as if the day itself was reluctant to begin. My body felt like it had been hollowed out and filled with bruises—every muscle sore, every breath heavy. Fear had soaked into my bones so deeply that even the gentle rocking of the marina made my stomach twist.

For a few seconds, I lay still, listening. The slow, rhythmic lap of water against the hull. The clink of a loose halyard tapping the mast. The faint hum of a boat reversing somewhere farther down the dock.

Safe. For now. Away from Rafa. Away from Marcelo.

But also... not home.

Not when Charlie was alive, but fragile, still recovering at the vet's office. Not when the dolphins were somewhere out in open water, safe for the moment, but never safe enough. Not when CIMC, our home, our haven, was still owned by a man who would sell dolphins to a criminal if it suited him.

I pushed myself upright, every movement stiff. The cabin smelled faintly of salt, damp towels, and peppermint, the last thing I'd been able to drink the night before. I padded into the galley, my feet cold against the teak. For a moment, I froze.

Gabe had already boiled water. Steam curled from the kettle in lazy spirals. A clean mug waited beside it. Something in my chest softened and tightened all at once.

I poured my tea, inhaling the sharp, soothing scent. My eyes drifted to the painting from Rolando, propped against the bulkhead where the dawn light brushed it. The colors glowed faintly, sunset golds, deep purples, luminous blues. Seven dolphins. *Windy*. And Charlie with three legs.

The sight punched me in the ribs. Beautiful. But eerie. Like a prophecy I hadn't agreed to but had no choice but to live through.

Above deck, I heard Gabe moving, soft thumps, the scrape of metal, the stretch of canvas as he adjusted something on the boom. The normality of the sounds, after the chaos we had survived, felt surreal. Soon we'd go to the vet to see Charlie, learn how to manage his pain, hear the words "three legs" said out loud by someone who wasn't trying to comfort me.

And soon... we needed to decide where to go next. We couldn't stay in Puerto Rico. If Rafa or Marcelo was tracking us through satellite positioning, they could find us again. The thought made my stomach contract painfully.

One thought pulsed bright and clear under all the noise: CIMC is in danger. And until it's safe, we can't go home. I loved that Cozumel felt like home, and I hated that it wasn't safe to return.

Gabe came below deck, rubbing a towel through his hair. He reached for the coffee pot to pour himself another cup. His eyes flicked to the painting, lingering on the missing leg, then to me.

I swallowed. "Do you think he knew? Charlie. Do you think he showed Rolando... to help me? For when the time came?"

Gabe didn't even hesitate. "Anyone else would think it's crazy," he said firmly, "but yeah. I absolutely do."

The answer made my throat tighten. I wasn't sure which part hurt more, the grief or the strange, comforting magic of it.

"Rolando said he was happy in the painting," I whispered. "Possibly the happiest he's ever been." The words steadied me.

I sank into the seat at the table, wrapping my hands around the mug. The tea was hot enough to sting, exactly what I needed.

"I need to call Aunt Ann," I said, heart thudding. "I'm not even sure I've ever called her before."

Gabe sat across from me, leaning forward, elbows on knees. "Just do it, Marie. You'll never know unless you call. And if she says no, we'll figure out another plan." He said it confidently, but we both knew we didn't have another plan. Not one that didn't involve running forever.

I took a deep breath and flipped my phone over. Ann Whitestone's name sat there, tidy and innocent in the contacts. My thumb hovered. My stomach churned.

I pressed the button before I could lose my nerve. The phone rang once.

"Hello, Dear, are you okay?" Her voice was sharper than usual, an edge of fear under the politeness.

"Um... yeah," I said, trying not to let the shakiness creep in. "Why wouldn't I be okay?"

"You've never called me before, Dear. So I assumed you were in trouble."

I rubbed my forehead. Typical Aunt Ann—dramatic and blunt all at once. "Well... I do need to ask you for a huge favor."

"Oh." She inhaled sharply. "A huge favor. Well then. Go ahead. I'll help if I can."

I stared at my mug. My heart beat so loudly, I was sure Gabe could hear it.

"So..." I breathed out. "I'd like you to buy the dolphin research center where I work. CIMC."

There was a crackling pause, then—

"What? Why?" she practically shouted. "How on Earth would I buy your research center?"

"With my settlement money."

"Why don't you buy it?"

Her question landed like a stone in a still pond, perfectly logical, perfectly impossible.

"It's a long story, Aunt Ann."

"Well, start at the beginning," she said briskly. "I'm not going anywhere."

Gabe exhaled beside me, half encouragement, half anxiety.

I took a breath and started from the beginning.

I told her everything, really everything. The abandoned buildings when I first arrived at CIMC. The mildew smell in the empty lab. The way the dolphins met me, like they'd been waiting for me their whole lives. Meeting Rafa. The center slowly coming alive again. The first time Tursi pressed a button and said my name. The grants, the long nights, the soundboard Gabe built with his careful hands and big ideas.

"Oh, Gabe," Aunt Ann said gently. "I like him."

Gabe grinned from across the table, clearly pleased by that.

I almost laughed. "You don't even know him," I wanted to say, but something about the softness in her voice stopped me. Maybe me liking him was enough for her. Maybe that was all she ever wanted.

I looked up at Gabe, and I kept going.

I told her about finding Rafa's emails, my stomach dropping away. The hurricane. The dolphins breaking the rules of nature to warn us. Heading north while everyone else fled south. The calm, the fear, the chase, the nets.

When I reached the part about Charlie, my voice cracked.

"Aunt Ann... Charlie got hurt. They had to... they had to amputate his leg." The words scraped out of me like they'd been trapped behind my ribs.

"Oh, Dear!" she gasped. I heard her hand slap over her mouth. "Is he going to be okay?"

"I think so. He gets to come home today." My throat tightened again. "I'm just... worried. I want him to heal and still swim and play and have a good life."

"Yes," she whispered. "He's a good dog. I hope he can still have a good life too." Then her voice wavered, small-town practicality mixing with real worry. "How will he live on a sailboat now?"

The question punched me in the chest. Because I didn't know. Not really. But I couldn't say that to her, not when she was trying so hard to be kind and understand my life.

"I think he'll adjust," I said softly. "He's lived on *Windy* most of his life."

She hummed, considering that. Then I breathed out, nervous again. "Okay... so, about CIMC."

The words felt strange leaving my mouth, like speaking a dream before it evaporated.

"You understand that Rafa would never sell it to me," I said. "He'd see me coming from a mile away. But if you offered to buy it with my settlement money... he might say yes. He knows he made a mistake buying it. He only reopened when I promised grant funding. And now that he knows he can hunt the dolphins in the open ocean, the center is more of a burden than an asset to him."

She didn't answer.

My heart thudded painfully.

I kept going, stumbling over the offer. "And, Aunt Ann... you wouldn't have to move there. It could be in name only. But if you wanted, you could visit. You could keep an eye on things until it's safe for Gabe and me, and the dolphins, to come home. I'd still love for you to visit and see the center."

Still silence. I looked up at Gabe.

My palms went damp around the phone. Had I pushed too far? Asked too much? She'd lost her sister. She'd lost her family. She'd spent decades tucked into one tiny Illinois town, safe, familiar, predictable. And here I was asking her to buy a research center in Mexico and become the legal shield between me and two dangerous men.

Maybe I was insane. I closed my eyes, waiting for the worst.

Finally, she exhaled. "You know, Marie... I've been thinking I might need a change."

My eyes snapped open. Gabe gave me a cheesy thumbs up.

"I've been looking forward to visiting you in the new year," she continued, voice trembling but purposeful. "But maybe... maybe I'll visit sooner. And check out this center of yours."

My heart lurched. "Aunt Ann, I don't even know when we'll be able to go back," I said. "Probably not for months. Maybe years. Marcelo won't stop until he finds us. He wants the dolphins for his aquariums. We might not be able to return until... until we stop him. Maybe even get him arrested for illegal animal trafficking." The words felt heavy, terrifyingly real for the first time.

"I know," she said. "And that's even more reason for me to be there to watch over CIMC for you. Of course I can't do research. I don't know a thing about dolphins. But..." She cleared her throat, and when she spoke again, her voice carried a surprising steel. "...but I'm a tough old bird, Marie. No one will mess with Ann Whitestone."

A laugh burst out of me, half relief, half disbelief, because for a moment I didn't recognize her voice. She sounded braver than I'd ever heard her. Braver, maybe, than she'd ever been allowed to be.

"And who knows," she added, softening, "maybe I'll learn about dolphins. Maybe... maybe I'll even swim with one someday."

My eyes stung, tears blurring the edge of the cabin. "Oh, Aunt Ann," I whispered. "Thank you. This means the world to me."

I could almost hear her smile. "Well. Let's not get ahead of ourselves. First things first: get that dog of yours from the vet. Then we'll make a plan."

I nodded even though she couldn't see me. "I'll let Isabel know. We'll start figuring out details as soon as possible."

After I hung up, I pressed the phone to my chest, letting the quiet settle around me, the soft lap of the harbor, the distant clatter of halyards, the whisper of the kettle cooling. I let out a long breath.

For the first time since the chase, the storm, the nets... I felt something shift. Not exactly safety. Not yet. But possibility. A new path. A way home, someday, that didn't depend on running.

And in a few minutes, we'd walk to the vet and bring Charlie home.

The future was still terrifying. But we had a plan. I had support. And for the first time in years... I had family, real family.

Chapter Thirty-Eight

18° N latitude Puerto Rico

We walked slowly toward the vet's office, the morning sun warm on my shoulders, the air thick with salt and distant frying plantains. My stomach churned with worry the whole way. I wasn't ready to see Charlie. Not like this.

But when Dr. Ruiz led us into the recovery room, Charlie lifted his head the instant he heard me, eyes bright though the rest of him was heavy with medication, and thumped his tail once, twice, as if to reassure me that he was okay.

My breath caught. The incision was larger than I'd imagined. Angry pink curves sliced through his shaved fur. My heart twisted painfully, but I forced myself to breathe steadily. Charlie didn't need my fear. He needed me to be strong for him, now more than ever.

Dr. Ruiz motioned toward two chairs. I ignored them and sank onto the floor beside Charlie, pressing my forehead gently to his, feeling the warm puff of his breath against my cheek.

"We'll go over everything," Dr. Ruiz said softly. "He's doing very well, given what he survived."

She talked us through cleaning the incision, keeping pressure off the wound, helping him stand, and supporting his weight. How his body would relearn its balance. How swimming, once the stitches came out, would be wonderful for his strength. A true gift that he loved the water.

"He'll begin walking tomorrow," she added. "Slowly at first. He'll wobble. He may fall. But dogs adapt. And he's a tough one. I'll need to see him again in ten days to remove the staples and sutures."

I swallowed hard. "Ten days," I whispered. "Until the sutures come out."

Ten days in one place. Ten days knowing Rafa and Marcelo wanted the dolphins more than ever. Ten days balancing danger and recovery. But Charlie needed those ten days. So we'd make it work.

A tech drove us back to the marina in a small van to spare us carrying him all the way. Gabe carried him tenderly aboard *Windy*, Charlie's head draped over his shoulder like a sleepy child. My chest tightened at the sight.

As soon as we set him down on the deck, Charlie circled once, wobbly, hesitant, and collapsed into his bed with a deep, relieved sigh. Within seconds, he was asleep, chest rising and falling steadily.

Gabe and I sat on the deck beside him, the warm boards under our feet, the harbor water slapping *Windy's* hull in a soft, rhythmic lullaby. Boats rocked gently around us. Pelicans drifted by like feathery buoys. A warm breeze carried the faint smell of diesel and mangoes.

But peace was never simple anymore.

"Rafa and Marcelo aren't going to give up," I murmured, watching a pelican dive with a sharp splash. "Do you think we'll really be okay here for ten days?"

Gabe exhaled slowly, eyes narrowed toward the horizon. "I think it'll take them a couple weeks to regroup. They'll have to get back to Cozumel, resupply, and plan a new expedition. We have a window. Not a big one... but a real one."

"Then where do we go?" I asked. The question felt like a stone lodged in my throat. "Island hop through the Caribbean?"

He shook his head before the words had even fully left my mouth. "No. Not far enough."

The breeze shifted, warmer now. The sun glinted off his hair as he tapped his finger to his chin, thinking. Always thinking.

"Then where?" I pressed.

He looked at me, something electric and terrifying in his expression. "Farther than they'd ever expect." A beat. "The Pacific."

My jaw dropped. "The Pacific?" I squeaked. "Can the dolphins even go that far?"

He shrugged lightly. "You're the dolphin researcher, Dr. Mercer."

I rolled my eyes at him because I had no answer. "How am I supposed to know that? No one's asked a dolphin to circumnavigate half the planet before. And we can't take them through the Panama Canal. It's freshwater."

"Exactly," he said. "We'd have to go around Cape Horn."

I stared at him, stunned. "Cape Horn. You want us to take a sailboat, with a still-healing dog and a pod of dolphins, through one of the most dangerous stretches of ocean on Earth?"

"Pretty much," he said, completely matter-of-fact.

"Are you insane?"

He grinned. "Probably a little."

"It's some of the roughest water in the world."

"And you," he said softly, "are one of the best sailors in the world."

"I am not." But the protest lacked conviction. Because even as he said it, even as I tried to reject it, some part of me recognized the truth: It was the best plan we had. Maybe the only plan.

Even the Strait of Magellan would put us too close to ports, patrols, and people asking questions, especially with dolphins following.

My gaze drifted over the water to where a few dolphins surfaced in the distance, just silhouettes, watching us, waiting. But I knew. I knew they were my dolphins. They had followed us through storms and nets and terror. And they'd follow us still.

"We're crazy," I whispered.

"Completely," Gabe agreed, his knee brushing mine. "And one more thing," he hesitated. "We need to turn off *Windy's* satellite tracking. I'm sure it's how they found us."

It was complete insanity. Only pirates and smugglers turned off satellite tracking. It was a safety feature that kept boats from hitting each other, and it allowed help to find a boat in an emergency. Turning it off was something I had never considered before. It was dangerous. And it was the only way to save the dolphins.

We fell quiet, the warm wind brushing over us like a promise.

Charlie snored softly in his bed, his breath steady and warm. The dolphins surfaced with gentle puffs of breath, lingering near the marina entrance like silent sentinels.

For the first time since the chase, since the screams and the nets and the blood in the water, I felt a thread of something fragile and fierce winding through my chest.

Hope.

And beneath it, an even deeper truth: The story wasn't over. Not even close.

But for now, for this moment, we were safe. We were together. We had a plan.

I reached down and stroked Charlie's soft ear, imagining him healed and strong, imagining *Windy* cutting through the deep blue Pacific with the dolphins dancing beside us.

"Okay," I whispered. "We'll go to the Pacific. We'll sail Cape Horn... with no satellite tracking."

Windy creaked gently beneath us, as if she'd already known.

And somewhere out in the harbor, a dolphin clicked, a sound that felt like yes.

Chapter Thirty-Nine
Epilogue

36° S Latitude, off the coast of Uruguay

The sea looked like a soft blue quilt, stitched with pale gold where the morning sun touched it. Warm southern-hemisphere summer air drifted across the deck, humid, sweet, and comforting, and I breathed it in like a gift. After weeks of moving south, slipping between weather systems, the Atlantic rising and falling around us like a sleeping giant, we'd fallen into a rare stretch of calm. No storms. No squalls. Just a gentle swell and a breeze that still carried the faint scent of Brazil far behind us.

It was Christmas morning.

Charlie hopped across the deck with his confident, jaunty three-legged gait, tail wagging like he'd never lost a thing. He'd taken to tripod life as if it had always been the plan, churning in circles when we let him swim, pivoting smoothly on his single front leg, pressing buttons on his soundboard with that determined little nose of his.

FOOD FISH. LOVE YOU MARIE. LOVE YOU GABE. His bright electronic "voice" drifted across the cockpit. I laughed. Yes, he said "love you" to Gabe too now, and it didn't make me the least bit jealous.

"You already had three fish," I said, scratching behind his ears.

He pressed two more buttons: FOOD WANT

Gabe groaned. "That dog has learned how to lie."

But I could hear the smile in his voice. Today, even the lies felt sweet.

Beside the boat, the dolphins cruised in lazy summer arcs. Solana closest, rolling to flash her pearly belly, humming with a kind of warm, content glow. They'd hunted at dawn and deposited a neat pile of fish on the swim platform with the proud efficiency of housecats. They'd been almost giddy all morning. And Solana, fuller in the middle, slower to leap, kept drawing my eye.

"Still think she's pregnant?" Gabe murmured.

I nodded. "Everything lines up. She's letting the other females bring her food."

He exhaled softly. "A baby. Out here. That would be... something."

"A new life," I whispered. "A new start."

A warm breath of wind brushed my hair across my cheek, and I tucked it back as I looked south, not toward the dark latitudes waiting for us, not toward the cold winds we'd eventually face, not toward Marcelo's shadow stretching somewhere behind, but toward the wide, glittering world holding us safe today.

Today was Christmas. Today, we were together. And that was enough.

By midmorning, it was time for our Christmas morning video call. I pulled out the laptop. I was grateful for my satellite internet plan. We kept automatic location reporting off. Marcelo wasn't getting a single breadcrumb from us anymore. But Mr. Gutiérrez knew our general route and checked in weekly. It made me feel safer knowing someone knew our location.

Isabel's face filled the screen first, hair pulled back, eyes bright. Behind her, the courtyard of CIMC glowed in Cozumel sunshine, new planters, fresh paint on the dolphin mural. Aunt Ann stood beside her, wearing a turquoise blouse and a proud, slightly shy smile that was new to me. Isabel's parents leaned into view from the other side, festive *papel picado* fluttering behind them.

"Merry Christmas!" they all shouted.

My throat tightened instantly. Gabe squeezed my hand.

Aunt Ann waved too enthusiastically. "I signed the papers, Dear! CIMC is ours." She laughed nervously. "And... I think I'm staying here. In Cozumel. For good. It's amazing here."

Tears blurred my vision. "I'm so happy for you."

"You should see Ann!" Isabel chimed in. "She's reorganized everything. The office is back in tip-top shape."

Warmth bloomed in my chest, relief, pride, love all tangled together in the middle of the ocean.

A second call lit up: Ana and Mateo, Turtle Bay. Bright desert sunshine framed them. Mateo held up a plate of tamales. Ana had tied a tiny garland around their cat's collar.

"We made your favorite!" Ana announced. "We'll freeze some for when you get here."

"We're holding you to that," Gabe said.

Charlie trotted over to his soundboard and pressed: HAPPY DAY.

We all laughed. "It really is a happy day, buddy."

After everyone finished exclaiming over Charlie, we continued chatting for about twenty more minutes. The world felt small and close, like all the places we loved had stretched across the sea just to wrap us in a big, warm, salt-scented hug.

When the calls ended, and the ocean hummed around us again, Gabe cleared his throat.

"I got something for you," he said softly.

I blinked. "How? We haven't been anywhere long enough to buy anything."

He shrugged, smiling sheepishly. "Maybe we've been in the right places."

He handed me a tiny box wrapped in the corner of an old nautical chart, tied with fishing line and a little dolphin-tooth charm we'd found on a beach months ago.

My breath caught before I even saw the inside. The necklace was delicate but strong, silver on a slender chain. Three tiny shapes interlocked like puzzle pieces: a dog paw with perfect little toe beans, a dolphin in mid-breach, and a sailboat, its sail curved like a crescent moon. Handmade. Irregular. Alive. It couldn't have been more perfect.

"Gabe..." I whispered. "How did you—"

"I found a jewelry maker in Rio, we designed it, and I had him send it to Montevideo," he said.

"Montevideo! That's why you insisted we stop there."

"Yeah, a refuel stop. You were asleep. Charlie and I snuck off." He jerked a thumb toward the dog. "Some of us were very loud about it."

Charlie pressed two buttons: QUIET GABE.

I laughed through my tears. "It's perfect," I said.

Gabe fastened it around my neck, his fingers warm against my skin. For a moment, the world seemed to pause, the breeze holding its breath, the dolphins rising together in a shimmering arc, sunlight scattering over the calm sea like blessings.

By late afternoon, the deck radiated warmth under my bare feet. Uruguay was a pale smudge to the west. The dolphins glided beside us, Solana humming a low, contented note that vibrated faintly through the hull.

Charlie barked once and trotted forward with his jaunty three-legged stride. I watched him climb to the bow, not hesitant, not awkward, but proud and sure.

My breath caught.

He looked exactly like Rolando's painting. The same stance. The same tilt of sunlight. The same expression, joyful, free, impossibly brave.

Rolando's voice echoed in my memory: "He showed it to me. He wanted me to paint it. He said it was one of the happiest days of his life."

And here he was, alive, triumphant, standing at the bow like a king of the sea. Charlie turned back toward us, wind ruffling his fur. This was it—the moment of Rolando's painting. The sun was just right. My heart melted with joy.

Solana and the others breached behind him in a shimmering arc, their bodies catching the late-afternoon sun. The sea breathed gently beneath our hull. Our strange but perfect little family, human, dog, dolphin, sailed on into a warm, summery Christmas evening.

We still needed to face Marcelo. We still needed to brave the Horn. We still needed to fight for the dolphins and the future they deserved. But not today.

Today, Charlie stood proudly at the bow, just as he had in the painting of his happiest memory, and the world felt full of hope. And for one perfect Christmas day, that was everything.

Gabe slipped an arm around my waist. "I love working on the soundboard and learning about dolphin communication, but that's not why I came to Cozumel," he murmured, eyes warm.

"Well, I hope it wasn't really to divemaster either," I teased, "because now you're stuck sailing into the Pacific with me, my dog, and a bunch of bottlenose dolphins, and it might be a long time before you're in Caribbean waters again."

"I wouldn't have it any other way," he said, leaning over Charlie to kiss me.

And honestly, on this bright, warm, impossibly hopeful Christmas day, I realized I wouldn't have it any other way either.

Into the Pacific

Windy is headed west.

Marie, Gabe, Charlie, and the dolphins believe they've finally found distance at an isolated island in the Pacific, far beyond Marcelo's reach and Rafa's watchful eye.

The pod settles into the surrounding reefs. For the first time in months, Marie begins to imagine a version of life that isn't defined by running—a place where research, protection, and belonging might finally coexist.

Back in Cozumel, Isabel and Ana are quietly building a case against Marcelo's trafficking network, risking everything to expose what's been hidden for years. Each piece of evidence brings Marie closer to reclaiming the dolphins' home... and closer to a confrontation she cannot avoid forever.

The Pacific is vast, but it is not empty. Currents carry stories farther than anyone expects. Some truths rise slowly, like something long submerged. Others surface without warning.

For Marie, Gabe, Charlie, and the pod, Cozumel was only the beginning.

The ocean isn't finished with them yet.

Gratitude

I have many people to thank for helping *Windy Possibilities* come to life.

First, to the people of Cozumel, Mexico—especially the restaurant workers, shopkeepers, and the staff at Aqua Safari Dive Center—thank you. My trips to Cozumel years ago were truly magical, and the warmth, generosity, and strong sense of place I experienced there inspired much of this story.

To the Iron Eight Writing Group in Austin, Texas: thank you. When the idea for *Windy Possibilities* was first beginning to take shape, you offered encouragement, support, and belief in the story. Your enthusiasm helped turn a fragile idea into something I could never quite let go of, even as the years passed.

To the morning swimmers at the Kailua Pier: thank you. Our early swims and conversations about ocean conditions, marine life, and the rhythms of the sea quietly shaped parts of this book. I value my time in the ocean with you beyond words.

Laura Reid, I owe you my deepest thanks. Without you, *Windy Possibilities* would not exist. You convinced me that "now is the time" and encouraged me to join The Write Club. Through coaching, editing, and steady encouragement—along with invaluable guidance on the nuances of self-publishing—you helped bring this book into the world.

To every member of The Write Club: thank you. Each of you has been supportive, generous, and encouraging. The Write Club is a rare and special space for new authors, and I'm grateful for the camaraderie and care that define it.

To my beta readers—Laura, Ilana, Ingrid, and Greta—thank you. You read early drafts and believed in this story when I wasn't sure whether I had written a "good" book. Your enthusiasm for *Windy Possibilities* was one of the most encouraging experiences of this entire process, and your thoughtful feedback helped make it better.

Greta Friesen, thank you for the cover artwork. You understood this book and helped translate its heart into visual form. Your work captured the love, connection, and sense of wonder at the core of *Windy Possibilities*.

Thank you to Quintana Roo and Wichita for everything they gave me while I wrote this book. They were constant sources of inspiration for Charlie and Lilly. Wichita spent countless hours beside me while I wrote, and Roo made sure I took breaks. This book carries both of them in its pages.

Finally, I want to thank Jeff, my husband and lifelong dive buddy, who supports all of my wild ideas with unwavering love and shared those early Cozumel adventures that helped make this story possible.

About the author

Heather A. Herrick is a marine-science educator, lifelong ocean lover, and novelist who believes curiosity is its own kind of compass. The story that became her debut novel lived and grew quietly in her mind, shaped by her years teaching oceanography, her Master's degree in botany and wetland ecology, and many trips to Cozumel. There, scuba diving, exploring the island, and time spent in San Miguel with the people she met deepened her connection to the island and its waters.

Her writing is rooted in her passions for science, the ocean, and the remarkable bonds between humans and animals. Her dogs—Quintana Roo, whose spirit inspired

Charlie, and Wichita, who "speaks" using word buttons—both played a role in bringing the novel's ideas to life.

Heather now lives in Hawai'i, where she spends time swimming in the ocean, surrounded by the nature that continues to inspire her work. You can connect with her on social media at @oceanstoriesbyheather.

About the Cover Art

The cover of *Windy Possibilities* features an original painting by artist Greta Friesen.

Created specifically for this novel, the artwork captures a moment at sea from the deck of *Windy*, the sailboat that carries Marie and Charlie toward an unexpected new life. Charlie stands watch as dolphins leap alongside the boat.

Greta's painterly style brings warmth, motion, and intimacy to the scene, mirroring the emotional landscape of the story. The composition was designed to evoke both wonder and companionship: the vastness of the ocean balanced by the steady presence of a loyal dog and the unmistakable intelligence of wild dolphins choosing to draw near.

The author is deeply grateful for Greta's collaboration and artistic vision in bringing this world to life.